The wrath of
MAHABONE

(Book Two)

by

ROBERT BARNES

i

R. L. Barnes.

**Other Books
by Robert L. Barnes**
in this series

Rings of the
DARK KINGDOM
(Book One)

Coming Next

The Coming of
OROBAS
(Book Three)

The wrath of Mahabone

Typeset in: *Bookman Old Style* (Body), *Algerian* (Chapter Title) and *Angelic* (Map)

Editing, Publishing by *Rowen Publishing*©
Copyright© R. L. Barnes 2023

*First Edition
ISBN – 978-1-7395157-2-0
Cover Design:
 Robert L. Barnes ©2024
www.robert-barnes.com

R. L. Barnes.

This book is dedicated.
in memory of my father.

Bob

Thank you for everything!
1929 – 2019

Preface

In another world, deep within the human mind, and where time has no meaning, there exists *Deawilder*, a supernatural dark kingdom warped by time.

***

Long ago, there were three *Ouroboros* rings on the handle of a mighty sword called *Shibboleth*, with a magical ruby pommel stone. Together, they made the sword so powerful, the bearer was almost invincible. Forged by magic in the mountain's belly, its sole purpose was to be used for good.

Sadly, during a fierce battle between good and evil, three evil sorcerers stole the sword, broke it into separate pieces, and concealed each object in various locations throughout the land of Deawilder and beyond.

These sorcerers quickly discovered that the ring's individual powers could be used for their evil deeds. Eventually, their deeds plunged *Deawilder* into an oppressed darkness.

However, a few of the stolen items were eventually returned to their rightful owner, along with one of the three Ouroboros rings that Gerald had snatched from Mahabone during his last adventure to Deawilder.

Remembering his past attempt to lift the family curse once and for all, where each first-born son had to enter *Deawilder* to retrieve heirlooms, or forfeit their souls', he later discovered he had failed.

With the passing of time, Gerald got on with his busy life at home and without him thinking too much about the consequences of returning home with one of Mahabone's *Ouroboros* rings in the past, its existence became much less important to him, and was eventually lost to memory.

However, because he had stolen and returned home with the *Ouroboros* ring, Mahabone, had not kept his word in lifting the curse, and still remains the reflection of Gerald's deepest fears.

Gerald must now delve deeply into his past once again to explain to his son what terrible things had happened to him whilst in that God-forsaken land.

Can he convince his son from his hospital bed, to help him find a way back to the supernatural land of *Deawilder?*

And can Mahabone be stopped?

ACKNOWLEDGMENTS

All my *Gerald Lindsell* books (*series*) are works of fiction/fantasy. There are so many people without whose help and support it would have been difficult, if not impossible, to write with a sense of authenticity. A special thank you to my wife and all my friends, whose belief and inspiration have never wavered.

I would also like to give heartfelt appreciation to author Michael K. Foster, who went that extra mile to show me encouragement and unqualified support in making a difference to the book.

R. L. Barnes
County Durham, England
www.robert-barnes.com

R. L. Barnes.

'*Deawilder*' The ancient map of the kingdom

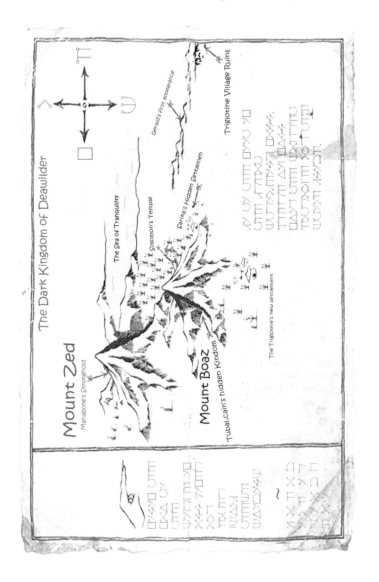

CHAPTER ONE

Present Day ...

David Lindsell woke with a start, his heart pounding in his chest causing him to sweat profusely as the blood drained from his face in panic.

Unable to clear the image of Mahabone's brother from his head, he could still hear the echoes of his evil laughter. How much longer would the nightmares continue? How much more could he take before he reached his breaking point?

Before making any hasty choices, he would need to sit down and have a heart-to-heart with his father about this Mahabone and his kin. That bastard in his dream is now never far from his thoughts.

***

Within Kings College Hospital, London, 75-year-old Gerald Lindsell lay exhausted yet relaxed in his hospital bed after his morning bed-bath. Gently lifting his head, he looked at the middle-aged auxiliary nurse who had just bathed him. She was of slim build and standing with her back to him whilst muttering away to herself as she put away the equipment she had been using.

'Excuse me, nurse,' he asked. 'What time is it, as I am expecting my son David to visit me again first thing this morning.'

'I bet you are both looking forward to seeing each other again, Mr Lindsell,' she quietly replied, knowing that other patients in the beds next to him would still be sleeping. 'Unfortunately, it's only seven o'clock. Dr Müller should start his morning rounds between nine and ten o'clock. Your son may come in the ward as soon as the doctor has finished.'

'Thank you, nurse. I understand. I'll just rest for now.'

Placing his head back on the pillow, he took a deep breath and closed his eyes.

***

David stood quietly at the Falcon Grove bus-stop just around the corner from his father's house in Afghan Road, London. He was pondering over his vivid nightmares and what his dad told him the day before. He wondered why his father was adamant that he visits again today.

'*God, it was hard enough to listen to his tales yesterday about his experiences,*' he thought. '*Let alone what I am to be told today. Obviously, it must be very important to him. I understand that he is looking out for me in his own way, by making me aware of what may be in store for me. And what he will he say when I tell him about my recent nightmares?*'

David watched as the number 319 double-decker bus pulled up at the stop. Standing to one side, David waited as several passengers alighted from the vehicle before stepping on the platform alongside the driver.

'Where to, lad?' asked the driver.

'A return ticket to Kings College University Hospital, please.

'You realise that's a forty-five-minute ride?' said the driver.

'Tell me about it,' replied David, rolling his eyes. 'But it's all I can do from here.'

'OK, that'll be three-pounds-sixty.'

'Thank you,' smiled David, who quickly found a seat at the back of the lower deck. He fell awkwardly into his seat as the bus pulled away.

***

'Hello Mr Lindsell,' said Dr Müller, looking down at Gerald. 'How are you feeling this morning?'

'I'm not in pain, if that's what you are asking. Other than that, I feel clean and relaxed, especially after my top-and-tail this morning.'

'That's wonderful Mr Lindsell,' smiled Dr Müller. 'We will continue to make you as comfortable as possible. And without giving you any unnecessary hope, we are constantly in communication with the cancer Therapy Research team to see if they have had any breakthrough in treatments.'

'Are you saying they might have a cure for me?' asked Gerald.

'Certainly not Mr Lindsell. I'm not saying that at all. What I am saying, and this may sound technical, is that there are cutting-edge technologies and innovators like CRISPR, artificial intelligence, telehealth, the Infinium Assay, cryo-electron microscopy, and robotic surgery that are helping speed up the progress against cancer. We are just grasping at straws now, but any news of progress might be helpful to us, and to you.'

'So why mention it at all?' scowled Gerald.

'It's to let you know what we are doing behind the scenes.' replied Dr Müller. 'We don't want you to think we are just leaving you here to suffer.'

'I'd rather not hear any of that, thank you very much,' snapped Gerald. 'I'd rather remain ignorant about these things, unless there is something positive to say.'

4

'As you wish,' Dr Müller replied with a calm and reassuring tone. 'I apologise if I have offended you. Please forgive me.'

Dr Müller gave a few instructions to the nurse and walked over to the patient in the next bed.

***

David stepped out of the bus near the hospital and walked toward the taxi rank for the last leg of his journey. It was only a ten-minute walk, but preferred to be lazy and pay for a taxi.

Walking into the hospital entrance, David quickly made his way to the lifts that will take him to the floor where his father's ward was located. Thankfully, he didn't suffer confined spaces like his father, but if he had, there would be an unmentionable number of steps to the top floor.

Just as he stepped out of the lift, the staff nurse he had met the previous day approached him.

'Good morning, Mr Lindsell, or can I call you David?'

'David will be fine. Is there something wrong with dad?'

'Not at all,' she smiled. 'Dr Müller asked me to keep an eye out for you. He would simply like to see you in his office to discuss any concerns you may have. You can ask questions for him to clarify before seeing your father.'

'Do you think there's anything I should be worried about?' he asked, looking a little pale.

'Not that I've noticed David. I'm sure it's just to let you know how things stand.'

'OK,' he replied. 'I take it the doctor is in the Same office as yesterday?'

'He is. I will let him know you are here. In the meantime, can you take a seat outside? I promise you he won't be long.'

Making his way to the doctor's office, he came across a row of empty seats and quietly sat himself down.

'This is awful,' he thought, whilst fidgeting in the seat. *'There is never anything to read. Why does it always seem like I'm waiting for ever in places like this? It's so boring.'*

'Hello David,' said Dr Müller, poking his head around the door. 'Please step inside?'

'Yes doctor, thank you.'

David sat quietly in front of the doctor's desk.

'How are you coping, David?' asked Dr Müller softly.

'I'm just taking things day by day, so to speak. Very upset at the situation with dad but looking forward to spending as much time with him as possible.'

'I understand,' replied the doctor. 'The reason for having you here is simply to ask if there are any questions, or if you would like any advice regarding your father.'

'Has there been any change in my dad's condition?'

'Not since yesterday, I'm afraid. However, I had a little heated exchange with him this morning.'

'What for?' scowled David.

'It was my fault, really. I was just letting him know we are constantly monitoring for new treatments. I didn't intend to give him any false hopes. My mistake! A slip of the tongue, I'm afraid, but your dad was feisty enough to put me quickly in my place. So, I must apologise for that. Now, is there anything else you would like to ask before you see your father?'

'Not for now doctor. I just want to see my dad.'

'OK! That's it then.' said Dr Müller standing up. 'But if you do think of anything that troubles you. Don't hesitate to come and see me. Now go and see your father.'

'Thank you doctor, I will.'

***

Gerald lay pan-faced whilst staring at the ward entrance in anticipation of his sons' arrival.

'*Where the hell is he?*' he thought. '*He's late.*'

'Hi Dad. Sorry I'm a little late.'

Gerald's face quickly burst into life as he watched David come sauntering through the ward doors.

'Where have you been?'

'Sorry dad. The bus was late, then I had to spend a few minutes with Dr Müller.'

'Why, what did he want?' asked Gerald.

'Nothing really. He just wanted to ask if I had any concerns or questions.'

'And did you?' asked Gerald, raising one eyebrow.

'Not really. I was more concerned about seeing you.'

Gerald plumped up his pillows and sat himself up in a comfortable position.

'Right David, now that you're here, can we start where we left off?'

'Just a minute!' insisted David. 'Do you think you can give me five minutes? I need to discuss something with you that is worrying me.'

'Sorry son, it's just me being impatient. Sometimes, my words can come across as cold and self-assured.'

OK, I must agree with you there. So, I have a problem.

'What is it son?

'I've recently been having vivid nightmares. But since you told me about Mahabone yesterday, the nightmares have become more intense.'

'How intense?' asked Gerald looking worried.

'Very,' replied David. 'In fact, they felt real. I was approached by a tall cloaked person who was chanting something I couldn't understand, but then he started to laugh and said he was looking for you dad. He said his name was *Orobas*, brother of Mahabone. Was it just my imagination running wild from what you told me?'

'What did this person look like in your nightmare?' asked Gerald. 'I have heard the name Orobas before.'

'He was enormous dad. Built like a brick shithouse. He was also holding a staff with a glowing light on top.'

'Christ,' said Gerald. 'It's already begun.'

'What's begun?'

'Can you remember what I told you about the family curse, where our ancestor made a deal with the necromancer Mahabone to get his deceased wife back, and that the first-born son of every descendant had to enter Mahabone's supernatural world, to reclaim all the family heirlooms he had taken from your ancestor as payment.'

'But what has my nightmare got to do with it?'

'It means our troubles are not yet over and that for some reason, it is now your turn.'

'I thought you said all heirlooms were collected to stop the curse.' scowled David.

'I did,' said Gerald. 'But something has obviously changed since I returned to *Deawilder*. Look son, I'm not being rude, but I need to continue telling you about the past when I had to return to *Deawilder*. It is imperative that you take onboard and understand the enormity of your task ahead. Let me remind you that this is deadly serious.'

'I understand what you are saying dad, but I am scared about what is to come.'

'Look David. You told me you are starting to have dreams, just like I did at your age. Now you are telling me you are having vivid nightmares about *Orobas*, the brother of Mahabone. All I ask is that you trust me. I'm not able to wait much longer. I need to tell you what happened to me on my last visit to Deawilder and why you never got the chance to know the rest of your family. You know we are the only ones left. Just give me the chance to take you back to the past and explain what truly happened. Don't forget, the family curse may not yet be over. I suspect things may still have to be resolved.'

'Now that you put it like that,' nodded David. 'I think you need to tell me!'

'I must ask you once again not to make fun of me when I start telling you. It may sound outlandish, but believe me, what I am about to tell you is deadly serious. The only way I can get you to understand what you will face, is by telling you what took place after I returned from Deawilder and why I had to go back. Therefore, I ask you to please listen with an open mind.'

'But what about our family?' asked David.

''You already know what happened to your grandad and his dad when I told you yesterday. Now I must explain what happened to the rest of your family, including your mum.'

David, now captivated by the sincerity of his dads' voice, pulled his chair closer to the bed.

'Tell me everything,' whispered David.

'As far as I can remember,' said Gerald, 'it all started again on my graduation day…

CHAPTER

TWO

Gerald's past - Graduation Day ...

Thinking back to his youth many years ago, Gerald remembered feeling very troubled as he precariously danced on the podium steps in his ceremonial gown. He was finding it extremely hard to hold onto his scroll while juggling to stop the wind from sending his mortarboard flying. The past had not been very kind to him as a teenager, however, it had been several years since he had restarted his studies and although it was hard work, his tenacity and perseverance eventually paid off.

***

Graduation day had finally arrived, and several of the students stood around with their faces glowing with the pride of self-achievement! It was not long before the band began to play along with the onslaught of family members, who by now, were eagerly starting to join in with the celebrations!

Looking around, he felt a little dispirited as the other student's parents huddled up to their sons and daughters. His mother could not make it for his special day, as his grandmother was not well, and he knew she had to be cared for. Knowing this, he didn't mind at all! He was very understanding and loved them both dearly.

He remembered it had been hard for all his family these past years, but if it were not for the books his father had given him as a young boy, he would never have had the courage or tenacity to succeed. As always, he was never a one to mingle in large crowds! He enjoyed the presentation of his graduation and was proud of his overall achievements but could not stay to celebrate any longer. He had to get home to help his mother and left quietly before anyone noticed.

On the bus home, he carefully laid his head against the window, watching the buildings slowly pass by! He had passed his driving test a few months before, but because he could not afford a car of his own, the local bus was his only choice.

It didn't take very long before his mind began to wander, thinking about what he had achieved these past few years with his university studies since his father passed away!

'I think my dad would have been proud of what I have achieved so far.' thought Gerald. *'I only wish he could have been here with me! I miss him so much.'* Gerald's eyes began to fill up with tears as he remembered his father's death.

'Are you OK?' asked the young lady sitting next to him.

'Sorry, I didn't realise you were watching me, but now that you ask, I am fine. I was just thinking about something personal and didn't realise I was showing my emotion.'

The young woman smiled with a caring glance and returned her attention to the magazine she was reading.

Gerald had missed so many years of his father's life! To be reunited with him through such profound and unorthodox circumstances in one hand, only to witness his father's life slip away shortly after, when trying to save him from the evil that pursued them on the other. All of which happened whilst he retrieved the final heirloom from his last adventure.

It had been so hard for his mother to listen to details of her husband's demise all those years ago, but as always, the great cliché, *'time is a great healer,'* came to bear. Thankfully, no-one ever mentions those days of darkness anymore and everyone has gradually moved on.

Wendy Lindsell (*Gerald's mother*) had spent most of her years as an unemployed single parent. Now she works as a Personal Assistant for a local pharmaceutical company.

It only took her a few years to get back into the swing of things, since her family was in peril. Thankfully, she now has a new sense of purpose with a career future, as well as enjoying the interaction with colleagues.

Due to Gerald's sleeping disorders, his mother had a tough time bringing him up. He had been inflicted with the family curse that had developed into her worst nightmare, an evil that had plagued their family for generations.

If it was not for her sons' heroic endeavours to bring back the family heirlooms, to hopefully break the family curse that had placed upon them, the family might never have survived the evil exploits of Mahabone. But in the past, when Gerald had stolen the first of three *Ouroboros* rings from Mahabone, as well as fighting him in the supernatural world of *Deawilder*, the consequences of such actions was unknown and ignored.

Thankfully, it is now all in the past and Wendy feels much happier that her family has transformed into an almost normal daily routine. She is so proud of her son and the man he has become. Not only of his achievements, but that he also reminds her so much of his father.

Now she spends her days enjoying her work and relaxing with family around the dinner table.

Both Wendy and Gerald are very aware that Kathleen (his grandma and Wendy's mother-in-law) is very frail these days, so much so that they have had to relocate and move in with her.

Kathleen had found it hard to deal with her ailments, especially living in the large house she owns at Wyer Forest, the largest native forest in England. Many a consultation with her doctors revealed she could not fully look after herself. Doctors then suggested she may have to go into a home. Her family fiercely opposed this suggestion. Wendy and Gerald moved in, keeping the family together under one roof.

Doctor Jachin, her primary consultant at the Temple Hospital, suggested that they also employ the services of a nurse, at least to cover the times when Gerald and his mother had to leave the household for work. They agreed to this, and with a few short phone calls, everything had been put in place.

***

Early one morning, while getting ready for work and making her breakfast, there was a quiet rustle at the kitchen door. Kathleen quietly entered, wearing nothing but her blouse, knickers, and a wrinkled old carrier bag.

'Oh dear, are we going somewhere?' said Wendy mischievously at her frail mother-in-law. Looking a little confused, Kathleen's sunken eyes glared across the room at Wendy, who by now stood there with a smile on her face.

'I, err... I think I've lost something!' spoken with a barely audible voice. 'I am, err... What time is it?'

Wendy knew Kathleen had had another turn and had come downstairs totally confused at her surroundings.

'Have you forgotten to take your pills again?

'I don't know,' said Kathleen, looking even more confused. Wendy gently took her hand and placed it in her own.

'What are you like?' said Wendy with a soft voice. 'You would forget your head if it wasn't fastened on.' Still smiling, she gently guided Kathleen back up the stairs to get properly dressed.

'Shall we visit Tom today?' whispered Wendy. 'Maybe, after you help Gerald go through some of your things in the attic, eh?'

Kathleen looked deep into Wendy's eyes and smiled, before gently nodding her head.

It had taken Gerald almost an hour to get back home the night before. After he had completed all his house chores and studies, it was late evening before he had the chance to crash out in his bed.

Using the tip of his fingers to remove the crustaceous material from the corners of his tired eyes, The familiar smell of bacon and eggs pleasantly greeted him.

'Ah! I can never get enough of that delicious smell. I don't know what it is, but it always smells and tastes better at Grandma's.'

Throwing the blankets from his bed, Gerald dragged himself towards the bathroom.

'Is that you up now?' echoed his mother's voice up the stairs.

'Yes! I'm up. I'm just getting washed and will be down in a moment.'

'Good,' she shouted. 'I'll put the kettle on then.'

Ten minutes later, Gerald entered the kitchen to find his grandmother sitting at the table eating her breakfast. His mother was at the breakfast bar sipping a fresh cup of coffee and reading the headlines from yesterday's paper.

'Oh! Good morning sleepy head, another late night I see!' said Wendy, peering over the top of the paper.

'Yep. I had to complete the study for my final job interview at the University tomorrow. So today, I'm off and resting,' grumbled Gerald, pouring himself a coffee and grabbing lashings of bacon and egg. 'There is a horrible smell of gas at the front door. Did anyone notice?'

'Don't worry,' said Wendy. Grandma said the gas man was out last week. They said there was nothing to worry about. The smell is the oxide coming from the copper piping. Anyway, I thought you could spend a little time with your grandma today, sorting out the last of the stuff in the attic. You know how she likes to remember things. It won't take too long, as I am only working half a day today. I should be back around noon. I thought it would be nice to take Grandma to see Uncle Tom this afternoon. I also asked one of the local groundsmen yesterday, if he could do me a favour. I asked if he could call in on Tom and let him know we will visit later today. I think it would be nice if you could help him again with a few bits he might want doing.'

'Jesus! Give me a break mum,' he replied sharply. 'You know I've got a busy day tomorrow.'

Kathleen lifted her head and looked directly at him. When he saw the reaction on her face and her eyes welling up, he realised his attitude had gone a step too far.

'Alright! I'll do as you ask if it makes you happy. I will help Grandma for a little while, then we will visit Uncle Tom.'

'Thank you dear,' said Kathleen. 'I so look forward to seeing Tom. He's not very well, you know!'

Wendy just smiled at her son and put her coat on.

'Well, I must get going. The sooner I get to work, the sooner I can get finished and come home.'

After waving goodbye to his mother, Gerald, and Kathleen returned to the kitchen and sat themselves down.

'Fancy another cup of tea, grandma?'

'Oh yes, please. I've always liked it when you make it. I don't know what it is, but it always seems to taste better. It must be because you have always been here looking after me these past few years.' Gerald simply smiled and put the kettle on.

'Yes grandma, I suppose you're right. How would you like to spend a little time in the attic this morning? We only have a few more things to tidy up and catalogue before it is all finished.'

Kathleen looked exhausted as she looked at him across the table, but when she smiled, her little face was glowing like a beacon at the thought.

'Oh yes, that would be nice, dear. I enjoy going through your grandfather's things... I miss him so much... and I know he is looking down on me.'

'Well, that's what we will do then,' said Gerald, carefully pouring a fresh cup of tea and placing a small plate of her favourite biscuits between them.

***

Later in the attic, the smell of old paper, along with the damp floorboards and rafters, made Gerald shiver. He had often found spiders and creepy crawlies running across old paperwork and out of cardboard boxes. However, he knew once this last session was over, he would no longer have to live amongst the things that made his skin crawl.

'Look at this Gerald.' Kathleen had pulled out a rolled-up cloth that had been wrapped around with a leather strap that smelled of rotten leaves.

'I have never seen this before!' said Kathleen holding out the wrapping for Gerald to look.

He had never seen it before, either. He had spent many an hour rummaging through his grandfather's things in the past. It was at that time he found a weird Key and Claw, hidden in the secret drawer within his grandfather's writing bureau. Instantly, Gerald felt a cold shiver run down his spine, as he remembered his battle with Mahabone and the death of his father. The memories of his past misfortune came flooding back. Finding the Key and the Claw led him on that unforgettable journey! A journey that changed the lives of his family forever! Memories he was not keen to remember!

R. L. Barnes.

Carefully untying the leather strap, he hesitantly unfolded the cloth to reveal a long wooden box fitted with a tumbler lock.

'*There is something heavy inside,*' he thought and fiddled with the six-digit lock. '*I can't get the damn thing to open!*'

Looking more closely, he noticed three faded letters on the back of the box...

T. H. L.

'What do these letters mean?' showing the box to Kathleen.

'Let me have a look.' Kathleen took the mysterious box from his hands and immediately smiled. 'It's your Uncle Tom's. THL stands for Thomas Harris Lindsell.

He must have given it to your grandfather for safekeeping, otherwise, why would it be here? We must give it back to him,' she said, rubbing her head. 'I suspect only he will remember the combination, or maybe not. It's been stored here a long time and I suspect his memory is not as sharp as it used to be.'

'Well, we can,' said Gerald. 'Mum plans to take us both to Tom's when she comes in from work. She said she would be back just after lunch. Maybe he can shed a little light on the box and its combination.'

Gerald often visited his Uncle Tom, who lived in a small wooden cabin. It is well hidden deep within the woods behind Kathleen's house. It takes an hour or so to walk there and has always been hard to find through the overgrown and never-ending pathways leading to his home. He could drive there with an off-road vehicle, that can deal with a very challenging terrain, but as he doesn't have one, walking is his only choice.

It is so remote out there. Even the post office refused to deliver his mail. So, he now has it sent to Kathleen's address.

Over the years since his family had somewhat pulled themselves together, Uncle Tom's health and mental agility had quickly deteriorated. It was becoming so bad that Gerald had to constantly attend to most of his basic needs when he visited. Not with feeding and dressing, or anything like that, but making sure that Tom had not forgotten to take vital medication, gather fuel, and the general upkeep of his smallholding that he finds harder to manage.

Uncle Tom was a mountain of a man. Standing over six feet tall with a beard halfway down his chest, he reminded Gerald of a typical caveman. However, the last seven years have not been kind. He now stands round-shouldered with a stoop, lost all his weight and his upper body strength and although he will not discuss anything about his health, his

23

family is getting very concerned. He now looks worryingly poorly.

Not watching how the time was passing, both Gerald and Kathleen were so involved with what they were doing in the attic; they did not notice Wendy returning from work, or that she had entered the kitchen, boiled the kettle, or even heard her calling to them from the kitchen.

Now standing halfway up the staircase, Wendy filled her lungs as much as she could, and shouted at the top of her voice...

'Hello. Can you two come down, before this tea gets cold!'

'Bloody hell, grandma! Have you seen the time? Mum's back. Come on, she's shouting up the stairs. She's even had time to make us a cup of tea.'

Grandma showed little urgency in her reactions. She continued to hold on to a bunch of papers, before moving slowly to her feet and making her way towards the attic door.

'Tea; Ooh lovely! Well, that's worth putting down what we are doing. Come on son, that's enough for today and let's get to that tea,' dropping the papers where she stood.

Gerald just shook his head, picked up the mess she had made on the floor and placed the papers neatly on the nearby table. He then slowly helped Kathleen down the stairs. Not by holding on to her, but by going in front of her, in case she fell.

Wendy was placing the tea and biscuits on the kitchen table when they both walked through the door.

'Hi, mum. Sorry, we didn't hear you come in. We were so involved with things; that we didn't even realise the time. Are we still going to Uncle Tom's?'

'Yes, of course,' said Wendy, putting the teapot back on the kitchen side. 'We will finish this tea first and then we will go. I have made a packed lunch to eat along the way. We'll have our dinner at Tom's when we arrive there.'

'Don't forget to take his post with us,' said Kathleen.

'Already done,' said Wendy. 'It's all in my bag.'

They quickly prepared for their journey to Tom's, and since driving through the forest wasn't an option, they had to travel on foot as usual.

CHAPTER

THREE

The sun was still shining when they entered the dense forest, but as they walked deeper into the foliage, the light quickly diminished. Gradually, the onset of midges filled the air, bombarding and nipping from all sides.

'The little bastards are everywhere,' sneered Gerald, slapping the back of his neck.

'We should have brought our midge nets,' said Kathleen.

'The *cart-before-the-horse* comes to mind, grandma. A little late to remember about them.'

'Well, we did leave in a hurry,' interjected Wendy. 'Never mind, we are third of the way now, too far to go back. We'll just have to put up with them the best we can.'

They were only thirty minutes into a ninety-minute journey, and it was already getting difficult to navigate through the overgrown track.

Both Wendy and Kathleen continued walking several yards in front of Gerald, who was by now remembering the fear he had experienced the first time he had walked this path several years ago on his own. He could feel the Sandye uneasiness of being watched. His mind was racing so fast, he imagined the dense forest leaning precariously towards him, whispering little secrets to each other as he passed.

As he looked from the rear, he could see that his grandma's legs were covered in little red whelps, and it was obvious she was getting tired from the way she was walking. Jogging to catch them up, he requested that they all rest for a while on a nearby tree stump in the small clearing ahead, at least long enough for his grandma to get her breath back.

'Just rest here for a while,' he suggested, guiding Kathleen to the remains of a once majestic tree. 'We still have a long way to go. Let us eat our lunch now. It will give us the energy to go the rest of the way.'

'I concur,' said Wendy.

'So do I,' whispered Kathleen. 'I didn't want to say anything in case I was stopping you both from going on.'

'Don't be silly,' smiled Wendy. 'We are not in a race. If any of us needs to rest, then we will. We are all looking out for each other and will arrive safely together in one piece in our own time. That's what really matters.'

After their well-earned rest, Wendy rose to her feet and started to pack the remains of their lunch in her backpack.

'Have you had enough to eat Kathleen, and are you OK to continue?' asked Wendy.

'Yes, I'm fine,' she replied. 'My legs were just getting a little shaky and itchy. I should have had more for breakfast,' she said, rising to her feet. 'I should now be alright for the rest of the journey.'

'Good,' said Gerald, still chewing the last of his sandwich. 'We had better get going then. The light will not last for much longer, as the foliage becomes heavier later. I would prefer we get there sooner than later! Even though I have walked to Uncle Tom's in the past, I have still lost my way occasionally. The longer mud track route is impassable by foot and is far too dangerous. I don't know what it is about this damn forest, but it seems to change from time to time.'

Wendy looked at him and scowled.

'Don't say that,' she said sternly. 'You will scare your grandma. Don't listen to him Kathleen, it's only because the overgrowth covers the trail in places, and when it gets darker, it is sometimes harder to navigate. Don't worry. We'll be there in plenty of time.' Gerald just shrugged his shoulders and gave his grandma a reassuring hug.

'Come on grandma, I was only thinking aloud. It just brought back old memories. Memories I care not to remember. That's all. Hey! Don't listen to me,' he said, smiling.

'That's OK son,' said Kathleen, smiling softly to her one and only grandson, which she loves so dearly. 'I understand more than you think. However, it would be nice if we could find an easier way to get to him. I'm not up to all this walking.'

Kathleen gently pulled Gerald's head towards her lips and whispered, 'Your mum is so overprotective. She is only trying to protect me. That's why I love her so much.'

Pulling away gently, he smiled back at her and put his arm around her shoulders, guiding her back on the path to Uncle Tom's.

***

The rest of the journey seemed to go faster now that they had eaten and, before long, they were standing just yards from the rough timber cabin hidden deep within the woods.

Tom's home looked more tattered and worn since Gerald had last visited. He could see that Tom had neglected everything, and Gerald was a little annoyed, especially after he had spent so much of his time putting things right. The yard was littered with bird droppings, leaves, and fallen foliage. It was a right mess.

'What on earth has happened here?' asked Wendy, picking up large pieces of fallen foliage to clear a path to the front door.

'I don't know.' Gerald was seething and shaking his head. 'I'm just getting tired of clearing it all up. He promised me he would at least try, but he has done nothing. I know I said I would help to take care of him, but he is trying my patience!'

'Don't take it to heart, my dear,' said Kathleen. 'Don't forget that your Uncle Tom is a sick man and is too proud to let anyone think otherwise. He does what he can, when he can. So, please give him a wider berth by having a little more patience with him.'

'As you wish, grandma,' he shrugged. 'I'll try my best.'

When all three were standing at the entrance, Gerald lifted his clenched fist, and with a little hesitation, knocked heavily on the rugged door. *Knock – Knock - Knock*

There was no sound at first, but soon heard the jangling of keys, followed by the distinct thud of locks and bolts behind the door.

'Hello!' said the grumpy voice through the gap as he opened the door. 'The groundsman said you would come today. It is about bloody time you got here.'

'I'm so sorry Tom,' said Kathleen, stepping carefully into his doorway. 'I had to have a rest halfway. You know I'm not as young as I used to be,' Tom grumbled a little before smiling at her. He then held her close and kissed her on the cheek.

'Come in,' he grumbled. 'Make yourselves comfortable.'

Gerald waited until everyone else was indoors before entering himself. Quietly closing the door behind him, he turned to greet his uncle.

'Hello again Tom,' he said, smiling. 'How are you today? I see that you have been changing a few things around!'

'Yes,' he replied. 'I was getting a little tired with how things were in my cabin, so I decided to make a few changes around the place. I'm sorry I didn't give much effort to the grounds outside, as it took all my strength to rearrange inside.'

Gerald looked around and could see that Tom had made a good attempt. Knowing that he was incapable of lifting heavy objects, he wondered how his uncle had moved so many heavy items of furniture.

'How did you move all these wardrobes?' asked Gerald and looking very concerned.

'Ah ... I pushed them along the floorboard with the help of that crowbar over there!'

'CROWBAR!' screamed Wendy, looking at the polished wooden floor.

Sure enough, on close inspection, both Gerald, and his mother could see the deep grooves and scratches in the wood, where he had forced the bar under the furniture and scraped them across the highly polished floorboards.

Kathleen scowled and shook her head. She slowly stood up from her chair and made her way across the room to take a closer look.

'Oh, Tom. What have you done to that lovely floor?'

'I tried to make it look better,' said Tom, lowering his head. 'I didn't have any wood filler or stain, so I did my best to stain them with a thick mixture of coffee.'

'So why didn't you wait until Gerald had come?' she said angrily. 'He would have given you a hand.'

'I'm sorry Kathleen. I wasn't thinking. I just wanted to prove to myself that I could still do things on my own. I know, I'm an old fool.'

Tom's eyes welled up with self-pity, but Wendy quickly held his face and kissed him on the cheek.

'You don't have to get yourself so upset,' she said looking at his eyes. 'We are always here to help. Don't be afraid to ask us. That's what families are for. We always stick together and help each other. Now sit-down Tom and make yourself comfortable. I will put the kettle on and serve up the food you have prepared for us.' He smiled softly back at her. Sweeping away his tears, he felt much better than he did before.

Tom was looking ever so old. Gerald could see the difficulty he was having in keeping his cheerful demeanour. He could see that he wasn't comfortable and was just being polite, as usual.

'Are you OK Uncle Tom?' asked Gerald, looking across the table. 'You don't look very well.'

'Well... I've been having a bit of a problem of late with the old waterworks, if you get my meaning!'

'Why, what's up?' asked Gerald, now leaning further towards him.

'I'm... Well, it's not the sort of thing I like to talk about, especially being personal. Please mention nothing to the girls, but I can't seem to pee very well.' Tom looked quite embarrassed about his sudden disclosure, but knew he had to confide in someone, and his nephew was as good a person as anyone. 'Yes, the flow starts and stops, you know, being quite painful.'

'Have you discussed this with Doctor Jachin yet?' replied Gerald with a sense of urgency in his voice.

'No lad. I think it will put itself right in a few days. If it doesn't, I will see him then. It's just a little uncomfortable today, causing me a few cramps, that's all.'

Wendy and Kathleen suddenly burst back into the room from the kitchen, holding cups of tea and all the food that Tom had prepared earlier that day. Placing everything on the table, Tom ceased his personal discussion with Gerald and promptly pulled his chair up to the table.

'Come on then,' said Tom, 'get stuck in. I'm starving. I've had nothing to eat all bloody day waiting for you a lot. Now, forget about saying grace, just eat.' Now, for the first time since his guests arrived, Tom forced a hearty-looking smile beyond his pain.

'Did mum tell you I have my interview at the university tomorrow?' mumbled Gerald, as he munched into a large slice of mince and potato pie.

'Aye lad, she did. I hope with all the studies you've been doing at home and the university, that you have learned enough to do well. It would be nice to see you follow in the footsteps of your father, wouldn't it, Kathleen?'

'Oh yes,' she replied. 'I was so proud of him. You know, the community respected him very well. It was such a sad day when he mysteriously disappeared and an even bigger shock when he passed away. Not only because he died, but the awful way in which he had lost his life.'

'Yes, it was,' whispered Gerald, who had stopped eating and was now staring into nothingness, remembering the last moments of his father's life as he was slain, all those years ago.

'Well, that's enough of that talk,' piped up Wendy. 'The past is the past. We are here to have a nice evening, so let us change the subject, shall we?'

Wendy was getting a little upset about the untimely death of her husband. She had never got over her loss and the way he had died. Gerald sensed this and squeezed her hand.

'Sorry mum. Now Tom, where do you keep that homemade wine of yours?'

'Oh. I believe I still have a little left,' winking back at him. 'I think I have a bottle in the bottom corner cupboard. Have a look.'

Gerald quickly sprang to his feet and made his way to the little wooden door. As he opened it, he began to laugh out loud.

'Ha! Just one bottle Tom, eh!'

There in the cupboard were at least twelve large bottles of his famous elderberry wine. Not at all what he was expecting when he opened the door. Nevertheless, it looked like it may be an interesting evening.

'Oh good,' shrilled Kathleen, as she watched Gerald bring the bottle to the table. 'However, we shouldn't have too much if we are having an early start in the morning.'

'Oh, you're all going to stay the night, then?' grumbled Tom.

'Of course, you nitwit. You don't think for one moment that we are going to try to get back in the dark, do you?' snapped Wendy. 'That would be ludicrous, not to mention dangerous.'

'Forgive me Wendy,' said Tom, looking very embarrassed. 'My mind is not quite with it today. I totally forgot what time of day it is. I'm so sorry, I should have known. You're right. Of course, you can stay.'

Gerald never said a word. He just sauntered slowly around the table, pouring wine into everyone's glass.

'Well, bottoms up!' said Kathleen, standing up from the table. 'Here's to our wonderful family and those of us who can no longer be with us.'

'Hear here,' they all whispered, raising their glasses in unison.

After consuming the entire bottle between them, Tom noticed it was getting late and raised himself from the table. He was a little unstable with the wine and had to hold onto Wendy's shoulders to find his balance.

'Are you OK Tom?' said Kathleen, looking at the surprised look on Wendy's face.

'Shush! Of course, I am,' he said with his finger on his lips. 'Just a little too much wine, that's all.'

'Oh, I've just remembered,' sprouted Gerald. 'I found this box at Grandma's with your initials on it with a combination lock. She said it had been there a long time and that you may remember the combination. Can you? So that we can see what it is.'

'I believe it is *526360A* I think!' slurred Tom. 'However, please leave it in my bedroom and I will explain later when my head is a little clearer.'

'OK,' replied Gerald looking a little disappointed.

'I think we had better call it a night then,' said Gerald winking at his mum. 'Don't forget I have my interview tomorrow and if we are to get an early start, I recommend that we all go to bed now.'

'I agree,' said Wendy.' 'I will help Tom to his room if you could help to make up the spare bed and couch, Gerald. 'Your grandma and I will have the spare bed, and you can have the couch.'

Kathleen cleared the table while Gerald sorted the beds. After struggling to see who was going to use the bathroom first, it wasn't long before they had set their alarm and were fast asleep.

***

The sound of wind rushing through the tops of trees, accompanied by a morning chorus, made Gerald open his eyes. He could clearly hear it coming through the window, that he had left ajar in the living room the night before.

Moments later, the the alarm clock in the spare room sounded, accompanied by the silent movements of others grumbling.

Peeling off his warm blankets and stepping out into the chilly air of the room, Gerald made his way to the bathroom, got dressed and quickly made his way outside to do a few small chores. Meanwhile, Wendy and Kathleen put all their bed linens away, before making everyone's breakfast. There was still no sign of Tom, so being a little curious, Wendy quietly checked on him to see if he was awake, but found him snoring. She decided not to disturb him and let him sleep.

Putting Tom's breakfast to one side in the kitchen, she wrote him a thank-you note and placed it next to his breakfast.

Gerald had finished clearing up the yard area and quickly returned to eat his breakfast.

'We must leave now, mum. I must get back in time to get things ready for my job interview.'

'OK son,' said Wendy. 'We are all done here. I have also packed a few little snacks for along the way. I have put Tom's breakfast in the kitchen and left him a thank-you note, as he is still fast asleep.'

After making sure everything was secure, they put on their coats, stepped outside, and closed the door quietly behind them.

38

CHAPTER

FOUR

The sun was brightly shining through the window when Tom eventually raised his head from the pillow. His head was pounding, and he had a niggling pain across his chest.

'Oh dear,' he thought. *'I think I had a little too much last night! My mouth feels as if I've been chewing dry sawdust. I feel awful.'*

Getting up to make his breakfast, Tom noticed the note Wendy had left and stretched over to get the breakfast she had kindly prepared for him. However, as he turned, he almost blacked out, feeling very dizzy. He immediately placed the food on the kitchen table and made his way over to his comfy sofa. Clutching at his chest in pain, he slumped down in the nearest chair.

***

Later that morning, Wendy and the others had returned to Kathleen's house. Gerald only had

39

a few hours to get himself ready and was soon well underway to attend his interview for the lecturer's position at the University College London on Gower Street, London with Professor Wyatt, a respected physicist. It is the Sandye department his late father *Robert Lindsell* used to work in.

Normally on time for meetings, Gerald turned up twenty minutes earlier than normal. He thought this would give him enough time to compose himself, but as he sat there twiddling his thumbs with several other candidates, the professor's door opened earlier than expected, and out stepped a beautiful young secretary.

'Mr. Gerald Lindsell, please.'

'Yes, that's me,' said Gerald, feeling very nervous. Standing and brushing himself down, he took a deep breath and followed her into another waiting room just outside the professor's office.

'Just sit there Mr. Lindsell, Professor Wyatt will be with you shortly.'

Within seconds, the door frame was filled with the body of a large man. His suit was very ill-fitted, far too small for his middle age spread. The jacket was so full of wrinkles, it looked like it had been slept in for weeks.

'Please step into my office Mr. Lindsell,' said the professor in a deep, gravelly tone.

'Thank you,' replied Gerald, stepping slowly into his office.

The smell of expensive cologne and cigars filled the room, as this hulk of a man passed, finally resting himself in the chair at the opposite side of the desk.

'Hello, I am Professor Shaun Wyatt. I will be conducting this interview today. So, let us begin. What is your name?'

'My name is Gerald Lindsell sir.'

'Ah,' sighed the professor with a slight smile. 'The Lindsell family, eh? ... OK'

'Yes sir, my father was...'

'Yes, I'm aware of who your father was my-good-man,' interrupted the professor. 'I now know who you are. Now, let's see what we have...', as he searched through several candidate's applications.

'Ah, here's your file,' said the professor adjusting his glasses, before turning the pages of the form in front of him.

The interview seemed long and very intense. Some of the professor's questions were difficult and personal, yet Gerald did not take too long to feel confident in his responses.

'So, how do you think you would cope with thirty or so students, firing questions from all sides?' said the professor, clasping both hands in front of his nose.

'Not easy, I know,' answered Gerald. 'Like my father always taught me... large problems are better solved by breaking them down into smaller sections and solve them one at a time.

41

The same applies to the students! I can only answer one question at a time.'

'Ah! I can see that you have a lot of your father in you,' said the professor. 'I can see you following in his footsteps too. I remember him well. He was a brilliant physicist. He was a great asset and loss to this establishment. Never mind Gerald, you should be very proud of him and no doubt he would have been proud of you too, had he still been alive.

Look, I have a few more candidates to interview today. I will let you know if you have been successful by tomorrow afternoon. Any questions before you go?'

'No Sir.'

'Well, that's it for now then. It has been a pleasure meeting you, and I wish you luck.

'Thank you, professor, I look forward to hearing from you.'

Gerald then stood up slowly from his chair smiling. He then shook the professor's hand and promptly left the office.

***

Wendy was sitting at the kitchen table when Gerald arrived home. He took off his jacket and hung it on the back of the door.

'How did it go then?' asked Wendy.

'I think it went OK. I was a little nervous at first, but everything got better as we went on. I should hear by tomorrow, hopefully!'

'That sounds promising!' smiled Wendy. 'Oh, by the way, if you look out the kitchen window, I have a little surprise to show you.'

Gerald slowly made his way to the window...

'What the... Who owns that?'

Standing outside in the back yard, was a large red 4x4 Land Rover Discovery. Wendy stood up from her chair and stood alongside him.

'It's ours,' she said smiling. 'It's not a new one, I couldn't afford that. I thought about Kathleen's age and Tom's failing health.

After yesterday, however, and watching grandma struggle, I thought it better to trade my old car in and get a second-hand car, that can deal with that terrible terrain between your grandma's house and Tom's house. We will get there much quicker and much warmer in wet weather, by going via the off-road track. Especially if we need to get there in an emergency. At least we won't have to walk through that damn forest anymore.'

'Wow,' whispered Gerald. 'Does that mean I can drive it too?'

'We will see son. I'll have to upgrade the insurance.'

'That would be great mum, I can't wait.'

CHAPTER

FIVE

*Meanwhile, in the supernatural
kingdom of Deawilder ...*

The sound of clashing armour could be heard across the courtyard, as Mahabone sat quietly in his chamber shaving his partially bald head. Whilst removing what little blonde hair he had, he looked in his mirror at his grotesque scarred features and began to ponder about his plans for revenge!

The time difference between their two worlds meant that his adversary would not have gained as many years as he had, meaning that Gerald would still be physically younger and stronger than he had ever been! This was not acceptable. He knew he had to depend on his magic. If he was to succeed in defeating Gerald and his accomplices, he had to act now, before it was too late.

Looking out of his dimly lit window, he could see and hear his guards preparing for what was to come. Only the occasional growl from his caged griffins could be heard above his guard's clashing metallic armour, as each griffin devoured their share of scraps from the castle kitchen.

Rubbing his old scars from his last encounter with Gerald, who escaped his grasp all those years ago, began to set his blood on fire!

Tapping his finger against his temple, Mahabone knew he was ready to enact his revenge and claim back what was rightfully his. The toolbox, and his precious little bell.

Only the bell can give him access to travel between his world and the world of the living. Lugging his battle-torn body towards the entrance of his chamber, he filled his lungs to bellow out his orders...

'MASTER AT ARMS!' he barked. The senior guard who was sitting amongst his men, sprang to his feet and scurried over to his master to see what was needed of him.

'Yes master,' grumbled the senior guard, who was now out of breath and wheezing profusely. 'What is your command?'

'Tell everyone to prepare themselves,' snarled Mahabone. 'Gather the guards at the north gate of the castle. We ride out in one hour.'

Bowing to his master, the senior guard turned and prepared his men for imminent departure.

The hour had moved swiftly, as Mahabone headed his way towards the front of his elite guards. Turning to face his army, Mahabone raised his sword, and silence fell.

'No one shall return his blade to his scabbard without drawing the blood of the enemy,' barked Mahabone at the top of his voice. 'Is that understood?'

'Yes master- shouted all his guards in unison.

The guards quickly began to gather their momentum, marching both on foot and on the backs of their very highly trained, yet most unpredictable griffins, *(Creatures that are known for fiercely guarding their treasures and priceless possessions).*

Yard-by-yard, Mahabone's army made their way towards the first of Gerald's accomplices, King Tubal'cain and his hidden kingdom…

And so, the wrath of Mahabone begins! …

CHAPTER

SIX

Mahabone, the powerful necromancer who is determined to enact his revenge on those who assisted his greatest adversary to escape, continued marching his raging army towards his unsuspecting quarry. The first of which, is King Tubal'cain, who's kingdom is located at the top of Mount Boaz. It is a secret kingdom hidden deep within the mountain and whose entrance is heavily guarded. The entrance of which can only be entered by his subjects, or the other *Triglotine* people who live in the lower valley in his kingdom.

Everyone remembers that *Triglotines* are a kind people with weird looking features. They have a small chubby round body, around three feet tall. They have pointed ears and a very wide mouth, which houses a rack of horrible short, spiked teeth and a narrow set of small pig-like eyes. They are a large community, all of which are dressed in serpent-like skins. Today however, Tubal'cain was unaware of the

47

onslaught that was about to descend upon his people.

As always, the King was going about his business, making sure that his people were safe, happy and prosperous. It was the least he could do. They had all been through a lot these past years. Most of them had been slaughtered when Gerald had led them into battle all those years ago.

However, after Gerald had eventually escaped back to his own world with their help, the kingdom had taken King Tubal'cain and his people, years to recover.

Sarika, the Kings daughter, was a fragile young woman, but since the time of the great battle, Tubal'cain made sure she was trained well enough to assist him in his duties, including combat should she ever need to defend herself, the kingdom and their people.

'Excuse me father,' said Sarika, stepping out of her bathroom and holding tightly onto her bathrobe. 'Do I really have to go to my combat training tomorrow? I'm so tired, I just want a day off.'

'Why?' grumbled the King. 'You know how important it is to keep your wits sharpened.'

'I know father, but it seems as if I have been training every day now for weeks-on-end. I just want a little time to myself.'

'You have to understand,' said the King, gently wrapping his arm around her. 'I am your father and I'm only trying to protect the only family I have left. Your mother was taken away from us before her time and I'm not prepared to lose another.'

'I know father, but you must let me breathe now-and-then. Sometimes, I feel as if I'm trapped in my own home. I'm aware I lost my mother, but you must remember I also lost Gerald. Although his physical appearance is not like ours, he is still the only man outside our family I've ever had feelings for.'

After hearing such heartfelt words from his daughter's lips, his heart felt very heavy. He now realised how hard he had been pushing her and how much he had also missed the man who had made his daughter so happy.

Remembering how he thought of Gerald as his own son, he looked at Sarika and sighed.

'Alright, I understand,' he said, holding her face gently in his hands. 'Have this morning off, but I still need you to visit Vaylor at his people. I believe he is helping in the grounds, just outside the main gates. He would like your guidance regarding his food stores and clothing.'

'OK, if I must,' she replied, slowly moving her face away from her father and making her way behind the decency screen to get dressed. At least it will be relaxing. I love Vaylor and his people. They are so friendly and especially loyal.'

49

Tubal'cain watched as she threw her robe over the top of the screen, remembering how his late wife used to do the same. *'She is so much like her mother'* he thought, and with a gentle sigh, quietly left her chamber.

Vaylor, a fellow *Triglotine*, is a kind and gentle man, who has been a good and loyal friend for many years. Ever since he assisted Gerald in his escape, he had witnessed his own village being raised to the ground and a clear majority of his people being slaughtered by Mahabone.

Afterward, Vaylor was humble enough to ask Tubal'cain if he and the remaining survivors of his people, could serve under the Kings reign. This was immediately granted, because of his people's loyalty in recent years.

Vaylor and his people were very grateful of this. They also asked if they could rebuild their village near the border of Tubal'cain's hidden kingdom. Not so close to give away the entrance to the kingdom, but close enough to feel safe should anything happen.

After a long deliberation with his advisors to assess any implications regarding security protocols, including any concerns that his daughter Sarika may have, King Tubal'cain finished his pondering and finally sanctioned Vaylor's request. Sarika was now aware of her duties to oversee the needs of Vaylor's people and to assist them wherever possible.

A great deal has happened in her world since Gerald left to go to his own. However, Sarika still misses him dearly. Even though there is a time difference between their two worlds, meaning that she has aged more quickly, making her much older than Gerald. However, she still longed for his return.

She had given him a talisman many years ago in hope that one day he may use it to return. Nevertheless, she knows it is nothing but a lost hope. Acknowledging that she must keep her head out the clouds, she must concentrate on her own responsibilities to her own people.

***

Mahabone's army had stopped to rest and eat, while they fed and watered their griffins.

Looking across and above the heads of his subordinates, the senior guard looked curiously at Mahabone as he approached. He watched as his master climbed down from his ride, who then preceded to remove several objects from around his person, before slamming them hard against the large rock at his feet.

'Oh dear!' mumbled the senior guard to one of his men. 'Something has upset the master again. Do you think I should wander over... to see if he will tell me what's troubling him?'

'Better you than me!' squirmed the other guard. 'You know what he is like... he'll chew your balls off and spit them out, as soon as look at you.'

'Ay, maybe you're right. However, I think I still better go to him. I remember something I had witnessed about that Gerald. I had forgotten all about it until now. I might have some information that may, or may not be significant. You never know, it might cheer him up, or on the other hand, it may not!'

Putting his hand on the senior guard's shoulder, the other guard just sniggered and simply replied, 'Good luck.'

***

Mahabone sat with his back against the rock, chewing on his last piece of dried meat. The senior guard stopped and took a breath, before stealthily approaching his master with caution from behind.

'What do you want?' grumbled Mahabone.

'Sorry for interrupting master, but the guards have noticed that something may be troubling you, and I was wondering if...'

'Wondering what? You're a blithering idiot!' barked Mahabone, not even giving his guard the chance to finish. 'Be off with you and leave me alone.'

'Master, I was only hoping you could give me an answer to lifting the spirits of your men. You always said they fight better when they know you are happy.'

Mahabone was just about to bark again but then realised that his senior Guard was completely right.

'On second thoughts,' sneered Mahabone. 'As you are the only guard I trust, I will enlighten you, but you must never tell the others the truth I'm about to tell you. Should you betray me, I will tear your pitiful soul into shreds and return you to dust. Do you understand?'

'Yes Master, completely.'

'Good. Then after I have spoken, you should only raise their spirits by telling them something completely different instead. Do I make myself clear?

'Yes, master.'

'Over millennia, I have collected a selection of magical tools. These are the tools that allow me to travel from realm to realm. I placed them in a special toolbox. Many years ago, Gerald's grandfather stole it and returned to his own realm by using my little bell called *The Sleeper*. I won't go into too much detail, but this little bell allowed Gerald to escape with one of my *Ouroboros* rings and return to his own realm. The *Sleeper* bell allowed him to go home, but as the bell only works one way, Gerald can never

53

return with it. You see, Gerald could only enter this world through his dreams when his family was cursed. But since his family retrieved all the objects given to me, their curse was broken. Now the *Ouroboros* ring and *Sleeper* are lost in his realm forever, and I can't get them back!'

'Ah! That now makes sense,' said the senior guard. 'However, this has reminded me of something I had witnessed in your last confrontation with Gerald many years ago...'

'Reminded you of what?' barked Mahabone, who had now turned to face his trusted guard.

'You're telling me that Gerald would not be able to return to this realm. However, I distinctly remember the quiet rumours that Tubal'cain's daughter had been seen giving Gerald a Talisman for safe keeping. It was said she gave him this in the hope he would return, should he wish to do so. It was also believed that it was Tubal'cain himself, who had given Gerald the sword called *Shibboleth,* that was used to injure you.'

'Is that so?' said Mahabone. 'This is very interesting. In fact, now that I know he has the *Talisman*, should your information be correct, may become very useful indeed.

Although I can't get to Gerald's realm without my precious little *Sleeper* bell. Maybe there is a way I can use my powers to trick Gerald to use this so-called *Talisman.* I could get him to bring back everything.

Today I will exact my revenge on all those who assisted Gerald. Then I will also use my dark powers through this *Talisman* to influence the demise of all who love him. ...*His family*!

I shall ensure he uses his *Talisman* by influencing the mind of the one who loves him in my realm... Tubal'cain's daughter, Sarika. He will be given no choice, but to return with everything that is rightfully mine.'

'That sounds splendid master. Now what should I tell the others?'

'Tell them I am planning our assault as we go. Tell them I have been pondering on which way to give them a glorious victory and if they fight well with honour, I won't kill them.'

Mahabone snarled as he looked at all his guards spread across the expanse. Forcing his lips to produce an evil smile, he turned to his senior guard.

'I think that will make them eager and thankful, don't you think?' smirked Mahabone. 'I have been good enough to give them the opportunity to fight for their lives and feed on the spoils of battle... They should be grateful.'

'Yes master,' croaked the guard. 'I will inform them immediately.'

With this, the senior guard hurriedly made his way back to his subordinates, where he relayed the message and gave instructions for it to be passed around the camp.

This caused a fearful stir within the ranks, yet, none would dare to complain, followed by the odd false loud cheer to appease their master.

Resting time was obviously over, as the ranks watched Mahabone raise himself to his feet and re-mount his now restless griffin.

Once again, Mahabone addressed his army by lifting his staff above his head, sending shafts of lightning spiralling precariously towards the now darkened sky.

'We ride into battle!' barked Mahabone. 'Prepare to ride out.'

Within minutes, his battle-hardened guards were either mounted on their griffins or marching on foot, quickly tearing up the land or anyone who stood in their way as they advanced towards their first destination; King Tubal'cain's kingdom.

It was not long before Mahabone and his guards descended mercilessly upon the borders of Tubal'cain and his men. Metal clashing and the sounds of war cry, Mahabone, and his men plunged forward into Tubal'cain's unsuspecting guards. They didn't have a chance! Even the guards at the entrance to the kingdom were not prepared for the sudden onslaught.

One by one, the kingdom's defences were taken by surprise, where Mahabone's hoards entered the bowels of the underground kingdom and ultimately, to King Tubal'cain's chambers.

CHAPTER
SEVEN

Deep in the *Triglotine's* village, Sarika rubbed the dirt from the root vegetables she had been pulling up from the fields. She often helps the villagers and wasn't afraid to get dirty. They had grown to love her and have become accustomed by the way she rolls up her sleeves and how she simply forgets her royalty status, before getting to work as one of their own.

Just as Sarika placed the last of the crop in the wagon, a loud rumble could be heard in the distance, stopping everyone in their tracks. They looked around to see where the noise was coming from.

Moments later, one of the workforces started shouting out-loud.

'Over there Your Royal Highness. Look! Above the old oak trees! Over there on the north horizon!'

Sarika scowled, as she witnessed the plume of black smoke rising beyond the horizon and in the direction of her home.

Standing there, paralyzed and perplexed, the realisation of some unfortunate disaster filled her heart with fear.

Vaylor and his security men also witnessed the plume of smoke in the distance and raced his contingent quickly towards the princess.

She was still in shock as he and his men approached, so he carefully placed his hand on her shoulder.

'Come with me Your Highness,' said Vaylor in a soft, yet nervous voice. 'We need to get there as soon as we can. We don't know what has happened, but by the amount of smoke, it is obvious something disastrous has taken place.'

'Yes, you're right Vaylor,' she barked with a new sense of emergency in her voice. 'We need to get moving immediately.'

***

Mahabone slowly stepped over the blood-drenched bodies of his enemies, as he made his way towards the locked doors of King Tubal'cain's chambers. Raising the hilt of his sword within his fist, he struck three heavy blows on the doors.

'Come out you coward!' bellowed Mahabone, at the top of his voice, 'come and face your destiny.'

R. L. Barnes.

A moment of silence was followed by the sound of unlatching bolts, the clanking of keys and creaky locks. The worn hinges of the enormous wooden doors squealed in pain, as the king's inner guard pulled the doors ajar.

'Who goes there?' asked the guard in a trembling voice, knowing that it was a silly question, but it was his duty to ask anyway.

'Out of the way, you stupid idiot,' sneered Mahabone. Take me to that excuse of a man you call your king,' pushing the guard harshly to one side.

'Stand fast!' interrupted Tubal'cain. 'He is only one man doing his duty.' The King stepped forward into the light. 'I know who you are Mahabone and you are mistaken. I will not be afraid, nor shall I bow down to anyone in my own home.'

With this, Mahabone stepped towards the King and with a swift tap of his sword, used his deep magic to bind the king.

'You should be afraid.' said Mahabone. 'You should be extremely terrified,' slowly placing the tip of his sword to the king's throat.

Tubal'cain was helpless. He was bound so tight; he could barely breathe.

'I have devoured your kingdom and slain all your guards,' growled Mahabone. 'My sources tell me that it was YOU... who assisted Gerald in his escape all those years ago, with his last

60

heirloom and my *Ouroboros* ring, by lending him your enchanted sword *Shibboleth*.'

Gasping for every breath, Tubal'cain's face was turning a shade of blue. He was unable to answer. Mahabone totally ignored him and continued...

'I could have destroyed you with all my power. However, I wanted to enjoy watching the pain and suffering of your people... and the satisfaction of personally executing your death by my own hand. I am also a being with honour,' he said grinning. 'I will allow your daughter to live if only to see her squirm in mourning at her father's death.'

With this, Mahabone tightened his grasp on the hilt of his sword, carefully replacing the tip just below the prominence of the king's thyroid cartilage. With a victorious smile of satisfaction on his face, Mahabone pushed the sword to the back of the King's spine. With the snapping of bones and blood gushing from his fatal wound, Tubal'cain groaned and gurgled away his last breath, before slumping lifeless to the floor.

Mahabone stood menacingly above his quarry and looked pleased with his handy work. Wiping the blood from his sword, he took a deep breath and placed it back in his scabbard.

'One down,' he muttered, 'several still to go!'

***

Sarika ran as fast as her legs could carry her, as she looked upon the doors to her father's kingdom. There were bodies strewn everywhere and the smell of burning flesh filled the air.

'What the hell...?' she could barely speak. 'What has happened here?'

Vaylor and his contingent were only seconds behind and quickly ordered his men to protect the princess and scout the area for any survivors or evidence to what happened.

'Stay with us Your Highness,' said one of the guards, 'come this way until we know it is safe.'

Vaylor slowly made his way to the entrance of the underground kingdom, but the great doors were tightly closed. There was no sound of the great horns, nor was there a *Gate Keeper* to be seen! This was highly unusual.

'Where the hell is everybody? Surely someone is still manning the gates!'

With the sound of his men crying out from behind, Vaylor turned to see what they had found. There in the distance, he could see his men leading a handful of the Kings bedraggled guards towards him.

'Stop there!' shouted Vaylor at the top of his voice, 'I will come to you.'

Quickly running towards his men, he beckoned the guards who were protecting the princess to follow.

'Do they know what happened?' shouted Vaylor as he approached.

'Yes sir,' said one of his men, they said it was Mahabone. He came without warning and slaughtered everyone he and his men could lay their hands on. The remainder of his men took to hiding and insist that he is still inside the kingdom with his men. And there is very bad news!'

'What of the sad news?' ordered the princess as she approached with the guards. 'Tell me now damn it!'

The guard looked at Vaylor for support, but he only nodded for him to go ahead.

'I'm so sorry Your Highness,' said the guard looking very sheepish. 'I don't really know how to put this... I am...'

'Oh, for God's sake man, spit it out,' snapped Sarika.

'Sorry... I'm sorry to inform you that the King is dead.

'Dead! What the hell do you mean, Dead?'

'I'm so sorry Your Highness,' said the guard shaking in his boots. 'Several of these guards witnessed the King's lifeless body, as well as watching Mahabone bragging about how he did it. All his men were celebrating just before he took them all inside and closed the doors.'

Sarika slumped to her knees in a fit of screams and tears. Only Vaylor had the courage to put his arm around her shoulders, to console her the best way he could.

'We can't do anything here Your Highness,' whispered Vaylor. 'This means you are now our Queen. We must regroup back at the village to plan how we can retake the kingdom.'

'I agree' she said softly through her tears. 'We need to take back what is rightfully ours and kill that son-of-a-bitch!'

After leaving a few guards to keep an eye on the kingdom entrance, Vaylor, Sarika and the remainder of the contingent returned swiftly to their village and to gather the remainder of their people.

'Now listen up!' shouted Vaylor at the top of his voice. 'The king is now dead, and the princess Sarika is now our queen. Please gather around to hear what she has to say.'

All the people tightly gathered around to listen to the Princess. Sarika prepared herself, as she stood precariously on a large log to peer above the heads of Vaylor's villagers.

'People of the Triglotine village,' she shouted. 'An evil darkness has unfortunately fallen on my people, and many are now dead.'

The sound of everyone taking a deep intake of breath could be clearly heard across the listening crowd.

'Mahabone has descended upon us,' she shouted, 'He has taken over the underground kingdom and I need your help. I need to ask you all a great favour.'

The sounds of muttering fell silent amongst the people, as each ear attuned itself to what was coming next.

'Now that I am queen of what is left of my father's kingdom, would you do me the honour of becoming my subjects? We can come together and fight to regain what is ours. To defeat this heartless tyrant, so that he can harm us no more. What do you say?

The people of the village stood in silence, looking at each other for an answer.

'Well then!' Vaylor shouted as he looked over the heads of his silent villagers. 'Time is not on our side people. What do you say?'

After a few seconds of deliberation, there came a unanimous...

'AYE.'

***

Mahabone sat comfortably on his new throne, sniggering at what he had achieved. He had raided every corner of his adversary's underground kingdom and even got his hands on Tubal'cain's famous enchanted sword '*Shibboleth*.'

'It's mine!' he smirked. 'Now nothing can stand in my way.'

Raising *Shibboleth* into the air and with a few incantations, *Shibboleth* turned a bright red in recognition of its new master, before being placed back in the vault for safe keeping.

'It is now time for the next step in my plan to bring Gerald back to my world,' whispered Mahabone to himself. 'Time to make sad events happen in Gerald's world and time to plant the seed for Gerald in the mind of Princess Sarika, or should I say... Queen.'

***

Meanwhile, in the *Triglotines* village, Queen Sarika ordered Vaylor to gather his troops to prepare them for battle. However, Vaylor had advised her that their numbers were low and asked if there was any other way to find additional help.

'What can we do Your Highness?' asked Vaylor, looking very worried indeed.

'I'm not sure,' Sarika murmured while tapping her fingers on her forehead.

Not knowing that she was being influenced by Mahabone's dark magic, Vaylor watched as her face began to change. Her eyes became large and bright and her smile began to grow from ear-to-ear.

'THAT'S IT!' she shouted. 'Gerald. I can get Gerald to come back!'

'What do you mean Your Highness? He has been gone for years. He will never remember us.'

'Don't you remember Vaylor? I gave him that *Talisman*. The enchanted one that will allow him a one-way ticket back to me!'

'Oh Yes! I can remember Your Highness, but how will he know how?'

Sarika ran to her satchel and rummage around for a little while.

'Here it is,' and pulled out the other half of the *Talisman*. 'I can use this to contact him. If he has it in proximity, I will be able to reach him in his dreams.'

'Well then,' said Vaylor. 'What are we waiting for? Let's get started.'

CHAPTER

EIGHT

Back in Gerald's world ...

It had only taken a few days before Gerald received the news he had been waiting for. The professor's secretary had taken immense pleasure informing him that his application for a position at University College as a lecturer in physics, had been successful and that they seek his immediate attendance.

This is what he had always wanted, the opportunity to follow in the footsteps of his father.

His new position meant that he was now able to provide more for his mother, grandmother, Tom and of course, save a little for himself too.

Today was the big day. It was late morning and will be his first day at the university as a physicist. He had studied there several times before in the past, yet this time the feeling was very different.

'*I may have the responsibility of teaching twenty to thirty students,*' he thought, as the hairs on the back of his neck stood on edge.

Walking into the staff room on arrival, the adrenalin cascading through his body was now sending shivers up and down his spine, as a member of staff approached.

'Hello,' said the voice behind the smile of a beautiful blonde woman, holding a large pile of files. 'You must be Mr. Lindsell?'

'Yes, I am,' he replied nervously. 'However, you can call me Gerald if you like.'

'Thank you, Gerald. My name is Sandra Williamson, I am the senior archaeologist here. However, everyone here knows me as *Sandy*. You may call me that if you wish,' she said with a smile. 'I am one of Professor Wyatt's personal secretaries. Please follow me to the briefing room, where I will introduce you and inform you of your duties.'

Gerald's vision of the briefing room was not quite what he expected. It was a large area with sparse furnishings. Only a few chairs had been neatly positioned, to form a semi-circle around a small desk, which had been placed in front of the large blackboard on the wall. The rest of the area was completely void of furnishings, making each of his footstep's echo, as he walked across the room. It was a cold and lifeless place and made him feel a little uneasy.

R. L. Barnes.

'Just sit here Gerald,' said Sandy in a soft voice. 'The others will be here shortly.'

'Others?' he asked.

'Yes. All the lecturers meet here each morning to be briefed on their duties for the day. It also gives everyone a chance to debate their concerns, and to put the world to rights, so to speak,' rolling her eyes as she spoke.

'Oh, I see,' said Gerald, lowering himself into one of the chairs. Sandy smiled at him and took her position in front of the desk.

Excuse me for asking Sandy, but do I know you? Your face looks so familiar.'

'I don't think so. Where are you from?' she asked politely.

'I live in Kerrison Road, London. Just around the corner from the local Fish & Kebab shop on the corner with Falcon Road.'

'That's weird. I lived there a few years ago too.'

'You never did!' he said, looking surprised.

'I did. I worked as a cashier in the local corner shop.'

'I remember you,' he said smiling. 'You served me when I bought presents for my grandmother.'

'That's right.' she smiled. 'I do remember. I told you to have a nice day and hope to see you there again soon. You did say you were away visiting at the time.'

'Yes, I did think of you when I was away, but when I got back home from my visit, I went to the shop to see you. Unfortunately, the shop keeper said you had left for a new position at a university. I asked him which university, but he did not know. I was really gutted that I missed you.'

'Were you?' she said looking rather flattered.'

'Yes, I was. However, I had no idea it was this university.'

'I was studying for my degree back in those days,' she replied. I only worked in that shop in my spare time, until I was lucky enough to get a working position here in the university. Much like yourself.'

'So, what's your speciality.' he asked. 'What do you excel at?'

'I love to tinker around with unusual artifacts. Find out their history and origins. I also have a personal interest in mythology, parapsychology and demonology in my spare time.'

'That sounds interesting,' he smiled. 'So, how are you doing these days?'

'I'm doing fine,' she replied. 'I still look after my parents from time to time, but I also have my own place here on campus.'

'Married?' he asked, trying his best not to sound too forward.

'I'm afraid not. What with my career and parents to watch-over, I've never really had time to socialise.'

'I'm not married either. I've spent most of my time in books, but I'm so pleased I had the opportunity to meet you again. Maybe one day when you're free, we can grab a coffee together. What do you say?'

'I don't know Gerald, but I'll certainly give it some thought.'

'OK, just let me know if you change your mind.'

'I will,' she smiled. 'Thank you.'

One-by-one, the familiar and unfamiliar faces of his peers started to enter the room.

'Good morning everyone,' said Sandy trying to sound polite. 'Before we get started this morning, I would like to introduce you to Gerald Lindsell, our new lecturer in physics. I know some of you knew and worked with his father and as it is Gerald's first day here, I would like you all to make him feel welcome in his new role.'

The briefing seemed to take hours to complete. However, Gerald had now been formally introduced to his new colleagues and was fully aware of his duties. He had now been given his first class, which consists of twenty-first-year students, but with the memories of his own first year as a student, he knew what to expect!

With all his notes now in hand, he made his way to his allocated theatre, peered at his students through the window, took a deep breath and entered the room.

***

Wendy settled Kathleen in the garden, and with a nice cup of tea, sat soaking up the sun next to the pond. Just when they were getting relaxed, the sound of the telephone could be heard ringing through the patio doors.

With a few moans and groans, Wendy peeled herself from her comfy sun lounger, made her way back inside and took the call.

'Hello.' she said quietly.

'Excuse me, is that Mrs. Kathleen Lindsell?'

'No. This is her daughter-in-law, Wendy Lindsell. Can I take a message?'

The telephone fell silent for a few seconds before the voice on the other end began to speak again.

'I am sorry to be the bearer of sad news madam. I am Dr Bates. I am currently at the hospital with Mr. Tom Lindsell...'

'Oh, dear God no!' shrilled Wendy, almost dropping the telephone. 'My God, what happened?'

'He has had a heart attack, madam. It just so happened that one of the groundsmen needed to hand him a package. He thought it

73

R. L. Barnes.

strange when there was no answer, so he took it upon himself to look through his window and was shocked to find him lying face down on the floor with the room looking damaged in places, possibly from him falling. Currently there are no suspicious circumstances. However, the police will be conducting a full investigation just to make sure. I have a duty to inform you of his condition. Mr Lindsell was airlifted straight to hospital via helicopter. Mrs. Lindsell, we need someone from his family to visit him... Just in case!'

'Of course, of course...' Wendy tried to gather her thoughts... 'Where do we go?'

'Have you got a pen Mrs Lindsel?'

'Yes, doctor, please go ahead,' she replied.

'Good. The Heart Centre is based in Bartholomew's Hospital at: W Smithfield, London EC1A 7BE.' He then finished the call.

'Heaven's... Poor Tom!' she thought. *'What the hell do I tell Kathleen and Gerald?'*

'Who was that then?' quizzed Kathleen.

'I don't quite know how to say this...' whispered Wendy, finding it difficult to find the rights words.

'Say what?' demanded Kathleen, looking a little perplexed.

'It's Tom...'

'Oh dear,' tutted Kathleen. 'What's he gone and done now? I told him to be careful...'

'No Kathleen... He's had a heart attack!'
Kathleen almost collapsed on the floor.

'How? What on-earth happened? she
sobbed, trying her best to console herself.

'The doctor believes he had a massive heart
attack. Tom is barely alive and the doctor wants
a member of family to visit him in hospital.'

Wendy continued to explain to Kathleen
what they think happened and how he was
found.

Gerald suddenly walked through the front
door at the end of his first shift, only to find his
mum and grandmother staring at him with long
faces.

'Oh! what's with the long faces then?' he
asked sarcastically, putting his briefcase on the
floor. 'I've had a good yet frustrating day today,
but I'm pleased it's over. I'm absolutely
shattered. By the way, did anyone notice those
funny oxide smells again from those copper
pipes at the front door?'

'Yes, the gas man said not to worry,
remember? However, there is something more
important to say to you. I think you better sit-
down son,' said Wendy, holding tightly onto
Kathleen's arm.

'Why, what's up?' his face now looking a little
worried. 'What have I done wrong this time?'

'It's not what you have done dear boy,'
interrupted Kathleen. 'I'm afraid it is your
Uncle Tom. The doctor telephoned and said he

had collapsed with a heart attack and was all alone in that wooden cabin of his.'

Kathleen started to sob uncontrollably, burying her head into Wendy's chest.

Gerald's mouth dropped open. His mind was a total blank and was at a loss for words.

'I'm so sorry. I just don't know what to say! Who found him...? I mean..., what was said about the circumstances?'

'The doctor said there were no suspicious circumstances at the scene,' said Wendy wiping her eyes. 'However, they are going to take him to the hospital to confirm why he had the heart attack.'

'So, what happens now?' asked Gerald.

Wendy stood up and placed her hand on his shoulder. 'They have asked us to go and visit him. Will you come with me? I can't ask grandma to do this and I can't do this alone.'

'Of course, I will mum, it's the least I can do.'

'Thank you,' she quietly whispered, gently squeezing his hand. 'We must be there in an hour, so we had better get ourselves ready. Your grandma said she would like to stay here. She can't face seeing him in that condition you see! She would prefer to say get-well prayers for him.'

Kathleen sat rocking in her chair next to the open fire, while Wendy and Gerald got ready to visit Tom at the hospital.

Seeing them both off at the door, Kathleen indicated that she would keep herself busy, by having tea ready for when they returned home.

***

Arriving, both Wendy and Gerald approached the side entrance to the hospital leading to the acute cardiac ward. It looked cold and very unwelcoming.

Gerald was first to enter through the double doors, closely followed by his mother, who by now, had quickly hung onto his arm. There was an awful smell of faeces and stale urine emanating from several cubicles as they passed, that seemed to crawl over every part of their exposed skins, making them cringe at each other until they reached the nurse's station.

'Hello,' said Wendy. 'I am Mrs. Wendy Lindsell and this is my son. We have come to visit Mr Tom Lindsell who was brought after having a heart attack.'

'And what is your relationship to him?'

'I guess he will be my uncle-in-law,' replied Wendy.'

'Just a moment,' said the ward sister. 'Let me just check for you.'

'Is he OK,' asked Gerald, but there was no response from the nurse, who quickly turned towards them.

'Yes Mrs Lindsell,' she said. 'Mr Lindsell is in cubicle 4. Please follow me and I'll show you the way.'

The nurse guided them through another set of doors, that led down a narrow corridor. It seemed a long walk, but they eventually arrived at another set of double doors.

'You will find Mr Lindsell on the right, just next to the window,' smiled the nurse. 'I will inform the doctor you are here and he will be in to see you later.'

Wendy and Gerald walked towards the bed that was currently hidden by the large decency screen. Not knowing what they were going to find behind the curtain, they slowly pulled it to one side.

For a moment, you could hear a pin drop as the tears welled up in their eyes, whilst Tom lay there with wires and tubes everywhere. The silence was deafening.

'Well?' groaned Tom, who seemed to come across his usual arrogant self.

Wendy, who was tearful, angry and relieved all at the same time, quickly responded...

'Are you OK? What has the doctor said?'

'He said I'm out of danger apparently,' he replied. 'But I must take things easy. No more living my usual lifestyle. He said he would explain things to you when he finishes his rounds.'

'How many times have we told you about living in that cabin all on your own,' she said squeezing his hand. 'Now look what's happened to you. You either must live closer to us, or at least live where you'll have immediate access to medical attention, should you become ill again. So, tell us, what can you remember?'

'Not much really,' he sighed. 'I was making myself some lunch and walked through to the living-room. The next thing I can remember was having a terrible pain in my jaw, chest and down my left arm. I felt very lightheaded and dizzy and remember falling onto several pieces of furniture, before hitting the floor. Then I woke up here.'

'Jesus Tom,' whispered Gerald. 'We all thought we had lost you.'

'I'm sorry if I made you all worry,' said Tom. 'I...'

'Don't be silly,' said Wendy. 'We are just thankful that you are still here with us. We love you dearly.' Suddenly, the curtain was drawn back.

'Hello Mrs Lindsell, I'm Dr Bates. It was I who telephoned you earlier about his condition. Pleased to meet you.'

'I wish it had been under much better circumstances doctor. However, can you please explain to me the details and how you can help him?'

R. L. Barnes.

'Don't worry,' smiled the doctor. 'Tom is a tough old boot and he will be fine. It took us a little while to stabilise him, but we are happy with his progress now. He has been overdoing things and must learn to slow down.'

'We have been telling him that for years,' said Gerald. 'But he can be a little stubborn sometimes.'

'Yes, we can believe that,' smiled the doctor. 'He has certainly shown staff his determination not to change his point of view, on anything.

We have decided to keep him here for week for observations and if all goes well, he should be able to go home. However, may I suggest he doesn't return to his cabin in the woods.'

'I agree doctor,' said Wendy. 'We have been telling him more times than we can remember. We can make provisions at home, until we find him something more suitable.'

'That will be great Mrs Lindsell. Now don't worry too much about Mr Lindsell, he is in good hands.

'Thank you doctor,' smiled Gerald.

After the doctor left, Wendy and Gerald spent a few quiet moments with Tom, but when Wendy noticed he was getting very tired, she kissed him on the forehead and explained they would leave him to rest in the care of the hospital. She told him that the family are looking forward to seeing him in a week when he can hopefully come home. Tom simply squeezed her hand and smiled before closing his eyes.

Their little ordeal now over, Wendy and Gerald left the confines of the hospital. Both relieved, they huddled their way back to the car and returned home to Kathleen.

CHAPTER

NINE

It was almost four weeks after Tom had returned home, when a registered letter arrived that Friday, addressed to Kathleen.

She carefully opened the letter and noticed that it was clearly marked with a solicitor's logo. Looking bewildered at Tom, Wendy and her grandson, she silently read what was written within...

> *Oracle Solicitors*
> *Aviation House*
> *125 Kingsway*
> *London*
> *WC2B 6NH*
>
> *'Dear Kathleen Lindsell,*
>
> *I wish to introduce myself as Tom Lindsell's solicitor.*
> *I also wish to inform you, that Mr Lindsell has instructed me to carry out*

his wishes as a matter of urgency. I have therefore completed all the legalities regarding his wishes.

Furthermore, I am now asking his family to attend my office on this coming Monday at 10:00am to discuss his instructions.

Yours Sincerely'

*Ashly Mahoney
Solicitor.*

Tom just sat there smiling.

What's all this about Tom?' asked Kathleen.

'I have just been making a few decisions, that's all. I had a fright when I had the heart attack and wanted to sort a few things out in case it happens again. Hopefully what I have in mind will benefit all of us. However, I'm saying nothing more until you see my solicitor on Monday.'

'I don't want to travel all the way there. If we have you in our lives, that's all that matters.'

'Don't worry yourself grandma,' whispered Gerald. 'Mum and I will take care of everything.'

***

Monday morning arrived early at the Lindsell's home after a stressful weekend. Not knowing

83

what to expect at the solicitors, Gerald `stood fidgeting, whilst Wendy prepared the car for their journey to see the family solicitor.

Kathleen, bless her, just remained seated on the sofa next to Tom, who was quietly smiling from ear to ear.

'Are you sure you just want to stay here grandma?' whispered Gerald softly, placing his hand on her shoulder.

'Yes darling, I feel better keeping Tom company. He still needs a little TLC you know. Don't worry, I'll be fine. You two just go and see what it is all about.'

'OK grandma, if that's what you want.'

'Are we ready to go then?' asked Wendy. 'The car is warmed up and the sat-nav is all set up to go. We'll have to leave now if we want to find his office in time. I know Tom has instructed his solicitor, but we've never had to deal with him ourselves. So, let's get our skates on. If we get there well before 10am, we'll just find a café and get a cup of tea... Yes?'

Not a word was spoken, just the polite nod with a half-baked smile was observed.

It was 8:15am when they left for the solicitors, but after turning down several unknown streets and the stress of finding a free parking space, they did not arrive at his office until 9:50am.

'Damn!' said Gerald patting his pockets. 'I've left my pager on the kitchen table.'

'Don't worry son, your mother has left hers too and I don't have one! I could never understand the bloody things. All this new technology is far too complicated for the likes of me.'

'We'd better get in the solicitor's office right away,' said Wendy, gasping and wheezing her way up the stairs to his office.

'Welcome Mrs Lindsell. I am Ashly Mahoney, Tom Lindsell's solicitor.'

'Thank you,' smiled Wendy. 'And this is my son Gerald.'

'Pleased to meet you, Gerald. I take it Kathleen has not come with you then?'

'Sorry, No,' replied Wendy. 'She decided to stay indoors to keep Tom company.'

'OK,' said Ashly. 'Well let's get down to business. Please take a seat.'

It was a bewildering atmosphere, as they sat listening to the solicitor read out Tom's instructions. Everyone thought he didn't have a lot of material wealth, still, Wendy and Kathleen received £8,000 each. To Gerald's surprise, Tom had signed over his wooden home, the entire contents, the livestock, as well as the surrounding two acres of land to him.

Obviously, they all preferred Tom to keep it all for himself, but this was the secret behind his earlier smile.

The solicitor briefly explained that Tom wanted to make sure that everyone was catered for, in the event he had a serious relapse. It was also explained that Tom was going to take things very easy from now on, by finding a more suitable accommodation with the help of his family.

'In fact,' said Ashly. 'I hope you don't mind that I have listed a few properties for him to look at tomorrow, if that's convenient for you?'

'That will be great Ashly,' smiled Wendy. 'I can drive him to see them tomorrow. Thank you.'

After spending a few minutes gathering documentation and keys from the solicitor, they gathered their thoughts and left his office with a spring in their step.

'Are we going straight home?' asked Gerald. 'Or can we go to Tom's house to check it out?'

'I think we should go to Tom's,' said Wendy quietly. 'I would like to go and make sure the cabin is all secure.'

'OK' he whispered.

'I know it was Tom's, but we must remember he has now given it to you. It is now going to be your responsibility to look after it properly.

By the time they arrived at the cabin, the midday light was beginning to diminish because of the overgrown treetops.

'Heavens, you wouldn't think it was daytime...' said Gerald looking out the car window.

The bottom half of the surrounding forest was dark, but you could see the increasing glow of green foliage as one scanned towards the treetops.

'This looks without Uncle Tom,' continued Gerald.

Wendy turned her head slightly towards her son and mumbled quietly under her breath... 'It's only because things are different now. It will never feel the same without him living in it.'

'I suppose you are correct mum. I'm just getting flashbacks of our time together and the foraging we used to do here. He used to have a great time. But now that he has to take things easy, he could never come back here. It would be too much for him...'

'Here we are,' interrupted Wendy.

The car swung heavily into the gravel that encompassed the wooden cabin, creating a harsh *swoosh* as the vehicle came to an abrupt halt.

'What a day,' blurted Wendy aloud. Before we do anything, let's get inside, get the fire working and make ourselves a nice cup of tea. We will just take our time today. We can air the place out and secure it before going home.'

The cabin was freezing! The dark belly of the forest had starved the cabin of sunlight and heat. Looking around, nothing had been moved. Everything was in the same place Tom

87

had left it. There were dirty cups, plates, and clothing everywhere. It was a right man's cave.

Wendy walked over and stroked the back of Tom's favourite chair.

After making a brew, Gerald proceeded to get firewood from the shed. Thankfully, it wasn't too long before they could hear the familiar crackling of a well stoked fire. The heat was tremendous and very welcome.

'Now that the place is warm, aired, partially cleaned and secure,' said Wendy. 'I think we will leave the rest of the mess for another day. I think we have done enough for today... Do you agree?'

Gerald's face was buried in the glow of the fire, rubbing his chin...

'Listen mum... Why don't you go back home and leave me here? I have a few things on my mind I wish to clarify. I wouldn't mind staying here on my own.'

'Why is that dear?' she asked inquisitively.

'It has been a while since I was last here. I also have memories here from when Tom instructed me about past family matters. I just want to have a chance to remember it all. There are so many things here to remind me about our conversation, regarding those terrible things that happened to our family in the past. I just need a little time to myself. You know, to get things clear in my head. I don't know how to explain what I mean, but I hope you understand?'

'I thought we had forgotten what happened in the past?' said Wendy. 'However, if that's what you want son, I can't stop you. After all, this cabin does belong to you now.'

'I know mum, but there is something bothering me and I don't know what it is yet.'

'Well, just be careful then, OK?'

It was getting quite late. The afternoon sun had disappeared, and the need for car headlights was apparent. Wendy gathered her things together and made her way to the car.

'Take care son,' said Wendy. 'Be careful. Don't forget your Uncle Tom has never had a landline put in here and because you and I left our pagers at home, I won't hear from you until I pick you up sometime late tomorrow morning. Bearing in mind that I must take Tom to look at a few properties first. Is that OK?'

'Yes mum, I'll be fine. I'm a big boy now!' he said smiling sarcastically.

Standing at the door as the new owner of his Uncle Tom's property, he watched his mother drive her red Discovery away down the mud track.

That night, Gerald sat comfortably on the old chair in front of the blazing fire, where his eyes became lost within the flames. His left cheek had become so red from the heat, he proceeded to rub it gently to take away the pain.

His eyes remained transfixed within the flickering light, as he tried to remember all the past adventures he and his uncle had talked about, as well as where all the objects were hidden.

He was now feeling very drowsy and far too tired to think clearly. Looking at his watch, he thought it best to have an early night.

'Maybe tomorrow I will think a little clearer,' he thought... 'Time for bed....'

***

A narrow shard of sunlight poked its way through Gerald's bedroom window like a laser beam. It was uncanny how it immediately found its way to where he had laid his head, where its brightness woke him up instantly.

'Bloody hell... what time is it? Jesus, it's 11am,' he thought, sitting up sharply. *'Where the hell am I?'*

Still half asleep, he looked around the room and couldn't quite grasp where he was. He knew he wasn't in his own bedroom...

Then, like a flick of a switch, it suddenly became very clear.

'Oh dear,' he yawned. 'I'll have to get up and have a quick look around after breakfast before mum comes to pick me up.'

Taking his breakfast from the stove, Gerald sat quietly and poured himself a fresh cup of coffee.

'*Come on Mum,*' he thought, while chewing the toast he had just dipped in his coffee. '*It's almost noon. Where the hell are you? You said you would be here late morning!*'

Gerald looked through the gap in Toms old bedroom from the kitchen table and saw the small box he had handed to Tom previously with the six-digit combination lock. Quickly, Gerald entered the room and picked it up from the bedside.

'*We never did get to open this,*' he thought. '*What was that combination number he mentioned. Was it 632506?*' whilst trying the combination lock. '*Damn-it. Come-on Gerald, get your thinking head on. What was it he said? Oh! I remember, it was definitely: 526360A.*'

Carefully, he dialled in the numbers.

'Eureka!' as the box sprung open. Inside the velvet lined box was a small security key with a label marked - *Safe.*

'*Safe. What Safe?*' he thought. Then he remembered when his Tom had explained about the hidden artifacts from the supernatural land of *Deawilder.* He said he had placed within the fireplace and the hidden safe behind the picture frame. However, before he had the chance to check them out, the sound

91

of tyres rolling over gravel stopped him in his tracks.

'Oh, thank God for that,' he said out-loud. 'It's about bloody time!' and put the security key in his pocket.

Before Gerald could look out the window, several loud knocks resonated from the door.

Thinking it was his mum; he undid the latch and quickly opened the door saying...

'Where have you been? ...Oh!'

Gerald stood there looking very confused at the police officer, who had parked his big 4x4 on the drive and was now standing directly in front of him.

'Yes, can I help you officer?' he asked looking very perplexed.

The officer took a few steps forward, removing the hat from his head.

'Are you Mr. Gerald Lindsell sir?' asked the officer with a soft voice.

'Yes, I am. Why do you want to know?'

'Can I please step inside to explain?'

'Certainly, come in,' said Gerald with a now nervous voice. 'Make yourself comfortable. I thought it was my mother, she was supposed to be picking me up by now.'

The officer made his way to the kitchen and placed his hat on the corner of the table.

'Would you like a coffee?' asked Gerald.

'No thank you sir, but I would like you to take a seat, if you may.'

Gerald sensed a heavy lump in his throat. He knew something was amiss and sat nervously next to the officer.

'I'm sorry to be the bearer of sad news Mr. Lindsell....'

'Oh no, what has happened?'

'I'm afraid there has been a terrible accident...'

'Please, not my mum and grandma! Was it the car... are they...?'

'Sorry sir,' interrupted the officer. 'It is your grandmother... It wasn't the car sir; it was a gas explosion at her home.'

Gerald fell to his knees, crying out with pain.

'Oh no! What happened?... he said sobbing. 'That fucking gas man! He said everything was OK. He said we didn't have to worry... Was that the cause?... Are they OK?'

'Sorry sir, we have not ascertained the cause yet. Your grandmother sadly passed away, and your mother and Mr Lindsell is at the hospital now.'

'O, my God! I need to get there.'

'Unfortunately, sir, you might not be able to see your grandmother due to her injuries, but I am able to take you to the hospital.'

'Please, I need to go now...' begged Gerrald.

'Is there anyone else we can inform sir?'

'No, there is only my mother and my Uncle Tom left.'

R. L. Barnes.

Leaving everything where it was, Gerald and the officer secured the cabin and made their way to the police car.

CHAPTER

TEN

Wendy sat next to Tom in the hospital ward, staring at what remained of Kathleens body. She had over ninety percent burns to her body and could barely talk before she couldn't fight any longer. Because the heat from the fire had seriously damaged her throat. Kathleen had found it hard to breath until her last breath.

Before she died, Tom also heard the surgeon say to the nurse, that her injuries were critical and that there was a high probability of fatality.

The pain she must have been in was being suppressed by morphine, but it was too late.

***

Gerald and the officer finally entered the hospital reception area.

'Excuse me, madam,' said the officer to the receptionist. 'What room is the deceased. Kathleen Lindsell in?'

'Just a second officer, I'll have a look for you... She is still in room 135 on the second floor. The lifts are just to the left.'

'Thank you.'

'Excuse me, officer,' prompted the receptionist. 'Who's the gentleman with you?'

'Sorry, I should have said. This is Mr. Gerald Lindsell, her grandson.'

'Thank you, it's just for the records you understand?'

The officer smiled and beckoned Gerald to follow him.

The lift was only going up two floors but seemed to take forever. Gerald could remember how he felt about travelling in lifts as a child and shivered.

Stepping out on the second floor, Gerald stopped to compose himself, ready for what was to come.

'Are you ready?' asked the officer.

Taking a moment of thought, Gerald simply nodded and politely replied, 'Yes.'

'Come on then Mr. Lindsell,' whispered the officer, 'let us go and see your family.'

The shock of seeing his mother and Tom sitting there almost took his breath away. They looked distraught. And then he caught a glimpse of his grandmother. All the pipes and the life-support equipment were still around her bed. It was far too overwhelming to see his grandmother's dead body.

'Christ mum,' he said with tears welling up in both eyes. Did she get a chance to say anything to you before...?'

'I'm afraid not son.' interrupted Wendy. 'We were here by her side until she took her last breath. 'I don't even know if she could hear us talking to her. Tom and I were lucky we were not in the house. As it happens, we were signing papers in Tom's new bungalow. Had we been home, God knows what would have happened.'

Gerald just stood there motionless.

'With the number of burns she sustained... and the damage to her lungs, it wasn't looking too good for her,' said Tom. They had made her as comfortable as possible, but it was too late.'

'But I didn't have a chance to say goodbye,' said Gerald, putting his head in his hands.

'How can all this happen to one family?' he continued. 'Not only did I almost lose Tom, I also lost my father and my grandfather. Now I have lost my grandmother. Why is all this happening to us? What have we done wrong to deserve this?'

'They'll be sending us out shortly, so that they can take her away,' said Wendy. Say your goodbyes and try and remember her as she was. Not as she is now. Just remember all the good times.'

'Just get yourself back to your cabin for some rest,' said Tom. 'We have all had a

97

traumatic shock today. Give yourself a little time to digest what has happened. Your mum and I will see to the rest.'

Gerald kissed his grandmother's forehead and shed a tear. 'I will do, Tom.'

'Can I take your car mum'

'Yes of course you can,' replied Wendy. 'Tom and I will get a Taxi to Toms new bungalow. I will be staying with him for a few days or so to get him settled in, and to organise Kathleen's funeral. The Discovery is downstairs in the carpark at the main entrance,' passing him the keys.

Driving back to the cabin in the Wyre Forest National Nature Reserve, Gerald made a point of passing what was left of his grandmother's house.

'Christ!' he gasped. 'There's nothing left.' All that remained was the foundations and a large scattering of debris.

There is something wrong about all this,' he thought. *'And I mean to find out.'*

*****

After parking his mother's car on the gravel, he felt fatigued and made his way to the front door of his new gift from Tom. Once inside the cabin, he threw his black jacket and necktie across the room, changed into his old jeans, then threw himself on the sofa; feeling very despondent.

'What the hell do I do now?' he thought. 'Maybe, if I can just close my eyes for just a moment?'

Closing his eyes, he quickly drifted into a deep sleep.

***

Waking up some hours later, the lack of light through the window told Gerald it was early evening. It had been a stressful day and he must have been very tired.

Staring at the ceiling, the thoughts of all the past discussions he had shared with his grandmother, particularly all the things he wished he had not said.

'I wish I had handled things differently,' he thought.

Then he thought about the chilling dreams he had as a child, Uncle Tom, the artefacts and the past adventures he had to endure in a strange spiritual realm, where he sadly lost his father and grandfather. Gerald suddenly quickly sat upright.

'Where was it that Tom said he had hidden that damn toolbox? I remember I asked him to look after them for me when I came back from Deawilder all those years ago. He said he had hidden it up inside the chimney breast.'

99

Making his way to the fireplace, he gently placed his arm as far as he could up the chimney.

'I can't feel a damn thing...' he thought and pushed his arm a little further, by putting his head up the chimney too. 'Ah! wait a minute...' He could just feel something with the tip of his fingers.

Grabbing what felt like a corner, he pulled, dislodging a heavy box wrapped in a leathery material, along with a face full of black soot.

'Oh Jesus, that tastes foul.' he spluttered. Keeping his eyes tightly shut, he placed the box on the floor and fumbled his way to the bathroom to clean his now blackened face.

The wooden toolbox was much bigger than he remembered and was about the size of a large box file. It immediately unleashed many painful memories, regarding the terrible legacy his ancestors had to endure for generations.

Cautiously he removed the material and released the tiny lock. Very carefully, he opened the lid and uncovered its contents.

His mind raced as he peered at the strange, yet familiar objects and bottles, which were arranged carefully inside.

The right-hand side of the box, about one third in total, was divided horizontally into three equal sections. The bottom two contained a row of four jars, and a top row of four taller bottles.

All these items had different and strange markings engraved on them. Above that, a taller section seemed to contain bunches of dead herbs. The larger left-hand section of the box, which made almost a perfect square, consisted of several different long roots, a feather or two, a couple of different bird claws, and what looked like a bone from the shoulder blade of a small mammal, such as a rabbit.

Suspended in the lid of the box, was a small red spell book, a larger curled root and a ring with a chain, which had the tiny bell attached to the end, known as: *'The Sleeper.'*

To the left of these things, in a tall narrow compartment, was a strange piece of apparatus which appeared to be made up from a test tube attached to a small skeletal torso.

This had been the toolbox his grandfather took from the Necromancer on one of his quests, where he later failed and died. The quests that his ancestors and all their firstborn sons had been burdened with for centuries, in their dreams.

As Gerald was also a first born and only son, he also remembered his own quest to bring back his ancestors *'gold wedding ring,'* and that the tiny little bell in the toolbox in front of him, *'The Sleeper,'* had the power to bring its bearer back home.

'Just a minute,' he thought. *'Where's the large Ouroboros ring I brought back?'* Then he

remembered Tom had a safe hidden behind his framed painting on the wall.

Pulling the hinged frame from one side, he exposed the door of the safe and noticed a small keyhole halfway down the lefthand side.

'How the hell am I going to get in there?' he thought. Putting his hands in his jeans pocket, he felt the little key he had found in Toms bedroom before the police informed him about the accident.

'No, it couldn't be,' he whispered. Placing the key into the safe lock and turned it. *Click.* The safe door swung open to reveal the *Ouroboros* ring made from a beautiful dragon eating its own tail.

Memories started flooding back about all the characters he had met along his journey and the people he cared about - or didn't!

'What happened to the *'Talisman'* I brought back?' he thought out loud. 'Where the hell did I put it?'

Putting his feelings of despair about his grandmother to one side, he put the toolbox on the table and made his way to the bedroom.

Looking around the room, he immediately started rummaging through the draws and cupboards to find his *Talisman*.

Just as he was about to give up, he placed his hand under one of the draws and felt a solid object. Pulling it free from the corner, he unravelled the necklace and sighed with relief.

'My God, where have you been? I had almost forgotten all about you,' he said looking at the *Talisman*. 'You symbolise so many of my memories and I'll never leave you to one side again!'

Smiling and exhausted, he locked the *Ouroboros* ring and toolbox in the safe, replaced the picture frame, then put the *'Talisman'* and safe-key around his neck.

'I have to have time out,' he thought. *'I have taken a few days off to sort myself out.'*

Flopping on his bed, he took a deep breath and slowly closed his eyes.

***

The hospital had passed the remains of Kathleen to the corner for the post-mortem examination. As soon as he had meticulously completed his report, the death certificate was issued. However, because of the advanced decomposition of Kathleen's remains were accelerating, he swiftly planned to have the funeral carried out as soon as possible.

The funeral was an awful experience for Gerald and the rest of his family. They had discussed arrangements over with the vicar and instead of cremation, decided to bury his grandmother's casket in the large family plot, right next to where his father and grandfather were buried.

R. L. Barnes.

Standing at the graveside; Gerald threw a handful of soil on the casket, followed by Wendy and Tom dropping a few of Kathleen's favourite pink roses on the casket. The vicar continued to say a few kind words to all who those attended, before retiring from the graveside.

When everyone except Gerald had faded away, he found himself looking down at the casket. With his head full of memories and eyes full of tears, Gerald now realised like his father and grandfather, she was never coming back!

CHAPTER

ELEVEN

A week later, Gerald had been working very hard at his job as a lecturer in physics. He was proud he had stepped in his late father's shoes at the university and didn't disappoint his peers.

Lying in his bed one evening, Gerald held his precious *'Talisman'* tightly to his chest and for no apparent reason, started to think about how he received it in the supernatural kingdom of *Deawilder.* He remembered the friends he had made, especially Sarika, the kings daughter. Trying his best to recall what she had said to him about using the *Talisman.* Suddenly, the sound of someone shouting aloud broke his concentration. Not from outside the cabin, but from inside his head.

'What the hell was that!' he thought, listening carefully to see if it would happen again, but everything had gone silent. Suppressing his thoughts and putting them

aside, he lay back down and drifted into a deep and well-earned sleep.

Dreaming, Gerald looked across a land he had not seen for a very long time. Everything was almost completely void of colour. The familiar horizons across the grassy plains and the two notorious summits of *Mount Boaz* and the fearful *Mount Zed*, took him back to the days of his last quest.

'How the hell am I back in Deawilder?' he mumbled. 'This can't be right. It looks so vivid and disturbingly tangible.

Unconsciously increasing his grip on the *talisman,* he could hear a familiar voice cry out across the grassy plains in front of him.

'I know that voice,' speaking aloud. 'I do know, it sounds like... Sarika.

'Why am I here after all this time?' he thought

Often as most dreams tend to do, he was no longer standing looking over the landscape, but standing at the gates of his good friends' kingdom, King Tubal'cain.

Hearing the voice of the king's daughter, Sarika, he suddenly found himself standing directly in front of her.

'Qnndify dia lotty,' she said, showing her spikey teeth as she smiled, but he could not understand a thing she was saying. He could see her lips and body language, but her words didn't make any sense at all.

'I can't understand what you are trying to tell me Sarika,' shouting at the top of his voice.

He could see the frustration in her little round face. She looked a lot older than he remembered and by the way she was waving her arms around, he knew she was in trouble of some kind.

'Is this all real?' he thought. *'Or is this just some kind of weird dream I'm in?'*

Becoming conscious that he might just be dreaming, he woke up and immediately sat bolt upright. His bed was soaked in sweat where he had been lying and for the first time in years, had that awful cold, clammy grey skin.

'Shit! That wasn't normal. I thought I had left all that crap in the past?'

He then remembered the day Sarika had given him the *Talisman* and what she had said. She said:

> *'Please take this back with you and do not let anyone know you possess it. Keep it safe, but beware, it can only bring you back to me, should you wish to return. It will not take you back home! Just say these few words and it will guide you back to me wherever I am…The words you must remember are:- Redire me ut ordo ab chao. Say these and think of me."*

R. L. Barnes.

Remembering this *Talisman* is only a one-way ticket. He now knew how he had to hold it and the chanting he had to recite to make it work.

Depressed and despondent with his current loss, he pondered over the outlandish idea of trying to see if the *Talisman* works.

'*Do I dare try to visit Sarika once more?*' he thought. 'I have almost lost everyone in my family; I don't want to lose anyone else close to me. What happens if my dreams of Sarika are correct, in that she was seriously attempting to contact me. She did look very distressed... Maybe I should give it a try.'

But little did he know, his dream had been influenced through the *Talisman* by the necromancer Mahabone himself.

Knowing that he had to have a way back home, as he had so many times in the past, he knew he must take the little bell, known as the '*Sleeper*,' from the toolbox in the safe, as it is the only means to bring him back.

In the past when this bell was worn, he remembered the small ringer within the *Sleeper*, was held to one side with a leather strap to stop it from accidently ringing the bell. Used wrongly, the bell would send the barer into a never-ending sleep.

He remembered he had to carefully remove the restraining strap and ring the bell only three times to bring him home. Anything less,

108

it would do nothing. Anything more, would send him to a never-ending sleep.

'If I am going to do this,' speaking aloud, 'I must find out more about the contents of the toolbox and the secrets it may hold.'

Thinking he could take the whole toolbox and its contents to the university; he could ask his new friend and colleague Sandy, the archaeologist specialising in unusual artefacts. At least then, he may get some sort of inclination as to what they are and what superstitious powers they may hold (*if any*), or at least what they could be used for.

However, to do this, he would have to divulge the secrets of his past exploits and what his family had to endure to Sandy. Better still, she also has an interest in parapsychology and demonology.

Not wanting to look like he has a screw loose, he knows he must ask her to keep everything confidential.

***

Later the following morning, Gerald arrived a little late at the university. Carrying the toolbox in hand, he made his way through the main entrance, past the reception and into the staff lounge where several of his colleagues were happily drinking tea.

'Good morning.' said Gerald, trying to force a smile.

'Oh! Good morning.' sounded a very rustic voice from across the room. 'I didn't expect you to be coming in today.' said Brian Burges, who is the current Chief of Department.

'I know.' said Gerald. 'I haven't come to work today. It's my day off. I have come to seek a little advice from Sandy, has anyone seen her this morning.'

Scanning the room to see if anyone was going to respond, a voice made from silk, echoed quietly from behind.

'Here I am Gerald. I'm so sorry to hear about your grandmother. You have had a string of sad circumstances. Very tragic too. Please accept my condolences. How may I help you?'

Turning around, Gerald quickly fixed his gaze onto Sandy's beautiful eyes. She seemed to be leaning up against the doorframe provocatively in her tightly fitted pencil skirt and blouse.

'I was wondering, could I please have a word with you in private?' he asked.

'Sure, why not,' she whispered. We can discuss things in my office. Please come this way.'

Following from behind, he could smell her sweet perfume as she glided herself along the hallway to her office.

'Ghost?' said Gerald softly.

'Excuse me?' she said, turning quickly.

'Ghost,' he replied. 'The perfume you are wearing is Ghost, isn't it?'

'Yes! How did you know?'

'I would know that anywhere. I gave it to a friend once as a present and I loved it. It smells the Same on you too.'

'Thank you, Gerald, that is very sweet of you,' looking slightly blushed with his complement. 'Here we are then, please step inside.'

After making himself comfortable, he watched Sandy close the door and make her way to the other side of the desk.

Now, you said you wanted to discuss something with me. Oh, how rude of me, I forgot to offer you a drink. Would you like a tea or coffee before we start?'

'No thank you,' fidgeting with the toolbox in his lap, not quite sure on how to start. 'I wanted to ask your advice on your specialised subjects regarding unusual mythology and paranormal artefacts.'

'How do you mean?' she asked inquisitively.

'I have this toolbox with a few samples.' he replied. Carefully, he placed the wooden toolbox on the desk. 'I would like you to look at these.'

Sandy pulled the box to her side of the desk and opened the two brass latches and opened the lid.

R. L. Barnes.

'Oh my God Gerald, where did you get these?'

'They were given to me by my uncle. They have been in the family for generations.'

'They are exquisite,' said Sandy, almost drooling at the mouth. 'I have read about such things in my studies but have never seen any tangible examples. Are they real? Is this also the original toolbox?'

'That's why I'm here, you tell me if they're real?' not wanting to give too much away. 'I was wondering if you could tell me how they were used and what properties each of the objects may have.'

'What history can you tell me about how your family acquired them?'

Pausing for a moment, Gerald knew there was no other way to get the correct help... he would have to try and explain the truth to her, hoping that she didn't laugh and throw him out of the office.

'OK.' he sighed. 'There is no other way to say this... Sandy, I want you to listen to what I must tell you with an open and sympathetic mind, as it may sound a little far-fetched. Is that OK with you?'

Looking a little perplexed, but intrigued at his request, she nodded.

'Yes, of course.'

Gerald pulled his chair closer to the desk and took a few moments to gather his thoughts.

'I'll have to give you a general background as to where everything started. It's the story that has been passed down my family from generation to generation... So please bear with me.'

'OK Gerald,' she smiled. Just take your time... I'm all ears.'

'Well, it all started generations ago when one of my ancestors, my great-great grandfather, lost his wife. Their son and daughter had all grown up and left home, moving far away. His wife was the only thing that mattered to him and he was devastated when she died.

That night in his dream, he met a man who promised he would bring his wife back to life, if he agreed to play a game. Obviously, he wanted to have his wife back in his arms and agreed to play the man's game.

Now, unbeknown to my ancestor, the man in his dream was a *Necromancer*. An evil being who lives in the realm between life and death. This being can control dead spirits and told my ancestor to give him three objects that symbolised something meaningful in his life, in exchange for his wife's life.

The *Necromancer* continued to explain that each firstborn son from each generation would have to enter his realm. There, they would have to find and retrieve all three symbols, be it all at once or over generations. However, if they failed, or refused to participate, they would

113

belong to the realm of the dead for him to control for eternity.

If they were strong enough to outwit him and could return all three symbols to their own realm, the Necromancer promised to lift the curse that he had bestowed upon all the ancestor's descendants.

This was the price for the return of his wife.

Because my great-great grandfather loved his wife so much, he agreed to the conditions, and gave the *Necromancer* three of his most prised possessions:

- A Claw - which his son had given him.
- A Key – from his daughters 21st, and
- A Wedding Ring – that belonged to his deceased wife.

The Necromancer took all three from my ancestor, placed them in his pocket and said...

'It is done.'

The next day when my ancestor got out his bed, he heard a noise outside his window. Looking out, he couldn't believe his eyes. His wife was crouched down, picking flowers from their garden. His heart was so filled with joy, he forgot all about his dream and what he had agreed with the *Necromancer.*

Now that his ancestor's life was complete again, he continued to live happily with his wife until he died, leaving his wife to live out her years alone.'

'You're pulling my leg of course. Is this a joke?' she frowned.

'No, it is not.' he barked. 'I asked you to listen with an open mind. You are the only person I have spoken to about this. I thought I could trust you.'

'I'm sorry Gerald, my mistake. Please forgive me. You can trust me. Please continue...'

CHAPTER

TWELVE

'Several years after my ancestor's death, his first and only grandson was born. However, when his grandson was in his late teens, the *Necromancer* approached the boy when he was dreaming and explained the agreement his grandfather had made, telling him the rules and consequences of the game.

He was also advised that he had to pass on these rules to the first-born son of all future descendants.'

Sandy never said a word to him. She just sat there expressionless, looking to see if Gerald had anything else to say.

'I must tell you that I have also been subject to this family legacy in the past. In fact, my grandfather and I were the only ones to succeed in retrieving the three family heirlooms. My grandfather retrieved two, and I the third. Hopefully enabling me to end this terrible curse. Sadly, my father and grandfather lost their lives because of it. I know this may sound ridiculous to you, but because I came back with another artifact belonging to the necromancer, I think there may be some connections to the recent deaths of my grandmother! There is so much more, and so much to explain about what I have seen and done during this nightmare. I need to know as much as I can about this damn toolbox. I believe I still have something to do and I don't know where to turn.'

Tears welling up in his eyes, he stared deep into Sandy's and said: 'I need your help.'

'WOW,' gasped Sandy, feeling perplexed about his sanity, whilst trying to absorb everything Gerald had been telling her and not knowing how to respond.

'OK.' she said, taking the little bell from the case.

'Be careful with that!' he snapped.

'Why?'

'That little bell is known as the *Sleeper* and is very dangerous!' he replied. 'If you release it from its leather pouch, it can send you to sleep forever. My grandfather stole the toolbox from the *Necromancer* and used it to bring himself home.

When my Uncle Tom told me the story, and the instructions left from my grandfather for the bell, he gave it to me to help me on my journey. I had to use it to bring me home, after retrieving the third and final symbol from the *Necromancer* called *Mahabone*.

This is the only thing I know about the contents of this toolbox.

We thought that was the end of the legacy, as we had no more trouble since. However, I have my doubts with recent events. I need you to tell me what the rest of the contents may have been used for. I have no one else I can turn to and you are the only one I know that specialises in this sort of thing.

'I can't just give you answers right now,' she smiled. 'I will first have to look for any background information. Is it possible for you to leave these with me for a couple of days? I promise I will keep it under lock and key.'

'I'm not sure that I should.' he said cautiously.

Don't worry, I believe you,' said Sandy holding his hand with both of hers. 'You said that you can trust me, and you can. Although it all sounds a little weird, I am very intrigued with it all and promise not to tell a living soul.'

'OK, as long as you are true to your word,' he said looking a little concerned. 'I need to take the rest of the week off to sort things out in my head. I will see you in a few days to see what you have, or you can simply come over to stay in my, sorry, our cabin.'

'Well, let us leave it at that,' she said softly. 'I will get onto it as soon as I have finished my class and get back to you. Because of the sensitivity of this subject, I prefer not to leave any information around here. Therefore, I think it would be safer for me to call in at your home.'

'Yes, I agree with you,' he smiled. 'That will be awesome.'

He thanked her for believing in him and her understanding, before writing his address and directions to his home on a piece of card. He explained that she needs a decent off-road vehicle to safely navigate the mud track through the forest, but she assured him that she already owns a four-wheel drive and that she will have no problem finding her way.

Gerald left the toolbox with Sandy and left the office, while she placed the box in her private safe.

***

Sandy sat in her office after all the students and most of the lecturers had gone home. Knowing that she told Gerald she believed him about what he had explained to her earlier, she still couldn't get her mind to accept whether he was serious, or completely off his trolley.

Looking at the safe where she had placed the toolbox for safe keeping, she tapped her finger on the desk, wondering if she should really pursue his request.

'*Dammit,*' she thought. '*I so want to believe what he told me; I really do. I suppose it wouldn't hurt to try. I mean, I haven't got anything to lose if it turns out to be a crock of shit.*

I have studied about this man's work from when he was a student, even more so since he has been working here. I like the way he does his work. As far as I know, no one has ever mentioned he's the type of guy who would lie or exaggerate anything.'

Glancing at the keys in her desk draw, she picked them up and placed the appropriate key in the safe door. The toolbox was not very heavy at all. Although she had handled it earlier, it seemed different. There was an air of mystery, so tangible; she could almost feel its essence surround her. Taking a deep breath, she removed it from the safe and carefully placed it on her desk.

'Well, here goes.'

Later, after scouring through internet pages of tedious information, her eyes were sore and dry, so much so, that she found it increasingly difficult to concentrate on the task in hand.

Putting her hand on the lid of the toolbox, she noticed a few dull and almost un-legible markings around the inner surfaces. Earlier, when she had previously removed the contents for inspection, she had not noticed them.

Removing all the contents again, she noticed that the toolbox could fully open, so that both side of the toolbox lay flat on the desk.

Using a soft damp cloth, she gently wiped away the grime, to reveal a unique interpretation of an old Ouija board.

'Wow! I've never seen one like this before, it looks ancient. I wonder if Gerald has ever been aware of this,' she said, stretching her arms to the ceiling.

Sandy finished writing her report on the contents of the toolbox and sighed. Printing everything off, she lay back in her office chair.

'I'm so tired,' she thought. *'I'm so ready to go home. I think I have enough information for him now. I'll drop in to see him sometime tomorrow...'*

Sandy's report read:

- **Mammal shoulder bone:** Used to make a spiritual connection to the animal species within any realm he is present.
- **Test Tube** *Unknown*
- **Humanoid skull (on skeleton):** Also, used to connect with the species. (i.e.) An Owl skull to connect to owls. A wolf scull to connect with a wolf, and so on.

- **The Spell Book (The Witches Book of the Dead).** Has spells to conjure up and transform the spirits of the dead. Discusses the use of a humanoid skull in its representation of the dead.

- **The Ouija Board:** As far as records go, dating to the 19th Century. The Ouija itself was created and named in 1890 in Baltimore, Maryland by medium and spiritualist Helen Peters Nosworthy. It was made popular during the spiritual movement. Many people do not like the Ouija board as terrible things are often associated with it. It is stressed that if you don't use a form of protection, i.e., casting a protective circle with salt, or use the board flippantly, then you are asking for trouble. The Necromancer uses this as a tool as a means of connection to the spirits of the dead.

- **Herbs:** Used to heighten the Necromancers senses. To make magical ointments. Herbs such as *Mugwort, Wormwood* and *Dittany of Crete* are used in divination and dream control, usually as an incense, and communicating with spirits (alive or dead)

- **Feathers:** These are often used to focus concentration in spells. Feathers are used for magical undertakings and are mainly determined by the energy which is brought into the feather by the Necromancers concentration and thought. Feathers also have natural abilities. (e.g.) A Crow feather represents the souls of the dead. The Hawk feather has the active energy for hunters, and the Peacock feather to cast the evil eye.
- **Birds Claw:** Protection for the Necromancer from enemies.
- **Roots:** Such as Aconite (also known as *Wolfsbane* or *Monkshood*.) The Necromancer uses its dry root to serve as a tutelary spirit. The *Yew* (the death tree) is used for sorcery and dark magic. *Wormwood* is for summoning spirits, and *Mullein* (known as the Hag's Taper), used to make a torch for rituals. Also, a means to see and communicate in other realms and can be used as a talisman.
- **The Bell, Chain and ring:** brings the barer back to his original realm, or if used incorrectly sends the barer into a never-ending sleep.

R. L. Barnes.

***

Two weeks later Gerald sat quietly at his breakfast table thinking about his recent dreams with Sarika, and the possibility of his nemesis Mahabone, having something to do with his family's recent events.

'No, it couldn't be, could it,' he thought. *'It can't be! After all this time! I never gave it any thought. Now that I think of it, I remember Mahabone saying he would find a way to get to me, and I must admit, the string of events lately does seem a little weird. I wonder,'* rubbing his brow. *'I have no family left now, and it would be so nice to visit my weird little friends again. If I do try to go back to Sarika, should I take the complete toolbox with me? Whatever I decide, I must keep the Ouroboros ring hidden here in this world. Maybe Sandy will have some good news for me when she comes. If so, maybe I can give it to King Tubal'cain to keep safe deep within his vaults. Maybe the King could find a way to use the contents of the toolbox against Mahabone, giving Mahabone a good taste of his own medicine.'*

Thinking of this, he grabbed the *Talisman* around his neck, kissed it. *'There is something going on here. Why have all these thoughts come flooding back?'* he thought, then placed it down the front of his shirt.

124

CHAPTER

THIRTEEN

It had been two weeks since Gerald had given her the toolbox. She had now completed her report and had pre-set the satellite navigation unit in her car, making her way to Gerald's cabin along the rugged terrain to his cabin.

'Holy shit,' she said, frantically grabbing the steering wheel as it threw her from side to side. 'He wasn't bloody kidding was he,' screaming at the top of her voice. *'I know he said it would be a rough drive,'* she thought, *'but come on! I couldn't do this every day, that's for sure!'*

Gerald was outside gathering a few logs for the fire, when he heard Sandy's vehicle pulling across the gravel yard and coming to an abrupt halt.

'Home so soon dear?' he said laughing, while looking at the mud smeared all over both sides of her precious car. 'How did you find the journey then?'

'Don't even go there!' she scowled. 'It was the worst drive of my bloody life, that's what it was. What do you expect me to think?'

Gerald burst out laughing once again, before immediately invited her into the front entrance of his home.

'Would you like a coffee or tea, or would you prefer something a little stronger?' he asked, taking her coat and hanging it on the hooks on the back of the door.

'Thank you, a glass of white would be a good start, if that's alright?'

'Sure. Do you prefer sweet or dry?'

'Dry please, just a small glass if you don't mind.'

After pouring two glasses of wine, he made his way to where Sandy was sitting, handed over her wine and sat down beside her.

'You don't mind if I sit here, do you?' he said, realising that he should have asked her first.

'Not at all,' she said, pulling a yellow folder from her bag. 'I spent most of yesterday evening burning the midnight oil, looking for answers to the contents of your toolbox. Of course, I had to wait until everyone had left the building, but I did find a few interesting facts.'

'Oh, that's good, and what did you find?'

Sandy opened the file and handed it to him. His eyes began to grow larger and larger as he read the report.

'This is exactly what I wanted Sandy. Thank you so much. I may now be able to put them to good use.'

'You're most welcome,' she replied, smiling into her almost empty glass. Why would you want to put them to good use?'

'I will explain later. In the meantime, would you like a top up?' he said, not knowing what her plans were, 'or do you have other plans?'

'I don't have any plans this evening. However, I shouldn't really, because I'm driving.'

'Well, that's OK. I only asked because it is getting dark outside. The light here dies very quickly and it can be a little dangerous driving over that terrain. I don't want to be presumptuous, but you can stay here for the night if you wish. No strings attached and you can leave tomorrow morning.

It means you can have another glass of wine,' he said smiling, 'and I can tell you more about my plans regarding the toolbox.'

'Well, I'm not sure. Where would I sleep?'

That's ok, I have a spare bedroom. It used to be mine, but I have now moved into my uncle's old bedroom, it's larger you see. So, you are quite welcome to use my old room if you like?'

After giving herself a little time to ponder over his invitation, she drank the remaining contents of her glass, before stretching it out towards Gerald.

'I'll have another top up then,' smiling shyly, and exposing a delicate pink glow to her cheeks. 'Better make it a large one.'

'One large, white wine - coming up.'

***

The night had drawn in very quickly, while Gerald read through her report, paying much attention to what may be useful to his friends in the other realm.

'Tell me.' she asked, taking another gulp of wine. 'What is all this for? I know you gave me a brief story about your past, but I must be truthful and say it is a little tuff to swallow. However, because the subject interests me, I would like to know a little more.'

Lifting his eyes slowly from her report, he looked directly into her eyes and smiled.

'Look. Let's make one thing crystal clear Sandy. I would never put myself into a position that would make others think I had lost my mind. I came to you because we have a brief connection from our past encounter, but also your academic qualifications, and because you look like a person that I can confide in. Or am I mistaken?'

'No, you're perfectly right Gerald. I'm sorry, I didn't mean it to come across like that. I mean it's not like the things you told me happen every day in today's world. I am aware that there are

128

legends, fables and fairy tales, that people have recorded throughout time. I have researched many over the years and found there's always a small element of truth in each. However, there has been little proof of any off these ever-taken place, apart from the odd scroll, image, or engraving on some cave wall or rock or other.'

Gerald just smiled, placed her report back on the table and moved closer towards her.

'Right, let us start again, and this time I will continue with what I have in mind, but before we start, would you like your glass topped up?'

'Yes please.'

Gerald painstakingly re-covered all the ground they had talked about in her office, but this time with much greater detail. He explained about his father going missing when he was a child and that it wasn't until he found the artefacts in his grandmother's attic, that he was told about the dark family secret, a legacy passed down the generations.

He told her that he was sent to his Uncle Tom, who enlightened him further about the Necromancer. His uncle had explained why his father had gone missing when he was a child, and how his grandfather was the only one to recover two of the three heirlooms from Mahabone the necromancer. Gerald then explained to her how he had to enter the supernatural kingdom of *Deawilder* himself, only to find out about his grandfather's death and how he was killed by Mahabone. It was his friend King Tubal'cain who had explained everything to him, whilst trying to recover the third and final family heirloom.

He continued to explain to Sandy, that it wasn't until he himself travelled to the other realm, that he had found his father in a dungeon. But only after many trials and battles, was he able to return with the third and final heirloom, the *Sleeper* bell and one of Mahabone's *Ouroboros* rings.

Sadly, before he returned home, he had to watch his father sacrifice himself by getting killed by Mahabone, giving Gerald enough time to escape with the artifacts. He also explained about his close relationship with King Tubal'cain, his daughter Sarika and the *Talisman,* she had given him.

'That is so sad,' she said.

'No wait, there is more. On my return, I remembered Mahabone saying that he will find a way to retrieve what was his...'

'And what would that be?' she asked inquisitively.

'The little bell, called the *Sleeper*, the toolbox and his *Ouroboros* ring.

'What the hell is an *Ouroboros* ring anyway?' she asked.

'We understand an *Ouroboros* ring to be an ancient Egyptian symbol of a serpent or dragon circling to eat its own tail, but in Mahabone's world, they are a means of power.

'Right! I won't pretend I fully understand, but I'll soon catch up,' she smiled.

By the way, talking about toolboxes, where is the toolbox?'

'Oh, I clean forgot. It's in the boot of my car, wrapped in a tartan blanket. Would you be a dear and get it for me?'

'Yes madam,' he said smiling, with just a touch of friendly sarcasm. 'Immediately.'

Gerald soon returned with the toolbox and placed it on the coffee table in front of the sofa.

'Now Sandy, this is where you come in. Before I came to see you, I have been having vivid dreams about Sarika in the other realm. Not dreams like I used to get, but more like visions. I saw her frantically waving her arms around and trying to talk to me. The only thing is that I couldn't understand a word she was saying, because the words were in some other form of language. However, by the look on her face, I could tell she was in trouble.'

'OK, but where do I fit in all of this?' she asked.

'Please let me finish, I'm getting to it. Now that my family has gone and I am the only one in my family left. I know this is going to sound unreal to you, but I am planning to return to that realm with the toolbox, so that Princess

R. L. Barnes.

Sarika and her father King Tubal'cain, can make some use of it.

Whether you have given me the right information or not, regarding the contents of this toolbox, it is all that we have. At least it will give me some idea of its uses from an academic perspective.

'OK Gerald, I think I understand.'

''When I last visited Sarika's realm, she gave me this *Talisman*.' Showing it to Sandy. 'She said I could use it to bring me back and showed me how to use it. I must hold it across my chest when I go to sleep, along with any objects I wish to take with me, hence the toolbox and all its contents.

Once I am ready, I must utter the following words:

REDIRE ME UT ORDO AB CHAO, before letting myself drift into sleep.

'Yes, regarding those words,' interrupted Sandy. 'Correct me if I'm wrong, but I believe they are Latin.'

'Latin!' he said, looking a little perplexed.

'Yes, I am a little rusty. It has been some time since I have used Latin in my studies, but I believe your incantation in English says: *Return me to order from chaos*. Usually, with incantations of this kind, the words must be spoken in this manner for them to work.'

'OK.' He said rubbing his head. 'The second reason why I want to return, is that I believe

Mahabone, you know, the *Necromancer*, had something to do with the demise of my family. Don't you think it strange, that it all seemed to start when I began to think about my past adventures and dream about Sarika?'

'Surely Gerald, that could just be coincidence?'

'No, I think not. I know how Mahabone works. I want to put my mind to rest and find out if he had anything to do with it or not.'

'Well, if that's what you want to try, then go ahead. You seem to know what you are doing. I can't really have an opinion on this, as you were apparently there before and I simply do not know, or fully understand. So, what do we do now?'

'Nothing more,' he said smiling. 'I think that will be enough for one night,' picking up the wine bottle. 'I think it would be a shame to waste this half bottle of wine. Do you want another top-up?

'Maybe just one more,' she said almost losing her balance and stumbling towards the floor, but Gerald quickly dived forward and grabbed her by the arm, saving her from landing flat on her face.

'Oops! Silly me,' she said blushing, now standing face to face with him. 'You caught me just in the nick of time. Who said chivalry was dead eh? Thanks, young man,' and passionately kissed him on the lips.

Gerald stood there pleasantly surprised.

'Oops! I shouldn't have done that,' she said looking very embarrassed. 'I don't know what I was thinking, I'm so sorry.'

'Don't worry, it's OK,' he said smiling. 'It's a simple mistake anyone could have made, but it was a welcome one.'

'I'll have to blame it on the wine,' she smiled. 'I think I should go to bed before I regret doing something I shouldn't.'

'That's OK,' he replied. 'I have left a pair of shorts and a t-shirt on the pillow, and there is a clean dressing gown on the back of the door.'

Sandy, having consumed more than she normally would, had lowered her inhibitions. So much so, that when she had finished removing all her clothes, she only slipped on the dressing gown, opened the bedroom door and made her way towards an unsuspecting Gerald.

'Oh. Hello,' he said looking surprised and turned to face her. 'What's all this for?'

'Oh, I may have had a few too many,' she slurred, 'but it's the only time I have the courage to say how I feel about people I like, and I've grown to like you very much.', pulling him closer. I've never met a man like you Gerald and would love the opportunity to get to know you more personally.'

'That's very kind of you,' he whispered. I have to admit I've always liked you since I laid eyes on you all those years ago in that corner shop.'

Yes, I do remember,' she smiled, looking deeply into his eyes.

Sandy pulled his head towards her and French-kissed him full on the lips.

Initially shocked, Gerald soon reciprocated by returning the kiss and putting his arms around her tightly. Slightly pulling himself away to look at her, he searched the contours of her face. Staring deeply into each other's eyes, there was a moment where time seemed to stand still, where the world around them made no sense at all!

Hearts beating loudly in each of their chests, they were drawn together like two magnets in slow motion! The distance between their faces grew increasingly narrow and their lips became as one. Gerald moaned as he felt the warmth of her sweet breath and the softness of her lips pressing passionately into his, sending streams of erotic pleasure spinning down his spine and into his loins. Gently caressing the soft flesh of her inner thigh, she gently positioned herself to give him easier access, making her dampness ache for him to be inside her. Quickly losing themselves in a red mist of ecstasy, she frantically removed his clothing, dropped her dressing gown and rolled onto the floor.

Gently digging her nails into his back as he entered her, she arched her back in a series of

R. L. Barnes.

thrusts and explosions, before they rolled to one side in total exhaustion.

'Wow! That was mind-blowing!' she said, running her hand over his chest hair.

'Yes, it was. It was beautiful.' he replied, kissing her gently on the forehead, 'but it shouldn't have happened! I think we should get some sleep for now and discuss things in the morning, don't you think?'

'Perhaps you are right!' she said, pulling the dressing gown over her. Brushing her hand through his hair, she made her way to the bathroom.

Gerald still laying on the floor, pondered on what had just happened...

'I'm so pleased I came here tonight.' she shouted from the bathroom. 'However, I must get my head down before it falls off,' she chuckled whilst staggering through the door.

'If you need anything Sandy, just call out, my room is just next to yours.'

She closed the bedroom door behind her and within a few minutes, he couldn't hear a sound.

When Gerald returned to his own bedroom, he quietly opened his writing bureau and pulled out a clean writing pad. He was aware of the forthcoming dangers regarding his plans to return to Mahabone's realm and therefore started to write a set of instructions to the family solicitor, just as a matter of precaution. When he had finished, he addressed the envelope to his solicitor and placed it neatly on his dressing table. Quietly making his way into the lounge, he picked up the toolbox.

'Time for bed I think,' he whispered and returned to his bedroom.

Lying in his bed, he opened the toolbox to remove the ring and chain that held the little bell (*the Sleeper*). He placed the ring on his finger and held the bell in his left hand, before placing the toolbox under his right arm and gripping the *Talisman* across his chest.

'OK, I think I'm all set to go back,' he whispered, knowing he had to clear his mind before he started. Taking three deep breaths, he closed his eyes and uttered the Latin incantation that was given to him…

'Redire me ut ordo ab chao'

Gradually thinking more and more about the supernatural land, he had witnessed in the past. The look of an almost colourless environment. The enormous mountain top of Mount Boaz and the gigantic Mount Zed that overshadows all. Finally, the mystical looking creatures that lived around the lands.

As his mind travelled deeper into this vista, he could feel the room starting to spin. The memories of his past started to flood into every corner of his mind. Now he could feel his body temperature starting to drop rapidly.

Having no control over what was happening, his heart rate immediately reduced itself to an alarming rate! What was once a glowing face full of colour and life (*as it had done so many times in the past*), had become grey, drawn, and almost lifeless. He was now on his way to the dangerous land of Deawilder.

***

Sandy opened her eyes to find the morning sunlight stretching across her bedroom. It was much too bright and her head was telling her that she had far too much to drink last night.

'Oh, my head,' she thought. *'Never again! Why do I keep doing this.'*

Looking at her watch, it was almost 5:30 AM. She was still feeling very embarrassed about her actions the night before, and not wanting to wake Gerald, she decided to write him a thank you letter, for a wonderful, be it somewhat of an interesting evening. She again apologised for her earlier forwardness and left her private home telephone number.

After getting herself quietly dressed, she left her note on the mantelpiece above the fire and sneaked out the front door to her car.

CHAPTER

FOURTEEN

Gerald turned around and found himself back in the familiar landscape he knew so well. It was still almost void of all colours and what little remained was virtually completely washed out. He realised he was standing at the burnt-out remains of the *Triglotine* settlement, where he was accepted by his friend Vaylor, as an honoured member of their tribe.

Sadly, he remembered when Mahabone and his henchmen invaded the village expecting to find him and his father, to stop them escaping. But when Mahabone realised he was too late to find them in the village, he ordered his guards to kill all the villagers and reduce their village to rubble.

He remembered how he was stalked by one of the scouts guards the first time he had visited. The experience of it all was so bad, it had made him extremely vigilant this time around. Scouring the horizon to make sure it was clear, he walked stealthily towards the large bolder that was protruding several feet from the ground. He knew that the '*Sleeper*' was his only way home, and knew he had to find a safe place to hide it. At least this way, it couldn't be lost or stolen.

Looking around the surrounding area for something strong enough to dig a hole, he eventually spotted the old rusty remains of a sword and used it to create a recess under the boulder. Cautiously, he removed the ring on his finger, that connected to the chain and the '*Sleeper*' and placed them in the newly made recess.

Finally, he marked the spot so as not to forget its location. All he had to do when he was ready, was to return to the same place, uncover the concealed objects, ring the bell three times and go home.

Satisfied that it was well hidden, he started to walk towards Mount Boaz and any remaining friends that may have survived the onslaught from his previous quests.

The terrain was difficult as usual. The colourless grass and brittle reeds, seemed to grab his ankles, as if wanting to restrain him, or even a way of warning him to go no further. Nevertheless, remembering how difficult it was on his last visit, he forged ahead to the foot of the mountain.

It looked a lot smaller than he remembered, but there again, he remembered he was a little smaller in those days.

'*Well, here I am again,*' he thought, putting the toolbox on the ground as he rested.

The air had become damp and very thick around the base of Mount Boaz, alike a mixture of steam and sand, that began to rasp unforgivingly at his throat. The earlier clear visibility had deteriorated so quickly, he could only see across several yards, plus the murky backdrop of Mount Zeds larger summit had almost completely disappeared.

After only a few restful minutes, just enough to catch his breath, he picked up the toolbox and continued up the well-worn trails that had been cut out over the years, from the trampling feet of *Triglotines* marching up and down.

Surprisingly, after all these years, he still remembered where he was going and knew it wouldn't take too long for him to reach the boundaries of King Tubal'cain's fortress.

***

About an hour later, Gerald found himself in slightly unfamiliar surroundings. The path had become overgrown and the grey foliage had suddenly become very dense.

'Oh dear, I can't remember it being like this. I know I have been away for several years, but...' He then remembered the time difference between the two worlds and realised that time had moved on much quicker in this supernatural land. Remembering that he had spent months in this world before, only to find that he had only been gone for a day, or maybe two in his own world.

'Ah, that would make sense of all the growth then.' he thought. *'To these people, I have probably been away for many years.'*

Before he had a chance to start walking again, a rustle of branches caught his attention, making him spin quickly on his heels to face a small man brandishing a sword.

'My God, Vaylor! is that you?' he asked carefully. 'I can't quite believe how old you look! You have changed so much.'

'Who's asking?' asked Vaylor.

'It's me.'

Vaylor looked at him, slightly confused.

'It's me God-dam-it, I'm your friend Gerald. Don't you recognise me?'

Vaylor stood there pondering for a moment. Then his face began to change, exposing his short spikey teeth in his attempt to break a smile.

'Oh Gerald,' cried Vaylor. 'My dear friend, where have you been? You too look so different.'

'I have been in my own world living my life. I have so much to tell you...' but Vaylor quickly interrupted...

'I don't mean to be rude Gerald, but serious things have happened since you left. Mahabone started his uprising again, took over the kingdoms fortress and killed the King.'

'Killed the king?' shouted Gerald. 'You mean that my friend Tubal'cain is dead?'

'I'm afraid so,' squirmed Vaylor, who was now feeling very uncomfortable.'

'And what of Sarika?' asked Gerald nervously.

'Oh, she's fine,' Vaylor whispered. 'She has now been crowned Queen and is temporally living in our village, or often hiding at a secret location, at least until we can regain her fortress back from Mahabone and his henchmen.'

'You mean Mahabone has taken that too?' asked Gerald shockingly.

'I'm afraid so,' said Vaylor. 'Look Gerald, let us not stand here. Come back to my village where we can explain things in greater detail.'

The village was not like the old village at all. It was more like a shanty town with its small, misshaped structures made from large strips of tree bark, shrubs and what looked like mud. It looked and smelled awful.

'How long have you all been living like this Vaylor?' asked Gerald, who couldn't believe his eyes.

'Quite a few years now,' said Vaylor lowering his head. 'It took some time to gather all our

143

people who had scattered across the land. When Mahabone attacked, they had nowhere to hide, so they just ran in every direction to find safety. It took us months to find them. Even now, we have not found everyone.'

'Dear God!' Gerald gasped. 'Look, can you start from the very beginning. I need to understand exactly what happened?'

Vaylor took him by the hand and led him to a small group of handmade stools surrounding a large tree stump, that the villagers have been using as a table.

'Right,' said Vaylor. 'Sit yourself down. I'll get us a strong drink, and I will tell you everything as far as I know.'

Gerald made himself comfortable, placing his toolbox closely by his side, while his friend waddled back with two large goblets of the *Triglotines* favourite alcoholic beverage, crudely distilled from fruits and grain, but Gerald knew, that in his own world, the same substance would simply be known as, *Hooch* or *Moonshine.*

'Here, get this down your neck.' Vaylor passed the overfilled goblet to his friend. 'This will put hairs on your chest lad – Enjoy!'

After making himself comfortable, Vaylor prepared the words he wanted to say and pulled his stool towards Gerald. Taking another large swig from his goblet, he proceeded to tell his friend what he knew.

'Gerald, it was only a brief time after you had returned home, that everything started to change. We all thought that things would be back to normal after you had defeated and escaped the clutches of Mahabone, but we were so very wrong.'

We had all started to gather what was left from the ruins of our old village. Mahabone had retreated and left us to bury our dead. We couldn't rebuild what was left of the village and no one felt safe anymore. On hearing this, King Tubal'cain ordered his men to help us build a temporary settlement, until the king could make provisions for us to settle within the boundaries of his fortress.

Unfortunately, when Mahabone eventually learned about how the king had helped you, he and his men attacked the king without giving any notice to his intent or reasoning. The king and his people were slaughtered and the few that got away, now live here in this settlement, or protect the Queen in her hiding place.'

'Is Sarika here now then? asked Gerald.

'No!' Vaylor explained. 'She is presently in hiding, sending her men out to observe her father's fortress, to closely monitor the movements of Mahabone and his men.'

'What about *Shibboleth*' interrupted Gerald. 'The magical and enchanted sword, is it safe?'

'Of course, we were very lucky that one of the king's guards had hidden before his escape. He had time to steal it from the vault. It had been cursed with one of Mahabone's spells to serve him, but once it was back in the hands of its chosen people, it broke the spell and returned to serving its people as normal. It is now in its rightful place., hanging at the side of Queen Sarika.

Mahabone was hell bent on getting his revenge and something about retrieving what is rightfully his!'

Gerald picked up the toolbox and placed it on the table.

'Apart from the *Ouroboros* ring I stole from him on my last visit, I strongly think Mahabone will also be referring to this,' and opened the toolbox for Vaylor to see.

'Oh yes, I forgot you escaped with the *Ouroboros* ring, that would have really pissed him off. But what is this?' asked Vaylor looking at the toolbox inquisitively.

'It is Mahabone's toolbox. It holds the tools of his trade, possibly the essence of his dark magic! I'm not exactly sure, but that is why I have brought it. I was going to give it to the king. Now that I am unable to do so, I can only pass it onto Sarika, to see if she can put it to some use in her efforts against Mahabone.

I have come back because I had a dream that Sarika was in trouble, but not as bad as this. I thought I was having a troubled time in my world. As you will remember, when I last

146

visited, I had lost my grandfather to Mahabone, and after I eventually found my father, Mahabone killed him before I had a chance to get him home. Back in my own world, I then almost lost my uncle Tom who had a heart attack, closely followed by my grandmother in a house gas explosion. Something just doesn't ring true about any of this. The more I think about it, the weirder the occurrences seem.

Look my friend, is there a chance you can take me to Sarika? If Mahabone has had anything to do with all that has happened in both of our worlds, then I really need to talk to her.'

'Certainly, my good friend,' replied Vaylor, who's was now looking visibly stressed and was making him look older than ever. 'Unfortunately, we can't travel to her location while it is daylight. Mahabone's henchmen would easily track her location and that wouldn't be good for any of us.

Let us enjoy these next few hours before nightfall, then we will make our move. Is that ok with you?'

'I suppose so,' replied Gerald frowning. 'You're the one who knows what is going on more than I do... for now!'

CHAPTER FIFTEEN

It was quite dark when Gerald, Vaylor and his small contingent of *Triglotines,* started to move out towards Sarika's hidden location. They all had to move very slowly in complete darkness, so as not to give away their location, or direction of travel. The last thing they wanted to do, was to give Mahabone's hidden men, the chance to follow.

It was quickly getting cold and damp, as they stealthily made their way through the thickening foliage towards the location of their queen. The constant silence that surrounded them was deafening, so much so, it made every step and broken twig, scream like a homing beacon to the enemy. This, and the constant pressure to remain elusive to Mahabone's minions, made their efforts very intense, and fraught with danger.

'Gerald, we are almost there,' whispered Vaylor. 'We should be coming upon the entrance soon.'

Gerald just nodded his head to acknowledge he understood, while at the Sandye time, getting very excited about meeting his old friend Sarika.

***

Sarika sat quietly at her makeshift desk, pondering over several ideas on how she could take back her late father's underground fortress, but was quickly interrupted by one of her elite guards.

'Sorry to bother you my queen, but Vaylor has arrived with a visitor.'

'A visitor? Sarika snapped. 'Who is this visitor? Has he or she got no name?'

'Yes, Sorry your majesty. He said his name is Gerald.'

Sarika's eyes quickly opened wide, as her smile spread literally from ear-to-ear, exposing her full set of short and very spikey, pearly white teeth.

'I would never have believed it...' she gasped. 'After all this time. I know I was hoping he would respond to the *Talisman;* I gave him all those years ago, and I was also praying for him to return recently. However, not in my wildest dreams did I expect him to come! Send Gerald into my private quarters immediately, I wish to speak to him in private.'

'Yes, my queen, immediately.'

149

Gerald entered Sarika's quarters and sat on the large comfy chair next to the blazing fire. He slowly removed the toolbox from his backpack, laying it gently on the floor by his feet.

'Hello Gerald' said a voice from the shadows. 'I'm pleased you feel confident to make yourself at home again.'

Gerald turned his head to see the outline of Sarika standing in the dark side of the room. The odd flicker from the fire, sent splinters of light flickering across the contours of her face, exposing the familiar characteristics of her people. Her shape had not changed much, but due to the time difference, she looked a lot older than he remembered.

Standing up from his chair, he made his way towards her and guided her into the light.

'Hello pretty lady, how are you?'

Sarika's eyes filled with tears as she looked at his face. Not saying another word, she flung her arms around him and started to sob.

'I've missed you so much Gerald. I needed you when I learned about my father's death and prayed that you would come...'

'I missed you too,' he said, rubbing her head gently. 'I am so sorry to hear about the death of your father. I can sympathise with what is going through your head right now, as I have also lost a member of my family recently. We have so much to talk about. I dreamt that you were calling me for help. That's why I used the *Talisman*. The one you gave me to come back.'

'That's strange,' she replied.

'What do you mean, strange?'

'Strange that I never used any incantations to contact you!'

'Well, someone did!'

Listening to each other's evidence, it became suspiciously apparent, that Mahabone must have had something, if not everything, to do with recent events.

***

Several hours passed, while Gerald and Sarika explained to each other what had happened in their own worlds.

'I have also brought you this' said Gerald, opening the toolbox in front of her.

'What is it?' she asked, looking at the odd objects presented before her eyes.

'It is Mahabone's missing toolbox. My friend and colleague studied these artefacts and reported what she believes to be, the magical properties of each object.

I was originally going to bring these for your father, but now that he has passed away, I now present them to you, in that they may become useful to use Mahabone's own magic against him.'

'In other words' she said calmly, 'you are suggesting that we could give him a taste of his own medicine, for once?'

'Exactly!'

***

Mahabone stood on the balcony in his private quarters, looking at all his men drinking and staggering around the cobbled grounds in his courtyard. He watched as one of his men started running towards the outer door of his quarters. There was a *clash* and *bang* from the guard, as he entered the outer door. Mahabone sighed as he heard the elderly guard's chest wheezing, as he staggered up the passageway.

'Master,' the guard gasped. 'I have news that Gerald has returned and has been spotted several times near the *Triglotines* settlement carrying a small box.'

'Is that so?' smirked Mahabone, praising himself that his intervention with dark magic had paid off. He had successfully convinced Gerald to return with what is rightfully his, the toolbox!

'Now, did anyone see anything else on him?'

'I don't think so Master. Such as?' asked the guard nervously.

'Such as the Ouroboros ring he stole from me.' snapped Mahabone.

'No Master. Just a small box.'

'I see! Then I can at least get my hands on my toolbox and let them all suffer....'

CHAPTER

SIXTEEN

Gerald informed Sarika that he had hidden one of the objects from the toolbox when he first arrived, explaining that the small bell, called *The Sleeper* was his only means to get home. However, she reminded him that he had already explained about the bell when he last visited long ago.

Suddenly, one of the *Triglotine* scouts came rushing over to them.

'Excuse me Your Majesty, I must report that Mahabone's henchmen have been spotted close to the old *Triglotine* settlement…'

Gerald felt a cold shiver down his spine with the thought of them possibly finding where he had hidden his precious *Sleeper*.

'Shit,' blurted Gerald. 'What if they find it?'

'Find what?' she asked.

'The *Sleeper*,' he cried. If they find it, I will be stuck here forever. I need to take some of your guards Sarika. I must take a closer look and check that it remains safe.'

'I agree,' she quickly replied. 'Take six of my men with you. Go quickly, but with stealth. If they spot you, lead them away from here the best you can. Oh! and Gerald, please keep safe, I don't want to lose you a second time.'

Gerald looked deeply into her eyes and gently squeezed her hand. 'I will.'

When they arrived, Gerald and the guards watched as Mahabone's henchmen swarmed around the ruins at the old settlement. Then to Gerald's horror, the enemy left, making their way towards where he had hidden the little bell.

Following Mahabone's men as stealthily as they could, Gerald realised his worst nightmare as the enemy disappeared into the distance. They had somehow found his hiding place. The *Sleeper* had gone!

'We have to catch up with them,' barked Gerald. 'They have taken the bloody *Sleeper*. We must get it back, no matter what!'

In close pursuit of Mahabone's henchmen, it wasn't long before they could hear the distant sounds of chatter.

Unaware that they were being watched, Mahabone's henchmen had rested and had placed their weapons on the ground. This was an unexpected result for Gerald and his men who used it to their advantage. Quickly and without warning, Gerald and the *Triglotine's* descended upon the camp like ghosts, killing each of the henchmen silently by cutting their throats, whilst searching for the bell, but had not been found.

When the rest of Mahabone's henchmen finally realised what was going on, they fled into the darkness, taking Gerald's precious *Sleeper* with them.

With a sickly feeling in the pit of his stomach, Gerald sent all but one of his guards back to Sarika with news of what had happened, while he and the remaining guard continued pursuit of the bell.

The pursuit had continued for almost an hour through heavy foliage and in complete darkness. The sound of broken twigs could still be heard through the dense forest, but it was still impossible to see where the enemy was, or their exact location.

Suddenly, they walked into what seemed to be an open field. Gerald couldn't be sure because of the darkness, but up ahead he could see a shimmer of distant lights.

'STOP,' said Gerald to his remaining guard. 'I know where we are. We are now at the foot of mount Zed and those lights ahead of us are shining from Mahabone's stronghold. We now must be extremely careful. If you wish to turn back at this point, then do so. No one will think any worse of you, as I know you have a young family to care for.'

There was a period of silence while the remaining guard pondered on his request.

However, before Gerald could mutter another word, the guard decided to stick by his side and continue with him to the stronghold.

After completely losing sight of the enemy, both Gerald and the guard made their way to the side entrance to the stronghold. Gerald remembered this from his last visit and wondered if he still had a sympathetic friend inside.

'I know this is a bit late in the day,' mumbled Gerald to the guard, 'but, I still don't know your name.'

'My name is Hiram, Hiram Abiff. Why do you wish to know sir?'

'Well, saying that we are in this predicament together, I think it would just be nice to get to know each other a little better.'

'Oh! OK then sir,' said the guard rubbing his head and looking a tad perplexed.

'Look,' Gerald whispered. 'If we get to know each other a little better, then we will understand how each other might react in dangerous situations. It might give us that extra edge to save our lives. Do you understand now Hiram?'

'Yes sir.'

'By the way, don't call me sir. Call me Gerald.'

Yes sir, I mean Gerald.'

After waiting about half an hour, they monitored the movements of Mahabone's guards walking to-and-fro across the battlements. Eventually, Gerald had enough time to calculate that they had a ten second window to get across the open ground. Hopefully to the hole in the old well, that gave entrance to the dungeon below.

'Remember Hiram, Mahabone is not only a formidable opponent, but also a very smart one at that.'

Just as the guards disappeared behind the turrets, Gerald raised his hand and indicated it was time to run.

'Stay close to me Hiram. Don't make a sound and move very quickly.'

Running as quickly as they could, they just made it to the well, allowing them to crouch behind its low wall, just before the guards came back in view.

'Phew,' whispered Hiram. 'That was pretty close!'

Gerald looked carefully around the vicinity to see if there was anything he could use. It was a deep well shaft and would seriously hurt themselves if they attempted to just drop-in.

'Never,' mumbled Gerald. 'I can't believe it.'

Lying on the ground at the side of the well, was the same old rope that he had used on his past visit.

'What's up Gerald?'

'You'll never believe it. Obviously, nothing has changed here very much. This rope you see lying on the ground, was here when I last came several years ago, meaning that it has been here very much longer, due to the time difference between our worlds. See, it is still fastened to that large metal ring in the ground. Brilliant!'

'How's that going to help us?' asked Hiram, looking a little perplexed.

'Come-on silly. You strike me as being intelligent Hiram, surely you can work it out? Old well - deep hole - rope...!'

'Ah, yes, I see what you mean.'

Waiting until the guards disappeared again, Gerald threw the lose end of the rope down the well, where they both took turns to descend into the darkness.

The old shaft that gave access to the dungeons below, was very dark and smelt of damp algae. Not sure if the old rope would hold out, they quickly made their way down. It seemed to take forever, until their feet eventually touched the floor.

Only the flames from the torches around the outer stronghold walls, sent a narrow beam of light through the small well opening above. However, when their eyes became accustomed to the darkness, there was just enough light to make-out the outline of the inner dungeons, and the location of the stone spiral staircase.

'This is where I found my father,' whispered Gerald. 'He was imprisoned in one of these cells.'

'I was too young to remember,' said Hiram. 'I was only a child then. Unfortunately, I didn't get to hear the stories about you, until after joining the guards. I'm so sorry you lost your father to Mahabone.'

'That's OK.'

Gerald, being bold and audacious, quickly made plans to scale the winding staircase and take the chance to see if his old friend was in the kitchen.

'Hiram, follow me as quietly as you can.' He then proceeded to guide him up the spiral stairs, into the belly of the Mahabone's stronghold.

The walls were damp and covered in slime, as they made their way up the stairs. The sound of voices could be heard travelling through the winding corridors above. However, because Gerald had been here before, he knew exactly where they were coming from and wasn't too concerned.

'Stop here,' commanded Gerald. 'This is the kitchen door. Stay hidden here in the shadows. I need to try something.'

'Try what?' whispered Hiram.

'I think we need as much help as we can get. I must take a very dangerous risk, to see if my old friend Larna still works in the kitchen.'

'Are you sure?'

'Yes, I think it is very important. Listen carefully. You must stay hidden until I call you. If anything goes wrong, make your way back to the rope we came down, climb it and get the hell out of here. Do you understand?'

'Yes Gerald, I do.'

'Good, then here I go.'

Creeping his way to the kitchen, he put his ear to the door. He could here tiny little movements and running water and the odd clink of metal against metal.

'*She must be in there,*' he thought. 'Well here goes nothing,' he whispered and silently opened the door.

There, facing away from him in front of the sink, was a female dressed in cooks clothing. Gerald was sure it was Larna, but when he approached, the young woman turned and was startled to see a strange looking man coming towards her.

'Please don't scream,' said Gerald quickly. 'I am a friend of Larna.'

'How do I know that? Who the hell are you? Where the blazes do you come from and why do you look so ugly?'

'Look, my name is Gerald. I am from...'

'You mean, *thee* Gerald,' interrupted the cook. 'The same Gerald that came from another world, and who fought bravely against Mahabone?'

R. L. Barnes.

'Yes, the very same,' said Gerald, hoping that it was a safe response.

'What are you doing here? It's dangerous. Look, I am sorry, my name is Salindra. Larna was my mother.'

'What do you mean, was!'

'Unfortunately, she died a few years ago, trying to protect me from one of Mahabone's filthy guards, but not before she told me all about you.

You see, I am the product of another guard, who had raped my mother and when she saw another trying it on with me, she went like a hungry griffin at a bone.'

Gerald now knew it was safe to bring Hiram in and after explaining to Salindra who he was, he called Hiram into the kitchen.

'We are here to retrieve something from Mahabone,' said Gerald, 'and then return to your own people. I must help them regain your queen's kingdom.'

'What do you mean, queen? What happened to the king?'

'Mahabone killed him,' replied Hiram. 'The princess has now inherited what is left of his kingdom.'

'Bloody hell,' said Salindra. 'I've been enslaved here all my life. I've only ever known what my mother told me about my family and the *Triglotines*. No-one has said a thing here! I didn't know. So, what do you intend to do now?'

'I was hoping you could help us,' Gerald asked politely. 'We need you to be our eyes at the upper sections.'

'Oh! I'm not sure that I can!'

'Don't worry,' said Gerald reassuringly. 'Your mother carried drinks to the guards on a tray and when our route was clear, she warned us by dropping the tray. I only ask that you can do something along the same lines. Also, when we leave, you can leave with us too, if you wish?'

'That would be impossible,' replied Salindra. 'He would not stop until he found me and killed me. I wouldn't want any of the *Triglotines* to suffer his rage just because of me! I think it would be best if I just stayed here...'

'I understand what you mean,' interrupted Hiram. 'If you feel safer here for now, then stay. However, don't rule out the chance to leave later.'

'I hear what you are saying, but now is not the time.'

CHAPTER

SEVENTEEN

Mahabone had been back in his own stronghold for several hours now. He had left a large contingent of his men to monitor the movements of the *Triglotine* people. More importantly, to look after his recent prize, the kingdom of his deceased opponent, King Tubal'cain. But, when his henchmen had run away from Gerald, running gasping and wheezing back into their master's courtyard, Mahabone immediately confronted one of the guards...

'Why are you trembling and gasping for air you fool.'

'Sorry master, I couldn't see how many of them there was,' the guard gasped. 'Gerald and his men jumped us when we were resting...'

'JUMPED!' growled Mahabone. 'What kind of men are you? I'm surrounded by a bunch of brainless idiots. Where are the rest of your party?'

'Most of them are dead master. He surprised us when we were resting, we didn't know...'

'DIDN'T KNOW! bellowed Mahabone through gritted teeth.

'Sorry master, but we did find this...'

Mahabone watched in anger as the little guard pulled a chain from his pocket. When the guard presented the complete contents, Mahabone's face began to change.

There, in front of his red lifeless eyes, was the lost *Sleeper*. The special little bell that Gerald had taken from him, when he escaped his grasp, many years ago.

The *Sleeper* was still safely secured in its leather holder and still attached to the chain. Mahabone's eyes slowly closed, as he sighed with pleasure. Now that his bell has been returned, he can finally travel between other worlds, wherever and whenever he wanted.

***

Meanwhile, Salindra carefully carried the guard's food and wine to the upper battlements. They had been on duty for quite some time and she knew they would be hungry and thirsty by now. Normally the guards would take turns to have a break, however, when Salindra made their favourite gruel (*a sort of cold porridge with griffin meat*), they always let their guard slip and took their break together.

R. L. Barnes.

She had told Gerald and Hiram to wait in the shadows, then when the guards were settled, she would cough a few times when the coast was clear.

Gerald waited impatiently for Salindra to give the sign. He knew that the guards would have given Mahabone the *Sleeper* by now and had to find a way to get it back. After all, it was the only thing to get him home!

'Hiram, we must find our way to Mahabone's quarters without being seen. I have done it before in the past, except for the two guards I had to swiftly deal with.'

'What if we encounter any now?' whispered Hiram, his eyes almost popping out of his head.

'Don't worry, hopefully, most of the guards will be drunk by now. Saying that, if any do show up, we'll just have to deal with them as quietly as possible. You have killed someone before, haven't you?' Hiram just looked at him with glassy eyes, looked at the floor and never said a word. 'Oh-my-God,' Gerald whispered. 'You've never killed anyone before!'

'I'm sorry,' winced Hiram.' I have only pretended to kill things during training. I've never done it for real.'

'Jesus... Look, don't worry. I will stay in front. Just make damn sure you stay behind me and be my eyes at the rear. Should you see anyone coming let me know and I will deal with them the best I can. Is that OK?'

Hiram now looked like a young schoolboy, standing outside the headmaster's office.

'Yes, that's OK.'

Salindra, took the empty tray from the guards, as they hogged their food and drink. Knowing that they would be out of the way for a little while, she made her way to the top of the spiral staircase and coughed loudly a few times.

On hearing this, Gerald and Hiram quickly darted up the stairs. When they passed Salindra at the top, Gerald put his arm around her and gave her a little squeeze to say thank you. They then continued around the corner and out of sight.

'This way Hiram,' mimed Gerald.

Squatting uncomfortably behind the three-foot wall, that overlooked the large courtyard, Gerald could hear the main body of Mahabone's so called *elite* guards, exchanging their achievements and arguing amongst themselves. They were obviously getting drunk, relaxed and off-guard.

'We might be able to use this to our advantage,' whispered Gerald. 'While they are wasting too much time arguing amongst themselves, they should be so distracted, we should be able to creep down the side stairs and slip our way along the boundary wall. It leads right to Mahabone's chamber door.'

R. L. Barnes.

Just as he finished whispering to Hiram,
footsteps could be heard coming up the stairs.
One of the guards from the courtyard, had
heard something and was making his way
towards them.

'He's coming this way,' whispered Hiram in a
panic. Gerald quietly removed his blade from
its sheath and positioned himself just out of
sight of the approaching guard.

'Shush... Leave it to me!'

Just as the guard put his foot on the top
step, Gerald stood up and was almost nose-to-
nose with the guard, who by now was now so
startled, he was speechless.

Without another second to lose, Gerald
positioned the tip of his blade at the throat of
the guard and pushed it to the hilt. Not a
scream could be heard from the injured man,
only the horrible gurgling of a man, who has
just had his throat cut, accompanied by the
unmistakeable metallic smell of blood,
emanating from his lips. Gerald griped the
handle and slowly retracted the blade from the
neck-wound, allowing the guard to fall to his
knees and onto the cold stone floor.

'Help me Hiram, to drag his body over to that
recess. We must hide his body. They must not
find it, or they will raise the alarm. We'll have
to use his tunic to mop up the remainder of the
blood.'

After making sure that everything was cleaned away, they made their way down the short staircase and along the inner boundary wall, leading to Mahabone's chamber.

'This is it,' whispered Gerald. 'Keep your head low, while I try the door.'

Putting his hand and applying pressure on the large round knob, Gerald slowly opened the door.

'Follow me inside,' mimed Gerald. 'Look, stay here behind the door and keep it locked. Make sure no-one comes in. No-matter what you hear from now on, do not move. However, if you do see me running towards you, open it and run like hell. Do you understand?'

'Of-course I do Gerald, what do you take me for?'

'I know, I'm sorry. I just want to make sure before I go further. Stealing from Mahabone is not a walk in the park and that's if the *Sleeper* is even here at all!'

Leaving Hiram on the look-out at the entrance, Gerald quietly made his way along the hallway. He had been here before long ago, hoping everything was the same as he remembered.

As he approached the first doorway, Mahabone could be heard grumbling to himself at the far end of the front room.

'*Oh hell, he's still awake,*' cringed Gerald, trying his best not to make a sound, while making his way to the study at the rear of the building.

Feeling a sense of relief, that he had made it to the study without disturbing Mahabone, he made his way to the cabinet, where Mahabone usually kept his most valuable objects under lock and key.

As expected, it was locked, but only with a simple mechanism. Taking his blade from its sheath once more, he placed the tip under the weakest part of the lock and pulled. Gerald's heart seemed to stop beating, as the blade split the wood with a *crack*, sending the mechanism shooting noisily across the floor.

The silence that followed, seemed to last forever. Gerald listened for any movement from Mahabone's front room, but there was nothing, only the familiar mumblings as he had heard earlier.

Now that the cabinet was open, he carefully searched each compartment to see if the bell was there.

'*Jesus, there is nothing here,*' he thought, frantically searching each of the drawers without success.

However, just as he thought all was lost, he noticed one of the drawers was a lot shorter than the rest. Carefully removing it completely from its runners, he noticed a small finger hole at the rear. Sticking his finger through the hole, he realised there was a smaller hidden drawer.

He pulled the secondary compartment and to his delight, there, wrapped in a velvet cloth, was the grubby silver ring and chain, attached to his only way back home, the little *Sleeper* bell.

Now that the bell was safely under his tunic, Gerald heart was pumping so loud, he could barely hear anything else. With the adrenalin now pumping through his veins, he panicked and rushed uncontrollably towards the front door.

'Who's there?' boomed Mahabone, stepping out from the doorway. 'It's you! – Guard's – Guards.' Mahabone reached for his sword and lunged towards Gerald, piercing his upper arm. Hiram bravely stood his ground by throwing a punch to Mahabone's face, sending him crashing to the floor, while Gerald rose to his feet.

'Run Hiram,' shouted Gerald. 'Run as fast as you can.'

Without a second to spare, Hiram opened the door, pulled Gerald out and ran towards their escape route, thinking that Gerald would follow. However, by the time Hiram realised Gerald was not following him, he quickly hid behind the upper barracks wall and looked on in horror, as Gerald was being surrounded by guards near Mahabone's quarters.

Mahabone stood seething at Gerald, who now stood nervously in the centre of the surrounding guards.

Standing at the entrance to his quarters, Mahabone stretched out his hand towards Gerald.

'Hand the *Sleeper* back peacefully and I'll promise to let you live.'

Gerald put his hand inside his tunic, as if to comply, but as always, he had his own ideas.

Using his delay tactics, Gerald looked around for a way to escape and ran towards a small gap between the guards. Tragically, as he entered the gap, one of the guards tripped him up, sending him and the *Sleeper* flying.

Landing heavily on the ground, Gerald tried to forget the seething pain from landing on his wound. Scrambling to his feet, he realised the bell had landed several feet away, but by the time he tried to get to it, another guard slammed his large metal malice on the ground, completely crushing the *Sleeper* beyond repair.

'NO, no-no!' cried Gerald, realising his only chance of getting home had been lost forever. 'What have you done?'

Mahabone, not realising what had just happened, strolled over to where Gerald was standing.

'I knew I would catch you at some point,' sneered Mahabone. 'I always do, but what goes on here?'

'Your clever guard has just destroyed the *Sleeper* with his weapon,' cried Gerald. 'Now we have both lost out.'

'WHAT!' boomed Mahabone.

'I said your so-called elite guard, has just destroyed your precious bell and my only chance to get home!'

Mahabone's face looked like it was going to explode. Thinking about all the years he had tried to get the *Sleeper* back from Gerald and how the bell would allow him to go back to his old ways of tyranny, Mahabone finally snapped.

Without another word being said, he raised his sword above his head and swiftly brought it down on the guard, completely severing the guards head from his shoulders.

'Now let that be a lesson to you all,' sneered Mahabone to the rest of his guards standing nearby. 'Now grab this imposter,' pointing to Gerald, 'and fasten him with chains against that wall. I have something very special for him. He wants to be friends with the *Triglotines*, well, let us see what he thinks of this.'

Gerald stood fastened to the wall, while Mahabone returned to his quarters. No quicker had Mahabone gone out of site, he had returned with all his dark magic regalia.

'*Oh hell, what's he going to do now?*' thought Gerald, still wriggling at his chains. Mahabone had his hooded cloak on, plus a warlock's staff - never seen before. The stone imbedded in the top of the staff was a sapphire blue and flashed with shards of red.

'*That looks so weird,*' thought Gerald. '*I have never seen such vivid colour in their almost colourless environment before.*' He was now quickly starting to have a very bad feeling about this.

Standing outside his quarters, Mahabone raised his staff and started muttering incantations towards the sky. In less than a minute, Gerald could see dark clouds gathering above his head and the distant sound of rumbling thunder.

'*Oh God,*' thought Gerald. '*I hope he isn't going to cause something to happen at the Triglotine settlement. I hope Hiram has gone back to warn them about what has happened.*'

Little did he know, Hiram was still hiding and looking from behind the upper walls.

Hiram watched as the clouds above his friend's head became very dense. Not only were there rumbles of thunder, but flashing too. Then it happened!

Hiram's mouth fell open with disbelief and horror. He watched as Mahabone pointed his staff towards Gerald, followed by a sudden *Flash-Bang* of white lightning, passing down to the stone on Mahabone's staff, emanating a narrow shaft of intense blue light at Gerald.

Immediately, Gerald began to scream with excruciating pain, as the shard of light penetrated his torso.

Hiram on the other hand, watched intensely as he witnessed Gerald's hair and clothes vaporise, leaving him completely naked and bald. He then continued to witness the metamorphosis of his friend, watching his skin beginning to split, emanating a bright, white light from his deep lesions. Finally, Gerald gave out a loud blood-curdling cry, before finally shrinking into another humanoid form.

The Gerald he knew was now gone and, in his place, stood the unrecognisable, short rotund figure of a male *Triglotine*.

Mahabone, now puffed up with pride, strolled over to his new handy work. Smirking gingerly at the unconscious body lying at his feet, he looked at the expressions on his guard's faces, wondered if he had done enough to impress them!

'Dress him,' grumbled Mahabone to one of his guards. '...and put him in the dungeon. I will continue my work, once he is awake. Now that he is unable to return to his own body, that is sleeping in his own world, it will now rot and die. Now he is mine!'

On hearing Mahabone's words, Hiram crawled behind his wall as fast as he could, making his way back to the dungeon, hiding in wait for the return of his friend.

175

R. L. Barnes.

After the guards had dressed Gerald in a simple sackcloth, they carried him down to the dungeon and threw him on the floor, locking the cage door behind them.

Hiram, who was hiding in the shadows, waited until the guards had completely disappeared, before making his way to where his friend was held.

'Gerald. Gerald, are you OK?' Not a sound could be heard. He looked around for something he could use to prod his friend. He knew he couldn't shout but needed something to allow physical contact.

Looking around the dark corners of the dungeon, Hiram could see a metal pole. It was a lucky find and almost passed it by. It had been lying so tight against the inner corner, it had almost blended in with the moss-covered brickwork.

Taking the pole, he returned to where Gerald was lying and poked the pole through the bars at his unconscious friend.

'Gerald, wake up,' he said whispering '... wake up. We don't have much time...'

Gerald, suddenly started to moan, and rolled over on his back.

'Oh, what the hell happened? Where am I? My head feels like it's been hit with a train.'

'Mahabone used his dark magic on you,' whispered Hiram. 'However, I need to tell you something that you may not like, so don't flip out.'

'What are you on about?' said Gerald, now feeling a little better, bringing himself to his feet. 'Uh! I feel a little shorter than normal...'

'This is what I'm trying to tell you. Mahabone changed you into one of us...'

'ONE OF YOU,' shrieked Gerald, making his way to the door and putting his hands through the bars.

'Shush,' interrupted Hiram. 'You will alert the guards. Just keep quiet!'

When the dim light from the hole in the roof illuminated Gerald's stubby hands, he went berserk. He quickly put his hands on his now bulbous head and felt his pointy ears and spikey teeth.

'What the hell... Jesus Christ. What's he done?'

'Calm down... just calm yourself down...'

'Calm down! You got to be kidding me. I've got a head like a watermelon, pointy ears and fricking piranha teeth. How do you expect me to react?'

'Look, let us just find a way out for now. Maybe Queen Sarika knows a way to help. One thing for sure, we're not going to get anything done by standing here. Now get your head out of your arse and help me find a way to get you out.'

Gerald, still seething, knew his friend was right. He was not able to do anything here.

'OK Hiram, I get your point. As for getting me out, that's easy.'

'Easy!'

'Yes. When I found my father on my last visit here, I used a rod to lift the door off its hinges. They are such a bad design, anyone with half a brain could work it out. No disrespect.'

'None taken.

'I don't know if it will be strong enough but try using that pole you found.'

The pole was a little short for leverage, but Hiram placed the tip of the pole where Gerald had instructed, then placed his body weight on the other end.

'It's not moving Gerald!'

'Try bouncing yourself up and down...'

The sudden shrill of rusty metal moving on rusty metal filled the air, as both hinges gave way to the pressure. Bars vibrating, the door jumped off the hinges, and fell to the floor with a crash. The sound resonated all through the dungeon and up the spiral stairs to where the guards were stationed.

'Let's get out quickly Gerald. They must have heard that. They will be here in no time.'

With that, Hiram grabbed his friend's arm and led him to the rope, still hanging from the hole where they had first entered.

The sound of guards could be heard running and shouting, as Gerald and his friend started to ascend the rope, but three quarters of the way, the guards entered the dungeon and started to look around.

Holding their breath, Hiram tried his best to pull up the hanging rope below him, hoping the guards would not see it. Keeping perfectly still with pain shooting through their arms, they knew they must stay still and silent, until the guards either left, or spotted them.

The guards, being short and not too bright, looked around the floor area and the now empty cell.

'Quick. Go and tell the master that Gerald has escaped,' said the senior guard.

'Why me?' whimpered the junior guard. 'You know what he will do to me!'

'I don't care,' snapped the senior guard. 'Tell him that he must still be hiding in the castle somewhere. And that's an order.'

Luckily, not one of the guards had the sense to look at the ceiling, where Gerald and Hiram were hanging so precariously. However, with a huge sigh of relief, the guards finally left, allowing Gerald and his friend to continue their escape.

Once outside the well, the guards could be seen running around the top of the stronghold, but as soon as it was clear, both Gerald and Hiram made a dart for the heavy foliage at the boundaries, before heading towards Sarika's hiding place.

Chapter Eighteen

Sarika, sat very quietly at the window in her makeshift quarters. The fork lightening that she had witnessed over mount Zed an hour ago, seemed brighter than normal, yet, very unusual indeed. There was no indication that a storm was imminent. However, no sooner had it started, it was only a few seconds before it was over.

Her intuition had never let her down in the past and this time was no exception. She knew that something was afoot.

***

It was getting very dark, when Gerald and Hiram eventually entered the inner boundaries of Sarika's hidden camp and were immediately challenged by the *Triglotine* guards on duty.

'WOAH!' Hiram screamed, putting himself between Gerald and the guards. 'It is I, Hiram. We have returned from mount Zed.'

'What were you doing there?' said one of the guards. 'We have not been told anything about this!'

'You have obviously been on duty at the boundary for some time,' replied Hiram. 'Our troop had returned earlier that day, to inform the queen, that Gerald and I had continued to follow Mahabone's men.'

'So where is Gerald and who is this little fellow?' said the guard, poking Gerald lightly with the blunt end of his spear.

'Err, this might be a little hard to explain,' said Hiram, wondering if they would believe him. 'Well, there has been a bit of an accident...'

'What do you mean, accident?' said the guard looking a little perplexed and wondering why the strange little *Triglotine* was silent. 'Your friend is keeping very quiet!'

'Well, here goes nothing then,' scowled Hiram, who knew he had to just come out with it. 'Gentlemen, I take this immense pleasure, in introducing you to our mutual friend, ... Gerald!'

'WHAT!' shouted the guard. 'Excuse me Hiram, but we know Gerald and let me assure you, that is NOT him.' However, Gerald thought this had gone on long enough and stepped forward.

'Excuse me sir,' he interrupted, 'but I AM.'

'Impossible,' barked the guard. 'The Gerald we know is tall, brave and ever so ugly. So, who the hell are you?'

Gerald stepped closer to the guard and whispered in his ear.

'There has been an incident between Mahabone and I. Therefore, I strongly suggest you escort us directly to the queen immediately, otherwise, you will be held solely responsible for what she does to you next. I assure you sir; I AM the Gerald you know.'

Pondering on what had just been said and because he also knew Hiram, the guard turned towards his men with instructions to escort Hiram and his so-called companion, to the queen.

***

Sarika was still sitting in her quarters, when one of her guards asked permission to enter.

'Come in,' she said softly.

'Sorry to bother you Your Majesty,' said the guard. 'I must inform you that Hiram, the guard that went with Gerald in pursuit of Mahabone's men, has returned without Gerald. However, he does have a stranger with him, a *Triglotine* your highness, who also claims to be Gerald.'

Sarika's intuition told her that something was seriously wrong. *Why had Gerald not*

183

R. L. Barnes.

returned?' she thought. *'Yet Hiram was with a stranger who claims to be him!'*

'Bring them both here,' said Sarika, looking extremely perplexed and nervous. 'Oh, and make sure there is an armed guard to accompany me while they're here.'

'Yes, Your Majesty, I'll see to it right away.'

Several minutes later, the guard escorted Hiram into Sarika's private quarters, closely followed by Gerald, who had become very conscious of his appearance, knowing that Sarika would be unable to recognise him.

'Both of you wait here, until I inform the queen you have arrived,' mumbled the guard, while disappearing into the next room.

'God, I hope she believes me' winced Gerald. 'I have to keep calm when I tell her who I am.'

'Don't be in such a panic you fool,' barked Hiram. 'Look, leave it all to me. I will talk first and explain to the queen what I witnessed, so that she will be somewhat prepared. Only then will you be in a better position to explain who you are.'

'Yes,' sighed Gerald. 'I suppose you're right,' but before he could speak another word, Sarika walked into the room.

'Good evening gentlemen,' said Sarika beckoning the guard to stand a little closer.

'Good evening my queen,' bowed Hiram, but was quickly interrupted by Sarika.

'Hmm! Your name is Hiram, is it not?'

'Yes, my queen. I was the one who accompanied Gerald to try and retrieve the bell that Mahabone's henchmen had stolen. However, before I can explain who my friend is, I must first explain what had happened.'

'Carry on,' said Sarika, now looking intrigued, but a little perplexed.

'It's not a particularly pretty story Your Majesty. Therefore, may I be so bold as to ask you to listen carefully without interruption, so that I may concentrate enough to recall every detail.

'That is a little bold of you to ask such a thing,' she remarked. 'However, under the current circumstances, I find it acceptable. Please, continue.'

'Gerald and I continued to follow the guard to Mahabone's stronghold after sending the other guards back to you. We tried our best to catch up with them, but by the time we had reached Mahabone's stronghold, his henchmen had already disappeared inside.

Gerald had remembered how he got inside from his last visit, so we descended into the dungeons through the old water well, that now acted as a skylight in the roof of the dungeon Your Majesty.'

'Well carry on then,' said Sarika, pulling up a chair.

'Well, Your Majesty, Gerald left me hiding, while he found his way into Mahabone's

185

quarters. He had found the bell he was looking for, but as he left, I could only observe, as he was set upon by one of the guards...'

'Oh no! Is he alright?' scowled Sarika.

'Unfortunately, not altogether Your Majesty.'

'What do you me - *not altogether?*' she frowned.

'As I was trying to explain to you, Your Majesty, during the fight, Gerald dropped the bell on the ground and the clumsy guard brought his large weapon down upon it, destroying it beyond repair.'

'Poor Gerald, how will he get home,' she whispered to herself.

'That isn't the worst of it Your Majesty,' continued Hiram. 'Mahabone came from his quarters and when he found out what the guard had done with the bell, he killed him immediately. I watched as he had a few words with Gerald. However, when Gerald tried to move, Mahabone mumbled words, before raising his staff. Immediately, the sky filled with streaks of lightning, one of which went into the top of the staff and was directed towards Gerald.

I'm so sorry Your Majesty... Gerald's body crumbled and cracked, emanating shards of intense blue light. Within seconds... he was turned into one of us, a *Triglotine!*'

'Intense blue light! Surely not! There has never been such colour in these washed-out lands for centuries. So where is he now then?' barked Sarika.

'My Queen, please let me introduce you to Gerald,' turning slowly and pointing his finger to the odd-looking figure standing in the shadows.

'Is it really you? asked Sarika, looking intensely at his features. 'I'll ask you again! Is that really you Gerald? Step forward where I can take a good look at you.'

Taking several steps forward into the dim light, Gerald's greenish new features gazed into her eyes and smiled, exposing his new spikey teeth.

'I'm afraid it is true Sarika...'

'Prove it then,' she barked. 'What was the last things I said to you, before you left last time?' Gerald paused for a moment and then answered.

'First, you kissed me. Then, you whispered in my ear that you loved me and said that you would miss me. After that, you explained that there was another way back, should I wish to return to you. Finally, you gave me the *Talisman* and its own incantation.'

'And what was the incantation I gave you?' she said, thinking that this would finally prove his identity.

'It was... *REDIRE ME UT ORDO AB CHAO*.

Sarika's face was a picture, as the reality of his situation became clear.

'Can you all leave me alone with Gerald please. I need to speak to him in private. Make sure the door is guarded well. I don't want us to be disturbed. Do I make myself clear?'

Both Hiram and the guards nodded and left the room quietly.

'Gerald, I know I shouldn't mock your current circumstances, and believe me, I will do all I can to put things right. However, I must say you look so beautiful now. The change has done you good,' she said smiling. Trying her best to make light of the situation. 'Please, Come over here...'

Making his way over, Sarika never uttered another word, she just wrapped her arms around him, giving him a long passionate kiss.

'Wow! What was that in aid of?' he gasped.

'That was for remembering that I loved you. I couldn't say anything before in public, but now I can, and with someone of my own kind at that.'

'Yes, I understand all that Sarika, but I'd rather have my own identity back.'

'I know,' she said smiling. 'Look, maybe we can put that toolbox you brought to effective use. Maybe we will find something within it to help you. Let us rest first, then we can look at what we can do. It has been a harrowing time for you. First a little tasty food and wine, then you can lay by my side until morning.'

'That sounds so good Sarika, I could really do with a stiff drink and a good rest. I do appreciate your hospitality.'

'A stiff drink, I can agree with, but rest,' she smiled. 'Maybe later!'

CHAPTER

NINETEEN

Several hours had passed, before Gerald opened his eyes from the morning light. Momentarily forgetting where he was, he looked and realised both he and Sarika had been naked under the blankets all evening.

'Oh dear! What did we get up to last night,' he thought, while kissing her forehead and trying to recall the last several hours? 'I knew we had a lot to drink last night, but, dammit.'

Looking at the contours of her naked body, it was smooth, well-shaped, and yet, a pale shade of green. Apart from her facial features, everything seemed to be in the right place, but it just didn't look right. Then, as he shook off the remaining remnants of sleep, he looked at his own body and realised he was just the same.

'Shit, it wasn't all a dream after all,' he thought. *'The only means to get me home is lost forever and Mahabone had sealed my fate by*

*changing me into a Triglotine. What the hell am
I going to do now?'*

'Hi, good morning sleepy head,' he said as
Sarika lifted her head from her pillow of leaves.
'How's your head this morning?'

'I'm fine,' she said, sitting up and pulling the
blankets around her shoulders. 'And how are
you?'

'Well, I am still a little groggy,' he whispered,
'but I can't really remember to much about last
night,' 'he said with a nervous cough. 'Err, did
we... you know, did we do anything we might
regret?'

'Of course, we did! That's like asking if
griffin's fly, silly,' she whispered with a little
smile. 'You don't think for one moment, that we
lay naked together and did nothing. Don't be so
naive and don't worry if you can't remember.
You performed better than I expected and I
certainly do not have any complaints - so far.'

'So far!' replied a blushing Gerald, now
looking a little uncomfortable. 'You mean there
will be more?'

'Well, if you play your cards right,' rolling her
tongue around the circumference of his ear,
whispering, 'who knows. Maybe next time you
will be in a sober state to remember.'

'Well, let's just take things day by day for
now.' he whispered. 'I do have a load on my
mind and need to concentrate all my efforts on

solving our current problems. I can't afford to make any mistakes.'

'I understand, she said quietly. 'You are right. We can continue at a slower pace, if that's what you want?'

'It is. It's not that I don't want to, it's because the needs of your people must come before ourselves. You are their queen and that position comes with great responsibilities.'

'I agree.'

After leaving the comfort of the bed, Gerald dressed his bottom half and made his way to the toolbox he had left in her care.

'I need you to have a good look at this toolbox Sarika. I need to explain what I know about the contents and maybe the possibility for us to put it to effective use.'

'OK then, show me what you've got.'

He quickly put the toolbox on the makings of a crude table, and opened the lid, exposing the contents.

'What the hell is that?' Sarika asked, turning up her nose.

'These are some of the things that Mahabone uses to enact his dark magic on everyone. It's not all he uses, but by the way he is reacting, they must be worth something to him.'

'What are they then?' she asked.

'Well, I think the best way to explain their individual significances, I think it better to show you the report I got from my friend and work colleague Sandy, back home.

She could only make her hypothesis, based on our historical records of myth and theory. Her best guess!'

'OK, where is the report then?

'Here.' He placed his hand in a pocket of the lid, pulled out two sheets of A4 paper and handed them to Sarika.

Sarika took the report and picked up each item in turn as she read the report.

- **Mammal shoulder bone:** Used to make a spiritual connection to the animal species within any realm he is present.
- **Test Tube** *Unknown*
- **Humanoid skull (on skeleton):** Also, used to connect with the species. (i.e.) An Owl skull to connect to owls. A wolf scull to connect with a wolf, and so on.
- **The Spell Book (The Witches Book of the Dead).** Has spells to conjure up and transform the spirits of the dead. Discusses the use of a humanoid skull in its representation of the dead.
- **The Ouija Board:** Dates to the 19th Century and was made popular during the spiritual movement. Many

people do not like the Ouija board as terrible things are often associated with it. It is stressed that if you don't use a form of protection, i.e. casting a protective circle with salt, or use the board flippantly, then you are asking for trouble. The Necromancer uses this as a tool and is used as a means of connection to the spirits of the dead.

- **Herbs:** Used to heighten the Necromancers senses. To make magical ointments. Herbs such as *Mugwort, Wormwood* and *Dittany of Crete* are used in divination and dream control, usually as an incense, and communicating with spirits (alive or dead)

- **Feathers:** These are often used to focus concentration in spells. Feathers are used for magical undertakings and are mainly determined by the energy which is brought into the feather by the Necromancers concentration and thought. Feathers also have natural abilities. (e.g.) A Crow feather represents the souls of the dead. The Hawk feather has the active energy for hunters, and the Peacock feather to cast the evil eye.

194

- **Birds Claw:** Protection for the Necromancer from enemies.
- **Roots:** Such as Aconite (also known as *Wolfsbane* or *Monkshood*.) The Necromancer uses its dry root to serve as a tutelary spirit. The *Yew* (the death tree) is used for sorcery and dark magic. *Wormwood* is for summoning spirits, and *Mullein* (known as the Hag's Taper), used to make a torch for rituals. Also, a means to see and communicate in other realms, and can be used as a talisman.
- **The Bell and Chain** brings the barer back to his original realm, or if used incorrectly sends the barer into a never-ending sleep.

'Well, I think that has covered everything, but what does interest me, is the little red spell book and the little humanoid skull.'

'Oh! Why is that?' he asked, looking a little perplexed.'

'They look like the only things that may of be some use when used together. According to Sandy's report, they seem to be the only things that transform things. I think we may need some help. In the same way that you used your friend Sandy to gather information. I have the use of a very wise owl.'

R. L. Barnes.

'An Owl?'

'Yes, an owl. He can also speak. He also likes to be called Solomon. He lives in a small temple on the peak of Mount Boaz. We must go through the entrance between two pillars, across the checkered floor to its centre. There, he will appear to us. Only he may be able to guide us, on how to use these things correctly.'

'OK, when do we start.'

'Hold your griffins,' she said sharply. 'We must prepare. A hearty breakfast, weapons, tools and anything else that we might need along the way. You know, just in case there is a chance we run into any difficulties.'

'Point taken!' smiled Gerald. 'You are right.'

'I know I am!' whilst squeezing his shoulder and running her fingers seductively across his pale green lips. 'We will now decide for my guards to gather and prepare the equipment we may require. We should be able to start our journey by mid-afternoon. Is that fast enough for you?'

'Yes, it is. Thank you.'

'OK then,' said Sarika, gently holding his hands. 'Let us now use this morning to relax a little longer, whilst they do the work. We will have enough to do ourselves when we leave.'

Letting the guards continue with the orders she had given; Sarika took Gerald to a quiet part of the camp and asked him to clarify a few points about his family.

196

'I am fully aware that Mahabone killed your grandfather whilst here in the past, and later your father during your escape last visit. Yet, I am still a little confused! I mean, how sure are you that Mahabone had something to do with your uncle's heart attack and the death of your grandmother?'

'I don't know.' he replied. 'I just have the feeling that something doesn't add up.'

'What do you mean?'

'It just seems weird that everything who had something to do with that bloody toolbox, suddenly died without reason or cause. Uncle Tom is old, but he is as strong as a bull. There was nothing in his medical records to suggest his heart was faulty or anything else for that matter. Yet, he quickly became ill with a heart attack. Thankfully, he is on the mend.

As for my grandmother, well! It was only a brief time after the gas engineer called, there was a gas explosion. He had checked out the complete system and assured us it was sound.

After the explosion and fire killed my grandmother, I did curse the engineer at first. However, the more I thought about it, the more it didn't make sense. Something must have happened for the gas-pipes to fail. All this time I didn't realise why I was suddenly getting dreams about you being in danger. Don't ask me how or why, but I'm starting to believe

Mahabone had something to do with me coming here with his toolbox.'

'OK, that would make sense,' nodded Sarika rubbing her head. 'I know that I desperately needed help, but isn't it funny how the disaster with my father the king and my kingdom, coincided with what was happening to you in your world?'

'Look Sarika, if Mahabone has planned all this to regain his toolbox, then he must have other contingency plans drawn out. We must act as soon as we can. The more time we wait, the greater the chance he will catch up with us. We must make our way to your wise owl, Solomon.'

Sarika agreed and hurried the guards along. Within an hour, they were both fully equipped, and ready to roll.

As they stood looking up from the base of Mount Boaz, the rock-face looked steep, barren and extremely hard to navigate. Even the summit was partially obscured by the low clouds. It looked almost impossible to achieve, yet with everything he had experienced recently, it didn't seem to faze him at all.

'Come-on then, lead the way,' he said with determination, while gently squeezing Sarika's hand. 'I have no idea where I am going and you do. I hope?'

'Yes, I do!' she snapped. Although it has been some time since I visited Solomon, I am sure the route has not changed.'

'OK. I was only asking! Sorry, I didn't mean to sound harsh or offend you. I'm just anxious to get things sorted.'

'No offence taken.' She laid her head on his shoulder and kissed his neck.

'Right then young lady, please lead the way.'

CHAPTER

TWENTY

Gasping for breath after a few short hours, Gerald beckoned Sarika to rest on the final outcrop.

'Solomon's Temple is just beyond those dense clouds,' said Sarika, taking a drink from her flask. 'We will have to be careful, as the trail becomes extremely treacherous from now.'

'How treacherous?' asked Gerald.

'Well, let's just say, I highly recommend not to leave go of my hand. The visibility will be absolute zero for a while. Be warned, the slightest wrong move in the wrong direction, could send us crashing to our certain death. Even I must remember how to feel my way with my feet. Once we successfully pass through the dense cloud, it does become progressively clearer, exposing the entrance to Solomon's Temple.'

'How sure are you that we will be safe?' he asked nervously.

'I'm not! I can only trust my instincts. Trust me Gerald. Look, we are here for a reason, and we must accept that we may, or may not, make it. It's a chance we must take.'

'Why don't I feel too comfortable about this?' he said squirming.

'Look, it is something I have had to do every time I have visited Solomon. Just take my hand, keep calm and if you truly love me, then I hope you can trust me.'

'You know I can. What do you take me for?' he smiled.

'Then take my hand, and let's go!'

The time in zero visibility seemed to last forever, but as Gerald carefully navigated the uneven ground behind Sarika, following her tracks as best he could, he was fearful of taking a step in the wrong direction and falling to his death.

'Keep close,' said Sarika. 'This is the dangerous part.'

'Dangerous part!' he squirmed. 'How much further? I'm terrified here!'

'Don't be so impatient. The cloud cover will start to clear in a moment.'

'I bloody hope so. I can't even see the back of your head. You have no idea how much trust I've put in the touch of your hand.'

'Stop fussing!' she snapped. 'Look, I can already see something manifesting itself in front of us.'

Slowly but surely the mist began to clear, revealing two large pillars at either side of the entrance to a stone temple. The whole structure was tall and looked like it had been built from granite. The inside was surprisingly bright, and the whole floor was covered in black and white chequered carpet. There was nothing else in the open interior, except a large monolith in the centre of the floor. In its centre, there was a large inscription of a burning star.

'We have to place a hand over the star on the monolith,' instructed Sarika. 'It's the only way to summon Solomon to reveal himself to us.'

Without any further delay, Gerald placed his hand as instructed and waited with bated breath.

'Who do you think you are?' boomed a voice from behind. 'Coming in here unannounced!'

'I'm so sorry,' said Gerald turning on his heels 'We were...'

'It doesn't matter who, or what we are.' said the voice. 'Hello Sarika, who is this imposter?'

'He is no imposter, Solomon. This man used to be... I mean still is the Gerald I told you about. Mahabone has changed him which is why we are here. Furthermore, Gerald no longer has a means to return to his own world.'

Solomon, perched on a ledge at the top of the temple expanded his wings and carefully pruned his feathers.

'Mm, I see,' turning his head almost three hundred and sixty degrees. 'Tell me... How do you expect me to assist you against one of Mahabone's spells, prey tell?'

'I'm not sure,' claimed Sarika. 'The only thing we have to go on, is the contents of this damn toolbox.'

'A toolbox! Solomon replied. 'What is so special, that it has to be contained in a box?'

Sarika took the strap from Gerald's shoulder and carefully laid the box open on the temple floor.

'The contents you see before you,' she continued, 'is none other than Mahabone's very own tools, that he uses in his despicable trade.'

'Really?' responded Solomon, who quickly flew over to the contents on view. 'Let me see for myself.'

Using his claws and beak, Solomon started opening the bottles and surrounding objects, to see if they had any significance.

'Mm' grumbled Solomon. 'I'm afraid there is nothing here that can help you I'm afraid. A lot of this stuff is useless without Mahabone's intervention.'

'What do you mean?' piped up Gerald. 'There has to be something you can do to help me, surely?'

'I may be a wise owl dear boy, but unfortunately, I'm not a wizard. I can only give you advice and...' something caught his eye, a

R. L. Barnes.

corner of a little red book tucked in the corner of the toolbox. 'Well, I must say! What do we have here then?' slowly using his claw to pull out the little red book.

'Oh, we believe that's one of Mahabone's spell books,' said Sarika, hoping that it would mean something to Solomon.

'Let me see what it holds then,' asked Solomon. 'I have seen many of Mahabone's spells over the years. Maybe I will know some of these too.' He continued flicking through the pages. 'Nope that's no good, nope that's no good either... This spell means nothing. Oh... Just a minute,' he said looking a little perplexed.

'What's the matter? Have you found something?' enquired Sarika.

'This here!' pointed Solomon, holding one of his claws against the open page. 'It is a spell written in the ancient language.'

'Do you know what it says then?' barked Gerald.

'I think I can,' nodded Solomon. 'I have studied the ancient languages for generations. I am a little rusty, but I will try my best.'

'Yes, best is good,' agreed Sarika.

'Well, let me see... According to my understanding of the language, it seems to be a spell to reveal secret objects that have been hidden from sight. It says it allows whatever has been originally hidden by the spell, to be revealed to whoever recites this incantation.'

204

'Should we try to see what happens then?' asked Sarika looking hopeful. 'We have to try something, don't we?'

'I don't know if it would be wise to do so!' warned Solomon. 'I mean we don't have any idea what may be revealed. It could be dangerous.'

'We have to try,' begged Gerald. 'I think we should give it a go. It's a chance we must take to change me back, otherwise we have completely wasted our time.'

'OK!' chirped Solomon. 'If everyone agrees then, we will go ahead.'

In unison, everyone shouted 'YES.'

Solomon put the book on the floor and pondered for a while, trying to remember the syntax of the ancient language. When he was ready, he began to recite the incantation to the best of his ability.

'One is so hidden and time forgot,
Those who can see, shall see me not,
But should this be read in the presence
of travellers and brothers.
The power revealed will control all
others.
So let what was changed, now be seen
and revealed.
Release the spell, So, mote it be.'

There was an eerie silence to the air, not a breeze, nor a sound of the wild. Increasingly, the surrounding atmosphere became alive with static, making their hair and feathers stand on end, as if a thunderstorm was overhead.

A sudden rush of static air began to swirl fiercely in front of them, emanating small intermitting shards of electrical activity, then closely followed by an ear-piercing *bang*, sending everyone present to the floor.

'What the hell was that?' screamed Sarika, looking at Gerald and Solomon lying on the floor together.

Floating above her head was a sealed scroll. It was not hanging by anything! It was literally floating in mid-air.

Moving towards the others, she checked their pulses to make sure they were still alive.

'Phew, they are still breathing' she thought, and proceeded to try to revive them.

'What happened?' moaned Gerald, holding his head.

'You're not going to believe it, but look up there.'

Gerald couldn't believe his eyes, rubbing them in disbelief.

'Holy shit, where the hell did that come from?' he asked.

By now, Solomon was back on his feet and checking his wings for damage. 'Never mind me, I'm OK. What you need to be doing now, is grabbing that bloody thing before it disappears again.'

Sarika did as Solomon had asked and handed the scroll back to him. Carefully using his beak to break the seal on the scroll, he then proceeded to unroll it on the floor.

'What does it say?' asked Gerald impatiently.

'Wait a moment,' snapped Solomon. 'It is written in an even older form of ancient language, so have a little curtesy and grant me more time to decipher it, please!'

'Sorry, I didn't mean to be rude,' said Gerald sheepishly. 'I'm just getting a little anxious, that's all.'

'Apology accepted.' squawked Solomon. 'Now listen here. The text seems to mention something about a powerful source of dark magic.

It mentions the existence of a sacred artifact, that was acquired by Mahabone's ancestors, to be handed down through the bloodline.

Also, according to the text, it seems obvious that this is where Mahabone gets some of his power from. It also mentions here that the actual artifact is hidden in a secret location, deep within Mount Zed. Even better, the bottom of the scroll shows a map indicating the artifact's exact location.'

'How convenient, for us!' mumbled Sarika.

'Unfortunately, according to the map,' barked Solomon. 'The location of the artifact is dangerously close to the rear foundations of Mahabone's stronghold. As it is I, and I alone, who can decipher the map, I suppose I will have to help you more than I expected. I will have to come with you, to guide you all the way.

'That would be very kind of you,' said Gerald. 'I really appreciate it.'

Solomon looked him directly in the eye. 'I don't think you fully understand the sacrifice I am making here! I have guarded this temple for over four and twenty years, never leaving these walls. To leave here, is to leave the security I have enjoyed all these years. I will no doubt leave the temple in a very vulnerable position. However, due to the current circumstances, I am willing to take this chance and assist you.'

Gerald looked at him with tear-filled eyes and put his hand on Solomon's wing. 'Thank you.'

'Well let's get moving,' piped up Sarika. 'We must strike sooner than later. We must find this damn sacred artifact before Mahabone, and his men get wind of what we are doing.'

'I agree,' nodded Solomon, 'but I do strongly suggest that we take the toolbox with us. Although I found nothing useful now, doesn't take away the fact we may find something useful later. We may be able to use the power of the artifact to our advantage. Maybe even get

Gerald changed back to normal, or even home. But we need to go. And we need to go – Now!'

CHAPTER

TWENTY - ONE

The ancient trail towards Mount Zed was almost impassable due to the dense bracken. Obviously at this altitude, the old trails had never been trodden on for decades, or maybe even longer! Nevertheless, it was the only direct way for them to get to Mahabone's stronghold unnoticed. As time was of the essence, there was no other sensible way.

They both took turns to carry the toolbox, whilst Solomon soared in circles above them, constantly watching out for attackers and sending signals to indicate what direction to follow.

'Come on!' waved Sarika. 'Solomon is indicating that we have to go this way.'

'We've been walking for ages now,' shrieked Gerald, tripping on a tree root and stumbling into her.

'Hey! Watch where you are going,' she snapped. 'I've not come all this way to be jumped on!' her face turning from anger to a mischievous smirk.

'I'm so sorry,' he whimpered.

'Maybe you can try landing on me again?' she said with a thought-provoking grin. 'Providing we've completed our task that is.'

'I do hope that is a promise?' he remarked with a cheeky smile, while taking her hand to get back to his feet.

'Hey, you two,' twittered Solomon from above. 'This isn't the time for fraternising. 'Keep your voices low and concentrate on the task at hand. We still have an hour or so to go, but the closer we get, the greater the chances of being spotted by Mahabone's lot. Now follow me and we shall rest in a short while.'

'Sorry Solomon,' said Gerald. 'We were just trying to lighten the moment. I promise you; it won't happen again.'

Tired and exhausted, a further hour had passed before Solomon eventually landed on the trail in front of them, indicating that they should all rest.

'The skies are growing ever darker now,' whispered Solomon. 'We should rest here until all the light has gone. I think it would be prudent to continue from here under the cover of darkness. Mahabone's men will be everywhere from here on in. The less they can see, the better chance we have in reaching the stronghold,'

'Thank God for that!' gasped Gerald. 'My bloody legs are killing me. I just can't get used to these bony legs. I know they are not as muscly as my last legs, but come on, how do you people get around so much on skin and bone?'

'You will get used to them,' piped up Sarika sarcastically. 'To us, your last legs were fat! We couldn't understand how you could move with all that weight! Now you can see how others perceive things differently. So, stop griping and park your new skinny arse down here.'

'I suppose you're right,' he laughed, while Solomon just shook his head in disbelief.

'Here, grab some of these,' mumbled Sarika, as she passed Gerald a few berries she had collected along the way. 'Maybe they might give your spiny legs a bit of energy for later!'

'Oh, very funny-' he quickly answered. 'Very funny indeed.'

'Come on you two,' squawked Solomon. 'You are acting like two immature children. Get a grip, we can't afford to become complacent. We need to keep our wits about us, as we are very close to danger and in a very vulnerable situation right now.'

Solomon turned his back on them and flew high into the darkening sky. He had to see if there were any signs of movement in the vicinity, in preparation for their journey after dark.

'Where the hell is he going now?' whispered Gerald, licking his fingers and wiping the berry juice from his lips.

'Oh, he'll be checking to see if the coast is clear. Don't take too much notice of him. Although he always acts too serious, he has our safety at heart.'

'I see. So, he really cares then?'

'Yes, he does, so just relax and rest until he returns. We have a heavy night ahead of us and a very important artifact to find,'

'Yeah, if we can! We don't even know if the information in the scroll is correct. What happens if we get there and it has all been for nothing! A silly myth - a prank!'

'It won't be, just calm down and rest. Stop worrying. We will succeed, so keep eating your berries and close your eyes for a while. I'll keep first watch.'

Gerald for once, did as he was told and rested his head against a heavily moss covered bolder.

After spending time resting, Gerald woke up to find the air had become dark, damp and cold.

'Is he back yet?' he mumbled, rubbing the sleep from his eyes.

'No, not yet,' whispered Sarika from the shadows.

Gerald sat himself up against the bolder he had been resting on. 'Well, where the hell is he then? He should have been back by now!'

Just as Sarika was about to answer, there was a rustle in the distance and the sound of voices could be heard approaching.

'Quick,' she beckoned. 'Hide under this undergrowth.'

Gerald quickly shuffled himself along the ground to where she was hiding and squeezed his body close to hers.

'Who do you think they are?' he asked nervously.

'No idea, but I can bet they are something to do with Mahabone.'

Just as she finished talking, a handful of lanterns came crashing through the trees, followed by the silhouettes of Mahabone's men.

'This is where I heard a noise!' shouted one of them, 'but I can't see or hear anything now.'

'Whatever it was,' said another, 'it must be long gone now. Come on, let's take this bird back to camp, it will cook nice above the fire.'

Sarika looked on, to see Solomon trapped in a makeshift wooden cage, that was being carried on the shoulders of two more men.

'Oh no!' she whispered. 'They have Solomon. We must rescue him before they kill and eat him.'

'Eat him!' whispered Gerald. 'Well let's get going.'

***

Solomon sat quietly in the cage while he was being carried. As far as the guards were concerned, he was just a common owl of no significance. It was just by chance that they caught him while he was returning to Gerald and Sarika. If it wasn't for the sound of his wings brushing amongst the tops of the trees when he was landing, they wouldn't have followed and pounced on him so easily. He knew if he had landed directly at Sarika's location, they would have been captured too.

Listening to the men talk about cooking him, maybe it was better that he was the only one who was caught. At least they are concentrating on what they are getting in their bellies, rather than capturing his friends.

Gerald and Sarika stealthily followed the four guards from a safe distance. They both cringed at the thought of having to follow the men all the way to the stronghold, but as luck had it, the men stopped at their makeshift camp after only half an hour. Solomon, who was now quietly squawking to himself about being cramped in his small wooden prison, was abruptly put on the ground, whilst the men argued about who was going to collect the firewood and who was going to prepare the owl for cooking.

'Look,' whispered Sarika, 'they have left Solomon next to the tree in the shadows. The two guards that are guarding him will have to be taken out.'

'Where are the other two?' whispered Gerald.

'Over there,' she responded, pointing to two small objects moving in the distance. 'It looks like they are collecting branches, probably for the campfire.'

'Good!' he whispered. 'That means there are only two to contend with for now. If we sneak around behind them quietly, then we can take them out.'

'I agree,' she said, 'but the other two will know something is up when they return and will run back to Mahabone.'

'Oh no they won't,' smiled Gerald. 'I have a plan. After we finish off the first two, we can prop them up in sleeping positions against the trees. When the others look on, it will look like they are taking a nap. Then after we release Solomon, we can hide in the trees until they return. By the time they realise something is up, we can sneak up on them from behind.'

'Sounds like a good plan,' she replied, patting him gently on his back.

The two guards that were sitting and talking beside Solomon, were bragging about what they were going to report back at the stronghold. They were huddled around the only source of light they had; a small crystal jar full of glow worms. Because of the low light, these lamps were often used by Mahabone's men on scout duties in enemy territory.

While they were exchanging stories to each other, the dim luminescent light was just enough to show each other their macabre expressions and misshapen features.

Without further warning, both Gerald and Sarika stepped stealthily from behind the trees. The guards were so engrossed in conversation, they never heard a thing.

Immediately, and without hesitation, both guards were swiftly grabbed from behind, their mouths were covered quickly with one hand to muffle any screams, whilst their free hands pushed their blades through the side of the guard's necks, cutting their jugular veins and severing their windpipes.

Both Gerald and Sarika held on as tight as they could to stifle the guard's gurgling screams, while they slowly drowned in their own blood. Then, after a brief period of struggling for their lives, came the deafening silence of death.

Taking a few moments to confirm the guards were dead, they let both lifeless bodies slump quietly to the floor.

'Quick,' whispered Sarika. 'You prop them up against these trees facing each other, using those vines over there. Try and make them look natural, then clean all that blood off them. If you can't find any water to clean them up, find something! Even urinate on them if you must!'

'Yuk! that's so disgusting!'

'Look Gerald, just get on with it. We have not got time to mess about. If the other two guards suspect anything on their return, we will miss the opportunity to silence them. On the other hand, if they escape and run back to Mahabone, we will quickly become, very dead! Do you understand?'

'Yes, clearly.'

'Good, then get on with it. In the meantime, I'll go and free Solomon.'

***

Poor Solomon lay exhausted in his cage. He had been struggling for so long, he hardly had enough energy left to escape. He had been watching what Sarika and Gerald had been doing and although he never condoned violence, he felt great relief when Sarika's face appeared at his cage.

'Hello Solomon, have you missed us and are you OK?'

'I've felt a lot worse, but I must admit on this occasion, I really thought my goose was cooked. I am forever grateful for your heroic efforts and I'm so pleased to see a friendly face. Now, please get me out of here.' With a quick flick of her sword, she cut the vines that bound his cage.

The other two guards had now started to make their way back to their small makeshift camp, both carrying copious amounts of bracken strapped to their backs.

'I hope those two lazy beggars have plucked that bird for us. I'm starving.'

'Yeah, they better have. We haven't collected all this for nothing!'

'Yes, I know. I'll give them a piece of my mind if they haven't.'

'Piece of your mind! More like the back of my hand.'

'Yeah... That's funny that is,' sniggered the other guard.

'Oh, be quiet you fool, you sound as dumb as those two.'

Their heads now bobbing just over the horizon, the guards could just make out where they set up camp. It was still very dark, but because they knew where they were, they could just make out the dim spot of luminescent light, emanating from the lamp they had left with the other guards.

'I can see where they are. At least they haven't crawled their way back to the safety of the stronghold.'

'My belly's still grumbling,' the other guard mumbled.

'Pack-it in. Is that all you can do? You moan more than my pet griffin in heat. I get very hungry too you know, but you don't hear me complaining, do you?'

'I suppose not, but I still can't wait to get this fire going. I hope they haven't eaten it.'

'Eaten what?'

'The bird, silly.'

'What, a raw bird! Yew! Don't be such a idiot. Honestly. Now shut your mouth and get a move on!'

It took another fifteen minutes or so, for the guards to fight their way through the black terrain, tripping over unseen potholes and branches, like hidden man traps.

Looking at the luminescence light getting closer, they could just see the outline of the two other guards slouched against the trees. They were both crouched in a sleeping position, with their spears held firmly in their arms.

'Look at those lazy sod's,' said one guard pulling the bundle from his back and dropping it on the ground. 'They've both fallen asleep.'

'You know what,' barked the other guard, dropping his bundle next to the other one. 'Bloody Hell! I only asked them to do one simple job and look what they do... Oy, you two, what the hell do you think you are doing?'

There was no response. Both guards quickly ran over to where the guards were sleeping, to find both their necks severed and secured to the trees with vines.

'Shit! What the f...'

It was too late. Sarika struck first, closely followed by Gerald. Whilst the guards had been checking out their fellow companions, they had silently crept up from behind and readied their weapons. With two well practiced swings, it only took a moment to decapitate both guards, sending their bloody and mangled heads into the blackness of the undergrowth.

'Well, I didn't really think that was going to work,' sighed Sarika.

'Aye, well I'm pleased it's over.'

'You're not finished yet...' squawked Solomon. 'You will have to bury them and get rid of all the evidence. If other scouts come looking for them at dawn, they will assume they are scouting elsewhere.'

'He's right,' Sarika replied. 'We will have to bury them now and tidy up the rest as soon as we can see what we're doing.'

'Until then,' whispered Solomon, 'we shall get rid and rest to gain our strength for our journey tomorrow."

CHAPTER

TWENTY - TWO

The first early rays of daylight peeked over the horizon, turning the darkness to a lighter shade of grey. As soon as they could see their surroundings, they immediately began to get rid of any leftover evidence, burying it under the undergrowth.

Right, now that that's all done,' squawked Solomon, 'we can now get on our way and complete the task at hand.'

'After yesterday,' grumbled Gerald, 'I honestly hope that is correct. I certainly don't want to go through another session like that.'

'Oh, stop being so negative,' said Sarika. 'I have all my people to think about and I deal with these sorts of potential threats every day. Get a grip and think positive. We WILL, find what we are looking for.'

'Yes, we must hurry up now Gerald,' said Solomon encouragingly. 'We must leave before any other scouts arrive. If we start right away, we should be close to the stronghold by around midday. Then we can re-assess the situation and double check the map on the scrolls again.'

'Ok, I'm ready now,' replied Gerald. 'I was just getting a little anxious again, but I am fine now.'

Sarika leaned her head on his shoulder and kissed his neck. 'I understand, don't worry, we'll take care of you.'

'So, not a moment to lose,' interjected Solomon. 'Has everybody got everything?'

'Yes,' they said in unison.

Solomon immediately stretched out his wings, took a large breath, then soared just above their heads... 'Well, on we go,' he squawked. 'Follow my lead.'

'Well,' muttered Gerald, 'the man, or should I say, the bird, has spoken. Let's go.'

It was a difficult climb to the top of the mountain ridge. It overlooked a small valley, just before the last ascent to Mahabone's stronghold.

'Look just above the forest over there,' pointed Sarika, directing everyone's gaze to a ridge on the opposite side of the valley.

'Is that what I think it is,' asked Gerald. 'Is that the rear of the stronghold?'

'Yes, it is,' replied Solomon.

'Oh, I've only ever seen it from the front and side entrances. I've never seen it from this angle before. The walls look massive.'

'Obviously! snapped Solomon. 'It was made difficult for enemies to scale and penetrate his domain. Mahabone might be a tyrant, but he's certainly not stupid.'

'How long will it take us to reach there then?' asked Sarika.

'One, maybe two hours. However, we don't want to go there directly, we will be spotted without a doubt. I suggest we get within a few hundred yards and lay low until dusk. Plus, it will give us a little more time to study the map. Until we get close enough to the wall to study the terrain, we won't be able to pinpoint the exact location of where we can get to the artifact.'

'That makes sense,' agreed Gerald. 'The last thing I want, is to be caught again. My last experience turned me into this,' pointing to his *Triglotine* features.

'Charming!' barked Sarika, looking very upset.

'Sorry,' he said quietly. 'There was no disrespect intended. I wasn't trying to...'

'Hey, stop fussing you two,' squawked Solomon. 'Why is it every time you two speak, you always have a go at each other. It has been blatantly obvious that you have feelings for one another, and that you both aren't sure where you stand. So, can you please put all that to one side until later? You will end up getting us all killed. Now stop it and grow up!'

They both just stood looking at each other with opened mouths. They couldn't believe he had just told them off like little children. It was so uncomfortably silent; they could hear blades of grass rubbing against each other.

'I'm sorry,' she whispered, considering the lost look in Gerald's eyes. Gerald just smiled, before stepping forward and wrapping his arms around her.

'I'm sorry too. It came out all wrong. I should have taken your feelings into account. I wasn't saying that this body is a disgrace. I was simply saying it's what Mahabone turned me into when I was last there, that's all,' kissing her gently on the lips.'

'Right, that's enough of that!' grumbled Solomon. Now that that episode is over, we need to continue to get there in time. We need to be able to confirm the points on the map, while there is still daylight. So, let's get moving again. Please?'

The foliage in the shallow valley was dense and very tall. This was good, as it provided the perfect cover from prying eyes. If it had not been for Solomon hovering just above the canopy, they would have been going around in circles for sure, but as it was, it didn't take too long before they walked into the clearing at the foot of their last ascent.

'We'll make camp here, obviously no fires,' suggested Solomon. The stronghold is only fifteen minutes hike above us. You two stay here and I will take a casual fly-past the rear of the wall.'

'Is that wise?' asked Sarika.

'I'll be fine. Hopefully they will treat me as the other guards did. Just a simple owl, flying about my own business.'

'As long as you are sure?' she replied.

'What happens if you don't get back?' asked Gerald.

'Look, if I'm not back within the hour, then one of you keep low and look for me. I've already memorised the map, sort of. I just want to take a quick look to see if there are any obvious markers.' With all that said, he spread his wings once more and disappeared into the skyline.

Gerald undid the straps from around his shoulders, placing Mahabone's toolbox gently on the floor, along with the wrapped-up lamp he took from the dead guards. 'This thing might seem light to start with, but it is as heavy as hell after all this walking. I'm shattered.'

'Would you prefer me to carry it for you?' she offered.

'No, I'll be ok, but thank you for offering anyway. It is not custom where I came from, to ask a lady to carry heavy objects. However, I'm sure it will feel lighter again after a good rest. In the meantime, it will make an excellent seat for you,' he said smiling. He then placed the box near to where she was sitting.

'Mm, I wish the rest of the men hear would think like you. I've learned so much from you since you came into my life. It makes the others sound like Gowls.'

'Gowls! What the hell is a gowl?'

'Sorry, I forgot, you haven't seen one of them yet, have you?'

'Err, no!'

'There's very few of them left. They are small, wild and smelly. Covered in hair they are. They'll bite you as soon as look at you with their very long teeth, often running around in the forest undergrowth. Nasty little beggars they are. They don't think of anything but themselves, hence why I relate them to some of our male population.'

'Yes, we often have a similar problem with a certain class of people where I come from too,' he replied, then chuckled to himself.

CHAPTER

TWENTY - THREE

Solomon, eventually returned to where he had left the others resting. Only this time, with a sense of urgency and excitement in his voice. He had been circling well below the stronghold wall and spotted something intriguing.

'I've found something,' he squawked, trying to catch his breath. 'I think I have found a way to where Mahabone may have hidden something.'

'Take a minute to catch your breath,' suggested Gerald. 'Calm down and tell us what you have found.'

'I was flying around confirming all the landmarks from the map, but when I looked, I noticed a little recess hidden behind a very tall a mass of ivy, around thirty feet above the base of the mountain. Of course, the stronghold wall is over two hundred feet tall at that point, and because that section of the wall is built down the side of the mountain face, it is obvious its purpose is to support the structure. I therefore wondered why such a recess would be needed close to its base. So, I dropped down to take a closer look and found several symbols within the recess. They looked the same as what is on the map. It must be an entrance of some sort, as there was nothing else there.'

'Nothing else at all?' replied Gerald.

'Nope, not a thing. I couldn't fathom out what the map had indicated. If you look at the map,' he said, rolling out the scroll, 'you will see that is states the opening of the entrance is at the rear of the stronghold. If my eyes had not caught the sunlight rays casting a shadow from the edges of the recess, I would have not been able to find it. It was only because I was airborne. Anyone from ground level would have no chance of finding it at all. Now look at the symbols on the map. These exact symbols surround the inside of the recess, but no entrance is visible.

'Maybe the symbols are a key,' she said. 'Maybe we must read out the meanings, or do something with them to open up the door?'

'Sounds a little out-there to me,' mumbled Gerald to Solomon, 'but who am I to say what can, and can't be done! I mean, look what happened to me. In fact, she might be right. Obviously, the map and the symbols at the recess have some connection.'

'I have to agree,' nodded Solomon. 'As soon as the daylight has gone, we will make our way there, and use that luminescent lamp you acquired to see what we are doing.'

'Ok, that is what we will do,' she said resting her back against the tree. 'Now you need to rest after all that flying around. Here, take some of these berries.'

The vail of night had gradually fallen by the time Solomon had awakened. They had not wanted to wake him and let him sleep as much as he could. However, now that he was awake, both Sarika and Gerald swiftly gathered up their things, leaving Solomon to come around slowly.

'Right, we're all ready and packed,' said Gerald. We are ready when you are.' Solomon turned his head almost three hundred and sixty degrees.

'Ouch, my wings are so sore. I must have done more acrobatics than I realised. I'm not really used to this sort of thing you know!'

'It's alright Solomon,' whispered Sarika. 'Now that it's dark, you can ride on my shoulders until we get there. Give them poor wings a good rest.'

'No need to be sarcastic, but I'll take you up on that, if I may.'

'Certainly, my pleasure,' she said patting him between his ears and smiling.

The terrain was surprisingly light on this last stretch, not like the latter, which constantly ensnared the feet. It was dark, but not dark enough to obscure the outline of rocks and shrubs along the way. Nevertheless, it still looked eerie, and with the soft updraft of air from the valley filling their nostrils with a pungent smell of pine, that brought back memories for Gerald, when he used to walk through the forest to visit his late uncle Tom.

'We're almost there,' whispered Solomon. 'Just a little further to the left and beyond that large boulder.'

Within minutes, they were standing well below the recess in the wall, which from their position, looked as if it stretched towards the clouds, it looked enormous.

The recess itself looked far too high to reach. The foliage was now the only thing between them and the recess and was probably not strong enough to climb.

'Is that a crack in the wall at the foot of the recess?' asked Sarika.

'I believe it is,' responded Solomon, hovering just above their heads to take a closer look.

She started to untie the long rope that was wrapped around her waist and tied a few knots at one end. 'Here Solomon, can you fly up to that crack and place this knotted end of the rope within it?'

'I'll try,' he said, huffing and puffing as he struggled with the rope. Dropping it into the wider part of the crack, he wedged it down hard with his foot. 'It's in...' he squawked.

Sarika tugged hard on the rope, making sure it would support their weight. 'Yep, that will do. I'll go first,' she said, and one by one, they ascended to the recess.

Climbing onto the ledge, she gathered up the rope and wrapped it back around her waist. The recess looked far too small to be a normal doorway, but was deep enough to obscure them from any prying eyes.

Unwrapping the lantern from its cover, Gerald held it above their heads to gently illuminate the markings on the walls.

'These are not engravings Solomon, they are embossed. They look like individual stones embedded in the rock.'

'Well, I never,' whispered Sarika, running her fingers around the symbol, but when she put a little extra pressure on its surface, the symbol moved slightly towards the wall. 'Did you see that? I pushed the symbol, and it moved!'

'Don't touch any of the others,' barked Solomon. 'I think I know what they are. I believe these are a sequence of keys and have seen similar things before in ancient scriptures. They allow you to...'

'Yes, I know what they are too.' interrupted Gerald. 'In my world, they are known as combination locks. I just can't believe it, it's a god damn ancient door lock! How cool is that?'

232

'I've never seen this sort of thing before,' whispered Sarika. 'What the hell is a combination lock?'

'I wonder,' whispered Gerald. He opened the scroll again to reveal the two lines of symbols on the map. 'What if these symbols are the key to entry. What happens if we press the corresponding symbols in the order they are shown on the map?'

'We've got nothing to lose,' said Sarika. 'If you think that's what it is, then let's go for it.'

One-by-one, Gerald started to press the corresponding symbols in the order they were inscribed on the map, but when he had pressed the last one, there was an eerie silence, followed by disappointment.

'Nothing! I must have missed a symbol out,' he said through gritted teeth.

'Here, give me a go,' she suggested.

'No, it's OK, I'll try it again.'

He slowly started from the very beginning, this time making sure he pressed every symbol in turn, but again, nothing happened.

'What!' scowled Gerald. 'We must be doing something wrong, or we are completely barking up the wrong tree.'

'Why would we want to bark up a tree?' asked Solomon, looking somewhat confused.

'Forget it,' replied Gerald. 'It's just a well-used saying from my world. It means we must be looking completely in the wrong direction, misunderstanding the clue, or something like that.'

'Oh, I see,' she replied, still looking a little confused.

Looking more closely at the map, Solomon noticed what could be the problem. 'Hey,' he mumbled. 'Do you see how this text is written in the corner.'

'Yes,' they said.

'Well, I never took much notice before,' he continued. 'The incantation I read out from the little red spell book, when we made the scroll appear, was written both from left to right, and right to left on each new line of text.'

'And your point is?' asked Gerald.

'My point is the text in the corner of the map is written in the same ancient language. Maybe the symbols follow the same rules as the text!'

'How do you mean?' asked Gerald, now looking rather agitated.

'You have been entering the symbols as if reading from left to right. Maybe the second row of symbols have been written the other way, from right to left.'

Gerald meticulously entered each row of symbols as Solomon had suggested, before pausing at the final symbol.

'Hell, if this doesn't work, then I'm lost for ideas. Here goes...' He nervously pushed the final symbol until it couldn't move any further. There was a slight pause, then a click from within the wall, followed by a rush of damp, rancid air.

At the deepest part of the recess, an opening had appeared at roof hight. It was no bigger than two feet wide and about eighteen inches tall. Big enough for Solomon to get through, but would be somewhat of a challenge for everyone else. Nevertheless, they had to try.

Putting his arm within the opening, Gerald could feel the other side of the wall. 'I can feel the ledge at the other side. It seems to drop away to the floor and hopefully could be a larger space just behind this opening.'

'Are you sure?' asked Solomon, spreading his wings.

'I don't know for sure,' said Gerald. 'However, I do have an idea. Pass me your rope Sarika.'

Doing as she was asked; she undid the knot at the front of her loin cloth and unravelled the long rope from her waste.

'What are you going to do?' she asked inquisitively.

'I am going to tie the lamp to the rope and lower it into the void. That way we will determine if there is a floor, and maybe see clearly through the opening.'

'Good thinking,' she replied.

Gerald slowly lowered the lamp through the hole, letting it slide down the far side until it came to a stop. 'Yep, I am in no doubt, there is a solid floor. And by the look of it, it is on the same level as this side.

Now that the lamp is in there, I will have to ask Solomon to be the first to enter.'

Solomon nodded and perched himself within the opening. 'O dear, my feathers a sticking up on the back of my neck. I don't like this at all.'

'Don't worry,' whispered Sarika. 'You're a brave and wise owl. Just slip inside and let us know what you can see.'

Against his better judgement, he cautiously entered the small opening, and using his beak, he gripped the rope, descending to the lamp on the other side.

'I'm down,' he tweeted. 'It is a long tunnel carved through the mountain rock. It looks safe enough thus far.' Now feeling slightly alone and vulnerable, he asked the others to join him.

It took a little while, but after they both got their shoulders through the small opening, it was just a matter of falling a few feet to the floor.

'Well, that was a little awkward,' she said laughing, whilst patting herself down, but as soon as Gerald came through the hole, the opening quickly closed.

'That's it then,' he mumbled. 'Nowhere else to go, but onward. Hopefully there is a way out elsewhere.'

'I assume there will be,' said Solomon. 'When the ancients made tunnels, they would always make sure there was another entrance at the far side. Firstly, this was to let fresh air flow through as they worked on the excavations, and second, as a means of escape, should the tunnels collapse.

'OK, at least no-one knows we are here,' she said, wrapping the rope around her waist again. 'Hopefully no-one can follow us this way if they did.'

'Let's make a move then,' said Gerald, picking up the lantern and aiming it down the tunnel.

'It is far too narrow for me to fly in here,' mumbled Solomon.

'Don't fret, I've got you covered,' and gently placed him on her shoulder.

After walking the initial straight part of the tunnel, it seemed to go off at a tangent, curving its way in a sideways and downward direction. There was no immediate indication of any other passageways, until Gerald saw a dim light emanating from the wall on his right.

'Is that a reflection from this lamp?' he muttered.

'What reflection?' replied Sarika.

'Over there.' Pointing to the slither of light peering through the rock. 'I thought it was a reflection from the damp rock, but I now see it is not. Look, it's an unusual blue colour.'

Sure enough, as they approached this unusual light source, it became much brighter.

Eventually, the entrance to another passageway, opened into a vast underground cavern.

'Oh, this is different,' said Solomon. I've never seen colour as saturated as this before. It's hurting my eyes.'

'I've seen it before, snapped Gerald. Although I used to see colours like this every day in my home world, I have only ever seen it once in yours. It is the same-coloured light that emanated from the crystal on Mahabone's crooked staff., when he turned me into a *Triglotine.*'

'As it is the same colour as Mahabone's staff, as you say,' replied Solomon, 'then this could be a good indication as to where Mahabone's ancient source of power may be hidden. I suggest we follow this path.'

'That sounds logical,' said Gerald. 'If we are to find this power source, we must be prepared to check everything. Anyway, it seems to be the only lead we have so far.'

'I totally agree,' said Sarika, squeezing his hand.

The cavern was ginormous, filled with thousands of stalactites and stalagmites. Furthermore, the reflection from the unusual blue light was omnipresent, giving everyone no sense of direction as to its source.

'Where do we go from here then,' asked Sarika, pointing to the centre of the cavern.

'I'm not sure, it's my first time here to!' replied Gerald sarcastically.

'There was no need to be like that!' she replied. 'I was only asking.'

'I know,' he said smiling. 'I think it may be safer to keep to the left of the cavern, so if we get disoriented, we can turn back by following the right. If that make sense?'

'Wait a minute!' whispered Solomon. 'Did you hear that?'

'Hear what?' she whispered, pricking her ears to listen.

'I heard a rumbling noise,' he continued, 'from deep within the cavern...'

'That could have been something just falling from the roof,' interrupted Gerald. 'It is quite common for stalactites to break-off and fall to the ground. That's why it can be dangerous. In my world, we normally would have to wear a hard head covering for protection, as many people have lost eyes, or even been disfigured, by simply looking up at the wrong time.

As we have no protection, I strongly recommend we stay alert, especially when looking up.'

They continued to search along the cavern walls, to see if they could find anything that may lead them to the light source, but after almost an hour, there was nothing. Only the odd micro-cavern with no exits.

'This is getting ridiculous,' mumbled Solomon. 'We are not getting anywhere.'

'You're right,' said Gerald. 'I've just had a thought! Why would something that wanted to remain hidden, freely give us clues to its location? Surely it would want to remain hidden...'

'Yes, I think you might have something there,' said Solomon ruffling his feathers. 'It sounds like the perfect way to lead your potential thieves away from the real source. I think we've been led astray.'

'I agree,' nodded Sarika. 'Then thinking logically, we must return to the point where we first had a distraction. The first tunnel. I think we should have continued, instead of following the light.'

'Maybe!' Gerald grumbled. 'Hidden in a place we would least expect, I imagine.'

'Back to the tunnel then,' said Solomon, looking very annoyed at being hoodwinked.

CHAPTER

TWENTY - FOUR

It took another hour to find their way back to the tunnel. After spending so much time in the intense blue light, made it very hard to see in the dark. Even the light from their lamp didn't seem to do anything.

Further and further, they had to feel their way along the tunnel wall, until their eyes became accustomed to the dark. Only then did the low luminescent lamp become useful.

'That seems a little better,' she whispered. Sarika held the lamp well above her head so that she could make out the contours of the tunnel wall. 'There, can you see it?'

'See what?' squawked Solomon. 'What are we supposed to be looking at?'

'The tunnel has come to a dead end, but I have noticed on the left wall, almost at the roof level, there is a small opening. Can one of you go and have a look.?'

'I suppose that means me again?' mumbled Solomon. 'I knew I would end up being first.'

241

The tunnel was quite tall at this point, so Gerald got Sarika to stand on his shoulders, and place the lamp in the hole.

Solomon, fluttered up on her back, stepped off her shoulder and cautiously entered the opening.

'Yep, it is the same as before. There is a drop on the other side into what looks like a square room.'

'OK,' said Gerald, trying his best not to squirm under the weight of Sarika. 'Is there enough room for us to get in there?'

'Loads of room,' replied Solomon. 'Much bigger than the first opening we came in, just a little longer, that's all.'

One by one, all three made their way through the opening. It was a little awkward, as Sarika had to put her hands onto Gerald's shoulders and go in feet first. This allowed him to pass the toolbox up and to grab her hands far enough to grab the ledge.

All now inside, the dimly lit walls of the room revealed nothing but smooth surfaces on both walls, ceiling and floor.

'That was a waste of energy,' said Gerald, rubbing his hand along the surface of the wall. 'There is nothing here.'

'Oh, yes there is,' piped up Sarika. 'There is a small round recess in the far wall.' She held the lamp close to it and noticed it had a groove all the way down the inner left-hand side.

242

Placing her eye to see deeper into the recess, she could see a new engraved symbol at its base. 'Hey, it has another symbol engraved in it!'

'Where?' asked Gerald. 'Let me see.'

Gerald opened the scroll to see if it had any mention of the new symbol, but there was nothing.

'Now what do we do?' he said, rolling the scroll back up. 'It obviously means something.'

Just as he put the scroll back in his belt, he felt something on the end of the scroll. Holding the lamp next to it, he saw the embossed engraving of the new-found symbol, complete with a single embossed tooth at its circumference.

'I don't believe it,' he cried. 'It's been here on the end of the scroll all along.' Looking closely, he realised that the end of it was a similar dimension as the recess. Furthermore, the tooth on the outer circumference of the scroll, also matched the groove in the wall. *'It can't be as simple as that, can it?'* he thought.

Lining the tooth on the scroll, with the groove in the wall, he slowly pushed it down the recess, until he felt a small amount of resistance, proceeded by something in the wall clicking into place.

'What the hell is that noise,' screamed Sarika nervously.

The wall adjacent to them began to groan, as a hidden mechanism began to move the wall in a downward direction. Frozen to the spot, they all watched as it slowly revealed its secret.

A large Stone *Globe* stood motionless at the top of a five-foot pillar of granite. It was jet black, about the size of an average watermelon and was like staring into an endless cosmic universe, full of stars. It was mesmerising.

'I don't think we should move it,' instructed Solomon. 'I think we should do what we came to do, whilst it stays in place. Open the toolbox Gerald and pass me the red spell book.'

Putting the toolbox on the floor, he quickly opened the contents and placed the spell book in front of Solomon.

'Kneel on the floor over there,' instructed Solomon, pointing to the adjacent corner. 'If we are to attempt to change you back into the man you were and hopefully find you a way back home, then we have to be extremely careful in how we conduct this.'

Gerald walked slowly over to the allocated corner and knelt nervously on the floor. Solomon, still flicking through the pages to find a useful spell, hopped over to the globe.

'I think I have found the only appropriate incantation. It seems to have the correct instructions to...'

'YOU THINK?' interrupted Gerald. 'I need you to be certain, not just guess.'

'Don't worry,' whispered Sarika in his ear. 'Don't upset him. He can only try his best. Trust him, he always gets things right, well, most of the time.'

'Thanks,' he growled. 'Now that has really filled me full of confidence!'

Because Mahabone had used the power of the globe to change Gerald in the first place, Solomon hoped he would be able to use the same globe to reverse the original spell.

Standing himself on top of the globe, Solomon asked Sarika to hold the spell book in front of him, while he read from the book. He believed if he stood on the globe, the power would transfer through him and through his words. And so, he began.

The words he spoke, flowed effortlessly from his beak, but by the time he had getting halfway through the incantation, the stars within the globe began to spin, almost to the point where it looked like a ball of fire.

The air above Gerald quickly became static, sending shimmers of light flashing around the room, but something was wrong! Solomon's feet began to tremble from the vibration, emanating violently from the stone globe, followed by a blinding flash and the ear-piercing crack!

'What the hell happened there?' asked Gerald, still blinded from the flash and lifting himself off the floor. 'Did it work?' There was no answer!

As his eyes became accustomed to his surroundings again, he could see Solomon and Sarika still lying on the floor beside him. However, when he put out his hands to assist them, he gasped at what he saw. His hands were still the same pale green. Lifting his hands towards his face, he felt the features he was so desperate to leave behind.

'Oh no!' he sobbed. 'It hasn't worked!'

Moments later, Sarika and Solomon slowly opened their eyes to Gerald, still curled up in the corner and sobbing his heart out.

'What happened?' mumbled Sarika to Solomon. 'What's he sobbing for?'

Gerald lifted his head from his hands and faced them both. 'It hasn't worked!' he cried.

Solomon immediately turned his head and squawked in horror. There on the granite pillar, stood the stone globe in two halves. It had completely split in two and had become fully opaque. As for the toolbox and its contents, they had been totally obliterated. However, he could see there was something else neatly positioned between the two halves of the globe.

'What the hell is that? squawked Solomon.

'What is what? replied Sarika.

'I know what it is,' said Gerald. 'It's another God-damn *Ouroboros* ring.'

'Are you sure,' asked Sarika.

'I'm very sure,' he replied. 'It is almost the same shape and size as the last one I stole from

Mahabone on my last visit. Except, this one is in a shape of a different dragon. Mahabone must have been using the *Ouroboros* ring from within, using the globe as a disguise. We must take it and be quick to leave, as Mahabone will surely know something is up.'

'I agree,' squawked Solomon.

Gerald then placed the *Ouroboros* ring in his bag.

Looking for a way out, they could not find a second entrance, but found themselves back at the original entrance, which seemed to sense they had returned from within and opened the entrance by itself.

CHAPTER

TWENTY-FIVE

It was late at night when Mahabone slowly paced up and down his chambers. He had just turned towards his window, when he suddenly felt weak, causing him to fall to the floor. This was not expected at all, but he knew exactly what it was, as soon as it occurred.

Dragging himself across the cold stones, he pulled himself up and secured himself upon his chair.

'My powers!' he whimpered. 'What has happened?

For generations, his ancestors have basked in the power from the sacred artifacts hidden in the mountain, but he was now feeling very vulnerable, because he knew for some unknown reason, his connection with them had been severed.

Not wanting to cause unrest among his men, he knew he had to continue his powerful posture and go to his secret vault to check his greatest treasure.

'GUARDS!' he boomed. 'Prepare the lifting cage to descend the great rear wall.'

***

An hour had passed before his men had fully carried out his instructions. Mahabone, stepped nervously into the cage, instructing his men that he would descend the wall alone.

He commanded that the guards had to continue manning the mechanism that operated the cage, because he didn't want any of them to see what he was about to do, or find out the location of his secret vault.

'Lower me slowly,' he commanded. 'I will pull the rope three times to indicate when I wish to stop.'

All the guards acknowledged his instructions and immediately began to lower him down the great wall.

The cage continued to descend for several minutes, until the recess eventually came into view. It was situated well above ground level, where the recess stood just above the ivy that clung to the mountain side, making the recess very difficult to see from ground level. He waited until the bottom of the cage was in line with the recess floor, before pulling the rope three times, bringing the cage to a stop.

Stepping from the cage and onto the recess floor, everything looked just as it should be. The entrance was sealed and all the symbols were in their neutral positions.

One by one, Mahabone pressed the symbols in their sequence to open the entrance. Only this time, instead of it just revealing the small opening as it had done for Gerald, Mahabone pressed another few symbols to reveal a full-sized doorway, where he briskly walked into its darkness.

'The air smells quite fresh in here,' he thought. *'I would have expected it to be quite stale after all these years!'*

Being aware that he could no longer use his magic to light his way, once inside, he revealed an oil lamp from his tunic and struck a flint to its wick. The flickering flame wreaked instant havoc on his senses, cascading shadows and shards of light between the imperfections of the tunnel walls.

'Is anyone else in here with me?' he asked nervously, whilst hoping no-one would reply. *'Bloody hell,'* he thought. *'I know it's been a long time since I walked these passageways, but I can't remember them being this long.'*

'Hello, is anybody there?'

Feeling very vulnerable without his magic, he eventually reached the end of the tunnel, where he pulled himself up and crawled into the opening at the top of the wall.

The room with smooth walls, reflected and defused the soft light from his oil lamp, just enough for him to see a gaping hole from where the stone globe had once stood.

Instead of it projecting a beautiful dark universe from within, it now stood dull, grey and broken in two.

'No!' he screamed. 'It just can't be!' His screaming was so loud, even his men at the top of the stronghold could hear his feeble cries echo from the base of the wall.

'Who could have done this? What could...' He suddenly fell silent. After pondering for a few seconds, he turned his attention towards the entrance. 'It has to be that bastard, Gerald!'

***

Meanwhile, Gerald, Sarika and Solomon, continued to make their way back to the settlement as fast as they could. They were very aware it wouldn't take long for Mahabone to find out what had taken place.

Not wanting to take any chances in case Mahabone was in pursuit, they knew they must prepare their people for what may, or may not lie ahead.

***

R. L. Barnes.

Mahabone, now realising the source of his magical powers had been lost forever, had to quickly devise a plan to hoodwink his own people. He now knew he would have to reinforce his authority and instil more fear, by acting more aggressively than ever.

Running back to the lifting cage, he closed the recess entrance, pulled the rope three times and shouted new instructions to his men.

'Right, you horrible, useless sacks of slime,' he bellowed. 'Get be back up there immediately.'

It didn't take too long before Mahabone found himself pacing up and down his living quarters. He kept looking at himself in the mirror and started cursing Gerald aloud through gritted teeth. Even the inner guard, who stood diligently behind the entrance door, felt the atmosphere around him thicken, as Mahabone's anger grew.

However, the more and more he pondered about his predicament, the more his paranoia grew and the more irrational he became.

'How can I get my revenge, and make it look as if I haven't been affected? 'Curse them all!' he thought. Turning to face the entrance to his quarters, he shouted, 'GUARD.'

Immediately the inner guard jumped at the sudden outburst from his master. He was so afraid of him, he started shaking at the knees. Knowing what Mahabone was like, he cringed at what may happen to him. Taking a deep breath, he pulled himself together, before running to his master's aid.

'Yes, master,' he replied with a nervous croak in his voice. 'What do you want of me?'

'Get all the men ready,' he barked. 'We are riding out to kill Gerald and all who have supported him.' 'I want every able guard and griffin ready for battle within the hour.'

***

Sarika and Gerald, eventually escorted Solomon safely back to his inner sanctum, deep within his temple. Thanking him for all his help so far, they left him to settle in and started back to what remained of the *Triglotine's* temporary settlement.

'Surely Mahabone must know something by now?' asked Gerald inquisitively.

'I would have thought so?' she said, whilst concentrating to navigate the narrow trail. 'Normally, we would see or hear something to indicate his movements.'

'Like what?' he responded, holding on tight as she led him through the thick foliage of the trail.

'In the past,' she continued, 'when Mahabone wielded his magic through anger and frustration, we always saw and heard the crackling of thunder. Often this gave us some time to investigate or prepare for any imminent danger.

However, since we have destroyed the stone globe and taken the *Ouroboros* ring from within, there has thus far been nothing. If we are to believe what the scroll said about him receiving all his power from the globe, then we must assume he has not noticed anything yet, or, it is more likely that he has lost all power, and may already be in pursuit.'

'Then there is no time to lose,' he said, picking up the pace. 'If Mahabone has already started his march upon us, providing he has deduced it was us, then we must hurry. We must get the others prepared.'

'I am sure you are right,' she said. 'You forget Gerald, there are no other tribes that we are aware of in this small world.

Our people have never travelled beyond the brink of our horizons, to see what, or who, lies beyond. I could be wrong, but I think we are his only real adversaries and think we would be the only ones he would blame.'

'He may have thought it was one of his own men going against him!' interrupted Gerald.

'What! The chances of it being one of his men is ludicrous,' she said laughing. 'They can barely think for themselves, let alone come up with a plan like that. Why do you think Mahabone can manipulate all of them so well. He will know this and will be unlikely to hold them to account. Look, who else would have the intelligence and tenacity to carry out such a thing.

Gerald, he knows it could only be you. Only you have the experiences from your own world, and the capacity to carry it out.'

'Oh, I see what you mean!'

CHAPTER

TWENTY-SIX

The light of dawn crept silently across the horizon, allowing Sarika's hidden settlement to come into sight. It looked eerily quiet from where they were standing, but as they approached, they could see small groups of their guards walking around the perimeter.

'They don't look as if they are worried to much about anything,' mentioned Sarika. 'Obviously the lookout scouts have not seen anything to indicate any danger.'

'Yes, but if Mahabone is unable to use any of his magic,' replied Gerald, 'then they wouldn't see anything at all. In fact, if your scouts are unaware of what we have done, they will probably be looking for the wrong signals.'

'I agree,' she said. 'Plus, if Mahabone is planning a surprise attack, then he will not be spotted until he is almost upon us. We must assume he will attack from all sides.'

Gerald stopped walking for a few moments, turning to face the direction from whence they came. 'I think we should hurry,' he said. 'I suggest we prepare your guards to leave your hidden settlement and position themselves back at the main *Triglotine* settlement. You must protect the remainder of your people.'

'That means I will be seen by Mahabone's men back at my father's kingdom!' she barked.

'Yes, but if Mahabone is on his way, we must protect all your people. I'm sorry to be so direct with you, but if they are all killed, you will be Queen and ruler of nothing!'

'I must try and take back my father's kingdom...'

'I don't mean to be rude Sarika,' he interrupted. 'It is no longer your father's kingdom. It is yours! I don't want to sound heartless when I say this, but your father is dead! You must stop thinking like that. It is now your responsibility and yours alone. Your people need you. They trust you and look up to you for guidance and protection.'

Sarika fell suddenly silent. Her face turned very pale and her eyes overflowed with tears. Looking towards Gerald, she lowered her head and began to sob.

'I miss him so much,' she sobbed. 'I really have no idea what I am supposed to do! He was not only my father, but he was also my friend and protector. I'll never be able to fill his shoes.'

Gerald walked slowly up to Sarika and wrapped his arms around her. 'Don't cry,' he

257

whispered in her ear. 'It upsets me when I see you cry.'

'I can no longer do this alone Gerald. I may act hard at times by putting on a brave face, but inside, I'm still that little girl my father knew, and I'm very scared.'

'Don't worry, you are a lot stronger than you think you are. Besides, you have your guards and your people to support you and of course, you have me.'

Sarika slowly raised her eyes to meet his. In doing so, she expressed a little strained smile, kissed him gently on the lips and whispered, 'Thank you.'

'No, thank you,' he whispered.

'For what?'

'For simply being who you are. Not the Queen Sarika, but simply the woman who resides within you, the one I have grown to love and admire.'

'Do you really,' she asked, with her lips quivering, whilst her heart fluttered with gentle palpitations.

'Yes, I believe I do. Now, before Mahabone might get any closer, let's finish what we started. Let us show Mahabone, that the *Triglotines* have teeth and are not afraid to use them. However, if we are wrong and he is not on his way, then it will do no harm for us to be prepared.'

'But what about finding a way to change you back into a human?' she asked hesitantly.

'We can deal with that later,' he replied. 'However, we have more important things to take care of first. The return of your kingdom is paramount and I intend to stay by your side until it is done. As for my needs, they will come last.

'Thank you,' she replied. '

***

Meanwhile, back at the stronghold, Mahabone left the comfort of his quarters and quickly mounted his prize griffin. With his thighs gripping tightly to both sides of its bony ribcage, he turned to his guards. 'Mount your griffins,' he commanded. 'Foot soldiers - eyes forward and stand inline.'

All his men turned and came to attention in unison, making the ground rumble as they slammed their feet on the ground.

Riding his griffin to the front of his men, Mahabone raised his staff into the air, gesturing as if he still had magic. When he was sure his men suspected nothing suspicious, he commanded his army to ready arms and follow his lead.

Deeply filling his lungs, he shouted his final command:

'Forward!'

259

**

Sarika and Gerald finally entered the hidden settlement to find everyone going about their daily duties. Only when the guard in charge spotted them, did he run towards his queen.

Standing in the centre of the small settlement, she promptly called everyone else towards her.

'GATHER AROUND EVERYONE,' she bellowed. 'I have some vital information for you all.'

All her guards gathered around as tightly as they could, to try and hear every word she said, but all the pushing and shoving they were doing to get closer, annoyed her very much.

'WILL YOU JUST STAND STILL AND LISTEN?' she barked. The guards were shocked, as she hadn't spoken to them in this tone before, so they quickly fell silent. 'This is a matter of life and death,' she continued. 'We had gone to Solomon's temple for his wisdom, to see if we could help Gerald. Solomon had somehow summoned a hidden scroll, by using the tools that Gerald had brought. In doing so, the scroll led us to the location of a sacred artifact, hidden deep within Mount Zed, under Mahabone's stronghold.

According to the scroll, it mentions that the artifact was the source of Mahabone's power.'

'What do you mean – *was the source?*' shouted one guard.

'Unfortunately,' she continued. 'When we tried to use the artifact to help Gerald, it exploded, sending us across the floor and making us unconscious. However, when we came about, the artifact was destroyed.'

'Does that mean Mahabone's powers have been destroyed, along with the artifact?' shouted another guard.

'We think it could be,' interrupted Gerald. 'If it is true and Mahabone has realised what has happened, then we think he could have guessed it had something to do with me. I must also mention that when the artifact fell apart, there was another artifact left from within, known as an *Ouroboros* ring. This is the second of three rings I have found and must be kept safe from Mahabone. We are afraid he could be on his way to find me to retrieve this. He will no doubt want to kill me for taking it, as well as anyone else who gave me assistance. If he has lost his powers, we believe he would have hoodwinked his own men in believing he still has his magic and convinced them all to fight at his side.'

'We all have to get back to the main *Triglotine* village as soon as we can,' shouted Sarika. 'We must prepare for any eventuality. If we can convince the others to help take back my father's kingdom...' she quickly looked at

Gerald piercing eyes. 'Sorry, I meant *MY* kingdom, then we will regain our own stronghold. Just pick up all your weapons and leave everything else as it is. We must leave right now!'

The guards never spoke another word, they just ran around like ants, grabbing everything they could find.

***

Vaylor, who left the hidden settlement immediately after introducing Gerald to Sarika a few days ago, had returned to the *Triglotine's* village and was looking over many of the queen's ideas to regain what was her father's old kingdom.

Ever since King Tubal'cain was slaughtered by Mahabone's henchmen in his own chambers, a small contingent of the enemy had remained sealed behind the kingdom's large slate doors in preparation of their master's return.

Vaylor looked long and hard at her plans, but knew it was virtually impossible to regain access to their stolen kingdom. Only a few guards appeared occasionally at the top of the entrance doors, leaving little chance for the *Triglotine* guards to overcome them.

'*I can see where she is coming from with her plans,*' he thought, '*but the opportunity to carry them out, will be slim at best. Nevertheless, we do have to try.'* Suddenly, he was interrupted by one of the village guards bursting through the door.

'Sir,' said the red-faced guard, panting and wheezing. 'I have been sent to report,' he said trying to catch his breath, '...that there has been increased movement at the kingdom doors...and...'

'Take your time soldier,' interrupted Vaylor. 'Take a few deep breaths and start again from the top.'

'Sorry Sir. It's just that they said I had to get to you as fast as I could. The scouts watching the kingdom have noticed increased activity along the top of the entrance. They said they saw messenger birds flying in and out of the tower windows and that they could hear metallic sounds coming from behind the great doors.'

'Mm.' mumbled Vaylor under his breath. 'It sounds like they are up to something. Messenger birds you say?'

'Yes sir. It was after the birds started arriving, that everything started to happen.'

'Sounds like they may be preparing for reinforcements, or worse still... Mahabone!'

The guards face turned decisively pale. The thought that Mahabone may return, sent shivers down his spine.

'What shall we do now sir?' asked the guard nervously.

'Hide all the female villagers and children away from the village,' barked Vaylor. 'The safety of our women and children always comes first! Once that is done, gather all the guards, plus any able-bodied men who can brandish a weapon.'

'Yes sir!'

'You will all meet me outside these quarters for further instructions. Well, what are you waiting for man. Stop dilly-dallying and get a move on!'

'Yes sir!'

Chapter

Twenty-Seven

Sarika and her guards had successfully managed to make their way towards the *Triglotine* village. However, as they approached, they were just in time to see Vaylor briefing many guards, alongside a few male farmers from the village.

'Are we interrupting something?' asked Sarika.

'No, Your Majesty,' replied Vaylor. 'There has been a significant development at the kingdom gates.'

'In what sense?' asked Gerald.

'It has been reported that messages have been received at the kingdom via messenger birds,' explained Vaylor. 'Since then, Mahabone's men have been heard moving metallic objects behind the entrance. I think they are up to something.'

'That would make sense?' replies Sarika.

'How?' asked Vaylor.

'Because we believe we have destroyed his only source of power and because of that, we believe he is on his way to exact his revenge.

Sarika and Gerald continued to give a detailed explanation to Vaylor and his men, about where they had been, who they had met, and what they had done. Vaylor also explained to his queen, that he had recently been looking at her plans to take back the kingdom.

'Maybe this is the time to put your plans into practice my queen? Saying this, we must go over your strategy, as I think it will be very difficult to execute as it stands.'

'Meaning?' she barked.

'I don't mean to be rude,' replied Vaylor. 'We have been watching the entrance very carefully, where the enemy never presented us with any opportunities to gain entry.'

'OK then,' she replied. 'What do you suggest that can better my strategy?'

'Why don't we trick then to opening the doors?' interrupted Gerald.

'How do you mean,' she asked inquisitively.

'Isn't it obvious? 'If all the activity started after receiving messages, they could be preparing for Mahabone's return.'

'Interesting,' she muttered. 'Carry on!'

'Well, what is to say that Mahabone hasn't sent guards ahead of him, to clear the way, so to speak.'

'What are you saying?' interrupted Vaylor.

'We know that there is only a small number of guards defending the kingdom.' So, why can't we pretend to be a group of Mahabone's guards coming ahead of him and demand that they open the gates in preparation for his arrival.'

'That sounds so absurd,' grumbled Sarika. 'Yet, it sounds so ridiculous and dangerous, it might actually work.'

'What a brilliant idea!' smiled Vaylor. 'Why didn't I think of it before. When Mahabone and his men killed your father Your Majesty, all the uniform's from Mahabone's dead men, were placed alongside the weapons we recovered. We can use those uniforms to trick the guards at the gate.'

Sarika, looked across to Gerald and pondered the idea for a moment. 'Sounds very dangerous to me, but it looks like we have a plan. Get too it then, we haven't got a moment to lose. We will execute the plan as soon as you have it ready. If Mahabone is on his way, then we must act - and act now.'

***

An hour later, Sarika, dressed in men's armour, looked on hesitantly as shards of daylight fell intermittently through the clouds, casting numerous moving shadows across the two slate doors protecting her kingdom.

267

Now dressed in the enemy's uniform, she remained central to her men, as Vaylor marched his forty-strong unit towards the large doors.

'Halt! Who goes there?' shouted one of Mahabone's guard's from above.

'Open the doors,' shouted Vaylor. 'We have been sent ahead of the master. He will be with us shortly.'

'Then stay there until he arrives,' replied the guard, pointing his bow and arrow from above.

'We have been marching for ages,' said Vaylor. 'You can't expect us to just wait here. We need rest, food and water.'

'I don't give a damn!' was the guards reply, pulling the string of his bow.

'The master has sent us to prepare the way and help you prepare for his arrival,' shouted Gerald. 'Or would you prefer I tell him you personally disobeyed his orders and made us wait?'

There was a moment of hesitation and silence, before the first sounds could be heard from behind the great doors. Normally, the sound of the horns that operated the doors, could be heard from miles away. In the past, they were always blown from the battlement towers. Thankfully, on this occasion, they were sounded from within and were barely audible to those outside.

'*At least Mahabone wouldn't have heard them, if he's anywhere nearby,*' thought Sarika.

Slowly but surely, the creek and groan of the door hinges could be heard screaming their way to their open positions, until they came to a halt, by slamming against the black granite walls. There, in front of Vaylor's company, stood several of Mahabone's unruly guards, with bows fully drawn.

'Enter quickly,' ordered one of the guards, scanning the outer parameters. 'We don't want any of those *Triglotine* scum getting in.'

Vaylor almost swallowed his dry tongue, as he tried to respond to the guard's outburst. 'They wouldn't even try,' he said with a dry rusty throat. 'Not with all of us here,' whilst marching his men past the doors and into the great hall where Mahabone's guards were standing. 'Bye the way... How many of you were left here to guard the kingdom?'

'CLOSE THE DOORS,' commanded the guard, who seemed to be the one in charge. 'There was thirty of us, but since the master has been away, the *Triglotine*'s have been picking us off one by one. That's why we rarely let ourselves be seen on the look-out towers.'

'So how many of you are left,' asked Gerald.

'Only fifteen?' replied the guard.

'Only fifteen!' grumbled Vaylor. 'And pray tell, where are the remaining guards now?'

'As you can see, there are only seven of us guarding the gate, but the rest are on duty throughout the kingdoms many passageways.'

'Fine. Can you therefore summon the other eight to the inner gate? We are commanded to debrief all of you, complete a full inspection and report direct to the master on his arrival. Do I make myself clear?'

Mahabone's guards looked nervously at each other, before the guard in charge responded. 'If that is what the master commanded, I will summon them immediately,' sending two of his guards to collect the others.

While there were only five guards remaining at the gate, Vaylor took Gerald to one side.

'Tell the queen to spread her men around the great hall,' he whispered. 'There are forty of us and only fifteen of them. When the remaining guards arrive for de-briefing, surround them, then kill them all.'

'What about the five standing there now? They may suspect something as we move around the hall!' whispered Gerald.

'Don't worry about them, I have this covered.' With that said, Vaylor turned towards the five men. 'You men stand in line until the others get here. In the meantime, I will spread my men out to inspect the security of the hall, we can't be too careful where the master is concerned, can we?'

'No sir, we can't,' replied the guard who was in charge.

By the time all the other guards had returned to the great hall, Sarika's men had completely encompassed Mahabone's guards.

As soon as Vaylor got them to disarm themselves and stand in-line for them to be debriefed and inspected, the *Triglotine* guards closed in, drew their swords and decapitated the remainder of Mahabone's men.

'Hide their bodies down our waste-pit for now,' instructed Sarika. 'We don't want Mahabone to suspect anything when he eventually arrives. However, I am now in no doubt, that he will be knocking on these doors very soon.'

CHAPTER

TWENTY-EIGHT

Walking through the passageways, Sarika almost choked on the stench of rotten flesh, as she shuffled her way through all the remaining corpses of her own people, who had fought so gallantly to protect their king and kingdom

It had been so long since she lived within these walls, she hardly recognised the way to her old chamber. Every corridor was strewn with these decaying bodies of the people who had given their lives. *'How could they just leave them lying here like this,'* she thought. *'They could have at least put them to rest... Bloody barbarians!'*

The stench of rotten flesh had become so overwhelming by now, it had made her stomach retch in pain, sending her scurrying down another corridor.

Unaware of the direction she had taken, she suddenly found herself standing outside her dead father's chamber. Afraid of what she might find, she nervously pushed the large wooden door ajar. Peeking her head around the door, she could see that her father's room had been completely trashed.

Standing deeper within the doorway, she clasped her eyes on her father's robe. It was bundled in a heap on the floor, but as she looked closer, she burst into tears. There, mangled in a slumped position, was the decaying remains of her father. She could see what remained of the gaping wound in his neck. Running over to his side, she held him in her arms and screamed. Not only had she lost her mother to Mahabone in the past and most recently her father, she now had to re-live the physical pain of her loss, as she sat cradling the decaying corpse of her father.

'Mahabone, you bastard,' she sobbed, whilst seething at what he had done to her parents. 'If it's the last thing I do, I will make sure you rot in hell...', but before she could finish her sentence, the sound of horns could be heard echoing down the corridors.

'Hurry Your Majesty,' said a quiet voice from behind the door. 'Mahabone is approaching the entrance. He is asking for the guards to open the great doors!'

The guard waited patiently, while Sarika gently laid her father's body down and covered what was left of his face with his robe.

'Is he now?' she said sarcastically. 'We had better do as he says. Are all the men in place as we had planned?'

'Yes, Your Majesty,' replied the guard.

'Right, Tell the men to open the doors, not fully, but just enough to let a double file of his men pass. Don't forget to act as normal as you can. Mahabone will not come in straight away. As always, he has a backward way of doing things and will send in his best guards first to check things out.

Once they are inside, quickly close the doors as planned and kill them. The men we have on the lookout, will rain-down arrows on Mahabone and his remaining guards. This should stop them entering our great doors, whilst we massacre his elite.'

'Yes, Your Majesty.'

'Well get a move on man!' she ordered. 'The battle awaits.'

Mahabone sat impatiently on his griffin, waiting for the men he had left in charge to open the enormous doors to the kingdom. As predicted, he summoned his elite troops to the front of his army and ordered them to enter as soon as the doors were ajar.

The rumbling sound of stone grinding upon stone filled the air, as the great doors slowly opened, before coming to a grinding halt, that left an opening around ten feet wide.

'Why has the doors stopped?' boomed Mahabone to the guards standing above the doors. Sarika's men, who were still dressed in disguise and standing at the top of the doors, responded immediately.

'For security master. The local *Triglotines* have been attacking the entrance from time to time. So, we only open the doors enough to let troops through. Should the *Triglotines* attack during this time, it is easier for us to close the doors more quickly.'

Mahabone was very surprised by his guards unexpected strategic thinking, thinking it was a brilliant idea.

'*Mm, I'm very impressed,*' he thought. However, he had to make it sound as if he thought of it first. He couldn't have his men out-thinking him. That sort of thinking could breed adversaries within his own men. 'That's exactly what I had planned for you to carry out,' he boomed. 'I assume you know everything I always want?'

'No master,' the disguised guard replied. 'Please forgive my arrogance.'

Mahabone smirked at the guard's remarks, then turned to his elite guards. 'Go ahead of me,' he ordered. 'Relieve the current inner guards and secure the entrance to the kingdom. As soon as you have completed my orders, signal me and I will lead the remainder through the gates.'

Immediately, all his best guards came together, fell in-line and marched themselves through the narrow gap between the gates.

As soon as the last of Mahabone's elite guards passed the entrance to the kingdom, Sarika's men immediately jumped into action, by ordering the gates to be closed and the slaughter of all the elite guards. The elite were so taken by surprise, they never stood a chance to defend themselves. Their blood curdling screams could be heard resonating throughout the kingdom and beyond the great gates.

Mahabone and the remainder of his men, looked on in shock and horror, as the realisation of what was happening quickly sunk in.

'IT'S A TRAP,' boomed Mahabone. 'Take cover behind those trees,' pointing his finger towards the *Triglotine* village. 'Round up the villagers to use as a shield,' he commanded, 'until we assess what has happened.' However, as they entered the nearby village, it had the makings of a ghost town. Not a soul could be found, nor was there any sign that anyone had lived there for days. Little did Mahabone know, that all the villagers had already been moved to safety, well before they had arrived.

He was becoming so furious. He had not anticipated that the *Triglotines* had outwitted him this way.

'*Gerald must have known I have lost my powers,*' he thought. '*He must have told Sarika and the Triglotines! That's why they have the courage to do this to me!*'

Mahabone knew if the villagers had been taken to safety, without his magic, he would never be able to find them. Plus, he was aware that once the great gates were closed, the kingdom was impregnable. The only choice he had left to retain control over his own men, was to coax Sarika and Gerald from their hiding place and challenge them to a battle.

Gerald now stood over the corpses of Mahabone's decapitated men, wondering what to do with them.

'Take then to the top of the doors,' ordered Sarika, 'and throw them back at Mahabone's feet. Let it be a warning to him and his kind. Let him see that we are no-longer afraid. Inform him that we will no-longer be trampled upon and that his tyranny is coming to an end.'

'Are you sure we are ready to take that step?' asked Gerald. 'We have to be sure our men are fully aware of the consequences...'

'What consequences?' she bellowed. 'He no-longer has his powers, otherwise he would have used them by now. We already assumed he had lost them when we destroyed the stone globe. Let's be done with it. If we are to make any headway, let's not pussy-foot around. What is it that they say in your world Gerald... *Strike while the iron is hot!*'

'I suppose you're right,' he responded, whilst nodding his head.

One by one, each of the severed bodies were thrown from the top of the great gate as ordered, followed by Sarika's guards lining the upper walls. They had now discarded their disguises and stood proudly in their own armour.

When Mahabone saw what had happened to his elite guards, he almost burst a blood vessel, while trying to keep his composure in front of his remaining men.

'THAT'S IT!' he bellowed at the top of his voice. 'Surround the entrance to the kingdom!' he ordered. 'Collect our dead, and feed them to the griffin's, they've not been fed since we left the stronghold and we need them to be stronger than ever.'

Now sitting on his prize griffin in front of the great gates, Mahabone demanded to speak to whoever was in charge.

'Why do you hide behind those gates?' he shouted. 'Are you all scared of what I may do to you? Let me speak to the one who gives the orders, or are you all so weak that you must hide?'

'We are not hiding from you,' shouted a guard from the top of the doors.

'Then step forward,' ordered Mahabone, 'so that I can see who I'm talking to.'

'We all follow the orders of Sarika our queen. However, she is currently busy with important matters. Therefore, you are currently speaking to the one who has been the thorn of all thorns in your side,' said Gerald, stepping into view.

'Who the hell are you?' demanded Mahabone.

'Don't you recognise your own dirty work, you scum? It is I, your greatest nemesis, Gerald.'

Mahabone's eyes were now burning with fire. He was now aware that Gerald knew he had lost his powers, otherwise, why would he and the *Triglotines* be acting so brave.

'Then if you are not afraid of what I can do to you,' bellowed Mahabone, 'then why not show us your strength. Why not come and settle this once and for all?'

'If that is what you wish,' responded Gerald, 'then I grant it, but I must warn you, be careful what you wish for!'

Within seconds, the sound of retracting bolts and grinding hinges could be heard, as the great doors began to move, only this time, to their full extent.

Meanwhile, and unbeknown to Mahabone, hundreds of Sarika's men had exited the kingdom through secret passageways to the rear and sides of the kingdom. The time it took for Gerald to throw the bodies from the top of the gates, grab Mahabone's attention and have a conversation, Sarika's guards had time to manoeuvre themselves to a strategic position, encircling Mahabone and his men.

Suddenly, a smaller contingent of guards under the command of Gerald, charged from within the open gates and made their way directly towards Mahabone's position.

However, as Mahabone retaliated, he made the grave mistake of sending all his men to engage. For as soon as his men were concentrated at the kingdom gates, the remainder of Sarika's guards, who were lying in wait, moved in swiftly from the rear. Mahabone was surrounded!

The clash of metal against metal echoed between the mountain sides and the blood curdling cries from fatal blows filled the air. It was becoming a blood bath. Griffins were biting the heads off fallen guards, no-matter what side they were on, while the inferior weapons used by Mahabone's men, proved useless against the newly improved weapons of the kingdom. Mahabone could see that he was quickly losing this battle and started to panic.

Throwing any bodies that were obstructing him to one side, he cleared a straight path to where Gerald was standing. Looking directly at him, Mahabone removed his helmet, raised his sword, then challenged Gerald.

'Are you prepared for this,' said Gerald. 'You know what happened the last time we had a battle. Are you sure you want to try again? Why don't you just use your magic? Oh, that's right, you haven't got any, have you!' With that, Mahabone screamed at the top of his voice and charged towards Gerald.

'You bastard,' he cried, bringing his sword down on Gerald's shoulder, but the blade glanced off Gerald's armour, sending his sword to the ground. Quickly, Gerald removed his sword from his scabbard and raised it above his head.

Mahabone's face suddenly turned very pale, as the sword that Gerald held in his hand, was none other than the famous '*Shibboleth*,' the sword he had once held after killing King Tubal'cane, which had mysteriously gone missing soon after.

Trying to turn away from the famous and deadly sword, Mahabone winced, as Gerald thrust *Shibboleth* deep into his left shoulder. Unable to move away quickly enough, Mahabone held his sword in the only arm he had left, then swung a bone crunching blow to Gerald's right knee.

'Bollocks,' screamed Gerald, dropping *Shibboleth* to the floor. 'That's the same fucking knee you cut last time.' But by the time Mahabone had a chance to serve a second blow, Gerald picked up his sword and drove it deep into Mahabone's chest, sending him wheezing to the floor.

Within a matter of seconds, the sound of the battle diminished, as everyone looked on to where Mahabone was lying.

'Use your magic master,' shouted one of his guards. 'Get up and finish him off!'

'He can't,' said another.

By now, all the fighting had subsided, as enemy and foe both encircled the wounded tyrant.

Gerald, who by now had managed to bring himself to his feet, hobbled towards Mahabone's groaning body.

'Listen to me, and listen well,' boomed Gerald. 'The Evil of this creature is no more! He has been leading you astray. You have been hoodwinked. Your master no-longer has the powers he claims he has. How do I know this? Because queen Sarika and I destroyed his only source of power several days ago.'

'Impossible,' shouted one of Mahabone's men. 'Prove it...'

'He speaks the truth,' interrupted Sarika, shouting from the top of the great gates. 'I witnessed it with my own eyes. Why not prove it yourselves? Ask your so-called master to perform the simplest of magic. If he can't, then there is your answer.'

Two of Mahabone's guards carefully approached his broken body and knelt by his side.

'Is this true master. Do they speak the truth?' Mahabone could hardly breathe, he just rolled his eyes in shame.

'Show us master,' said the second guard. 'Show them that you still have all your powers, and ...' Mahabone stretched out his hand and placed it across the guard's mouth.

'Shush,' he whispered. 'What they say is true. I am fatally wounded and can no-longer protect myself. It is true, my powers have all been lost. I have lied to you all, but now that I am done for, I have no reason to exist...'

'Does this mean you can no-longer make us do anything against our will?' asked one guard.

'Or torture us, when we disobey you?' said the other.

'This is true,' nodded Mahabone. With this, the first guard shrieked with glee. 'Now it is our turn you bastard. You will no-longer oppress our people. For the first time in our lives, we can now try to live our normal lives in peace, and not have to grovel. We will be free at last.'

Removing his sword from his scabbard, Mahabone's guard placed the tip of the blade at Mahabone's throat and pushed the blade until it stopped at his spine. There was a brief gurgling and spitting of blood, as Mahabone's life ebbed away. He was dead.

'We are free.'

Putting the tools of war to one side, Mahabone's men dragged his lifeless body across the ground, and placed it upon one of the griffins.

'We will return to our stronghold now,' said the guard who had just killed his master. We will burn his body so that he can never return.'

'That would be acceptable,' agreed Sarika. 'Maybe our people can now live in peace, even share things with one another from time to time?'

'Yes, that would be nice,' said the guard, 'but we will have to spend a little time to get organised. We'll also have to start getting used to a fresh style of life.'

'Well, you know where we are if you need anything,' said Gerald. 'Now take your dead and wounded, as we will with ours and let's start with a new day.'

The guard looked directly at Sarika and said, 'Agreed,' indicating to the remainder of his men to move out.

CHAPTER

TWENTY-NINE

Sitting comfortably in his chair, deep within Sarika's newly acclaimed kingdom, Gerald pondered about the events over the last few weeks. Now that everything seemed to be settling down in this world, he started to wonder what was happening in his own. Devastated that his chances of returning home was seriously hindered, he began to think about what he had left behind.

'Damn, I had a brilliant job at the university!' he thought. *'Although I lost members of my family, I had a home, fond memories and a few loyal friends, especially Sandy. Not only that, but I also still have the old me there, physically lying in my bed. If I don't return soon, my body in my own world will surely die. Is this all I am? Am I to spend the rest of my days as a Triglotine? Surely not. There must be a way Sarika can help me to get home. If only that guard hadn't destroyed the sleeper, the little bell that would have taken me home!' He began to*

R. L. Barnes.

rub his temples in frustration. 'Damn-it.' he mumbled, throwing himself out his chair and making his way towards the door.

Sarika, who was now overseeing the cleaning of her kingdom, shuddered at the amount of decaying bodies being discovered throughout the inner corridors. There was far too many to bury in the normal way, so she decided to pile them outside the great doors, with the intention to hold a mass cremation ceremony with all her kind.

Just as she instructed her plans to the guards, Gerald came storming out of the corridor to where she was standing.

'What's up with you?' she asked. 'You look very angry.'

'I am, sort of. Not so much angry, but highly frustrated at my current predicament.'

'What predicament?' she asked, looking a little perplexed.

'Bloody hell Sarika, you've got a short memory!'

'What do you mean?' she whispered, looking very concerned. 'I don't understand...' Then the penny dropped. 'I'm so sorry Gerald. What with all this going on and with you being the way you are for so long; I simply forgot and accepted you as one of us. I'm so sorry.'

'I'm not blaming you,' he said holding her arm, 'there is no need for you to be sorry. I just can't believe that there is nothing we can do to return me to my old self.'

'Well, what do you want me to do?' she said quietly. 'I haven't got a magic wand.'

'I know,' he said, 'but we must try something. I won't be able to rest until we have exhausted all ideas. There must be a way?'

'Look,' she said, looking deep into his eyes. 'Let us first get this mess sorted out, get the kingdom up and running as it was, then we can seriously look at what we can, or can't do to help you. However, I must say, I doubt we will be able to succeed, as we have already tried so much without success, but I assure you, we will try.'

***

For the next few days, Gerald put his concerns on the back burner. He knuckled down, helping the guards to pile up the bodies for cremation.

Later, he helped his friend Vaylor bring back the villagers from their hiding places and back into their homes.

'Thank you for all your help my friend,' said Vaylor. 'You have no idea how you have impacted our way of life.'

'In what way?' asked Gerald.

'If it were not for you and your ancestors, we would still be under the control of Mahabone.'

'Nonsense!' smiled Gerald. 'Eventually, you would have sorted things out by yourselves...'

'No, we wouldn't have. Because of you and your forefathers, we slowly changed our way of thinking. Some of the ideology from your world, taught us things we would never dream of doing. New strategies, techniques and innovative ways to simply grow as a community.'

'If that is the case then,' said Gerald, 'when all this tidying up is done, why don't we set up a daily class to teach all the villagers how to do things the way my people do back home.'

'What a brilliant idea,' smiled Vaylor.

'Yes,' Gerald replied. 'It would stimulate their way of thinking too. I really shouldn't interfere with your culture and how it evolves, but by what you have just told me, I have already made a difference! Look Vaylor, if I am to find a way back, and I do, at least I can try and make a difference before I go.'

'And what happens if you don't find a way?' asked Vaylor.

'Then I will cross that bridge when I come to it, and not before.'

While Gerald was helping Vaylor and the villagers, Sarika sent word to her trusted friend Solomon, telling him what had happened to Mahabone and about the small battle that ensued. She also asked in her letter, if he would be willing to visit the village and the possibilities of finding another way to help Gerald.

'*This is the only thing I can think of doing,*' she thought. '*I am completely out of ideas. Maybe Solomon can think of another way?*'

When the guard reached the owl's temple, Solomon was relieved to hear he was needed again. He got so lonely living there on his own, and did enjoy his little adventure with Sarika and Gerald.

'Yes of course I will,' he said to the guard. 'Go and tell your queen, that I am pleased to be of service again and that I will follow shortly. I still have a few loose ends to tidy up here first, then I will come.'

The guard thanked Solomon for granting an audience with him and promptly returned to his queen.

Sarika looked-on from the top of the kingdom gates. She could just make out the silhouettes of the villagers running around their little houses. Breathing a sigh of relief, she turned and saw Gerald making his way back towards the gates.

'Hello kind sir,' she shouted from above. 'You seem to have had a busy day, how are you feeling?'

'I'm doing fine,' he replied.

'Get yourself up here, I have something very important to tell you. In fact, don't come up here, go directly to my chambers, it will be more private there.'

Gerald rolled his eyes, wondering what she had in stall for him now.' 'Yes, young lady, immediately,' he frowned. *'Not that I've worked my fingers to the bone already and that I'm far too tired to be bothered,'* he thought, whilst marching through the gates and towards her chambers.

By the time he arrived, he could already hear the pitter-pat of her feet echoing down the corridor.

'Heavens, you came down from those gates in a hurry. What's the rush?'

'Step inside, I prefer a little privacy.'

'Oh yeah!' he said, grinning from ear-to-ear. 'What do you have in mind?'

'Shush, by you're getting to be a right dirty bugger these days. There is a time and place for everything Gerald, and it is not now.' Giving him one of her half-baked smiles, she winked and put her hand on his shoulder. 'Just be quiet you lump and get yourself inside.'

Looking a little embarrassed about his loose remarks, he lowered his head and whispered... 'Yes Ma'am.'

The sweet feminine smell of Sarika's perfume filled his nostrils as he entered her chambers. She obviously hadn't wasted any time making herself feel back at home. Almost everything was as it was, when he had first visited her and

290

her father. What had been recently damaged by Mahabone's men, had been cleverly disguised to look almost normal.

'This looks and feels very cosy Sarika,' he said softly. 'Now, what is it that is so important, that you had to request I come here?'

'I have spent days thinking about ways I can help you. Unfortunately, I was totally out of ideas. However, saying that, I have sent word to our friend Solomon. I have explained what has gone on since he last saw us. I explained about the battle and the death of Mahabone. I also asked him if he would visit us here, to see if he had any innovative ideas about helping you.'

'Oh!' said Gerald. 'Do you think he will be able to help?'

'I promised I would try and find help for you,' she replied. He is the only thing I can think of. If he can't help, then I'm afraid no-one can.'

'I know you promised,' he smiled, 'and I love you for this,' he said with a slip of his tongue.

'Really? That's the second time you have said you love me since you returned to our world. Do you really love me?'

'I, err, well, I suppose I do...' he mumbled. 'I mean we have done so much together,' turning his green skin a lighter shade.

Sarika fell silent for a moment, then started to quietly smile. 'Look, what will be, will be. I must say, I'm a little taken aback by your

291

sudden outburst of feelings for me, but on the other hand, I hoped this was the case. I like it,' she said blushing. 'Let me just say, the feelings are definitely mutual.'

'*Oh dear,* he thought. '*I better tread carefully here. I only want to get back to my own home world and don't want to get in too deep with her if I can help it. I do love her, but only as a close friend.*'

***

Solomon puffed and panted his way across the sky, as he flew over the *Triglotine* village and over the great gates of the kingdom.

'I have arrived as requested,' squawked Solomon to the duty guard. 'Tell Her Majesty that I am here to fulfil her request.'

Immediately, the guard scurried away to inform the queen of his arrival. Meanwhile, Solomon entered the great hall and made himself at home.

'Does anyone feel the need to offer their guest a drink?' he squawked. 'I've been flying around for bloody hours and I'm parched. What kind of reception is this?!'

One of the palace servants heard his outburst and quickly ran to his aid, carrying a suitable beverage.

'Mealworm and slug juice sir?' stated the servant. 'I do believe it is your favourite.'

'Why yes, how thoughtful of you,' said Solomon sarcastically. 'At least someone was doing their job right.'

'Thank you, sir. It has always been a pleasure to serve you,' replied the servant, bowing as he shuffled back into the shadows.

'Ah, pleased to see you again my friend,' said Sarika as she entered the hall. 'I do hope you had a good journey?'

'Yes, thank you. I got your message about the recent events with Mahabone! All I can say, is that it couldn't have happened to a better person, if that's what he was in the first place. Good riddance I say.

Finally, maybe after all these years of oppression, things might have a chance to get back to normal, eh?'

'Hopefully you're right Solomon,' she replied. 'Maybe this time, we can get it right.'

'Now, what's all this about Gerald and his obsession to get home,' frowned Solomon. 'Can he not just accept that any further efforts will be futile. We had probably destroyed any chances of success, when we destroyed that damn globe. Nevertheless, I will search the old grey-matter to see if anything comes to mind. Talking about the little demon, where the hell is he?'

'I don't know. The last time I saw him, he was wondering around the grounds with his head in the clouds.'

'Mm,' mumbled Solomon, 'it seems to me, that we have a problem.'

'I'm afraid so,' whispered Sarika. 'We must keep on trying, he just can't let it go.'

'If I get him to come with me,' suggested Solomon, 'we can try a few things from the temple archives. I suggest that Vaylor accompany us, for moral support of course.'

I agree,' she replied. 'I will make arrangements for them to travel with you to the temple.'

After Sarika finished explaining what was happening, it took a brief time for an excited Gerald and his friend Vaylor, to pack a few essential things for the journey.

The thought of him having a chance to correct things, had Gerald nervously dancing on the spot. For days now, he had been thinking about the *Sleeper*, the little bell that was destroyed in Mahabone's stronghold. He knows he really can't return home without it, but doesn't want to give up, at least until he tries every conceivable idea. The realisation that his body lying in bed in the real world, may soon die.

Although he is aware he's been in Sarika's for a few months now, his real body lying in the bed in his own world, has been there for approximately one-to-two weeks, due to the time difference between his world and this one. The point being, his real body in his home world, has had no food nor water and if he can't return to it soon, it will die of starvation. He knows if this happens, his soul will be stuck in this green body, in this world, forever.

'OK,' shouted Solomon, 'are you two ready for the off?'

'I think so,' said Vaylor. 'I'm just waiting for Gerald to finish packing his drink.'

'I'm done,' shouted Gerald. 'I just had to fill my water skin.'

'Yes, I heard,' scowled Solomon. 'Come on, we need to get a move on. However, I must remind you Gerald, that we are only going to investigate the possibilities of helping you. The temple archives hold many strange things from our magical past. We can only try, but I must warn you. If nothing works, then I'm afraid we will be unable to offer anything else. Do you understand my friend?'

The excitement slowly diminished from Gerald's face once more, as he looked over to where Sarika was standing. 'Yes, I do fully understand.'

CHAPTER

THIRTY

The journey started off well on foot, but it wasn't long before fatigue started to set in. Just as they were about to rest, Solomon squawked from above, that two stray griffins were grazing just ahead.

'Wow,' said Vaylor, 'they must have run away from the battle with Mahabone.'

'Solomon,' shouted Gerald, 'do they have any leather work on? Are they wild or trained?'

'They are still in battle dress,' replied Solomon.

'Good, smiled Vaylor. 'That means they won't run when we approach them.'

As predicted, both griffins just stood there. They weren't bothered at all, in fact, they seemed pleased to have the company and before long, were being rode eagerly towards Solomon's temple, cutting the travel time by hours.

'This was lucky,' said Vaylor. 'A great find for the kingdom. It will be nice to have some decent

296

transport for once. They are very hard to come by you know!'

'Yeah, just like a Ferrari,' smiled Gerald.

'A fergargy!' said a puzzled Vaylor. 'What the hell, are fergargy's?'

'A Ferrari, you nitwit and it is an *IT*, not a *THEM*. It is a fast form of transport from my world, but far too complicated to explain.'

'Then why say it?'

'It doesn't matter,' giggled Gerald. 'Let's just get to the temple.'

Once outside the temple, the precious griffins were carefully secured behind closed doors, before both men followed Solomon into the temple.

'Stand there you two,' ordered Solomon. 'I must open the secret vaults and I can't allow anyone to see what I do or the location for that matter. I hope you understand, for I am the keeper of the temple. You must wear these blindfolds and promise not to peek. Please don't break the trust I have with you.'

It's alright Solomon,' said Vaylor, 'we do understand,' pulling their blindfolds into position.

There was a moment of silence whilst Solomon disappeared into another section of the temple. Then, in a volley of clicks and bangs, the monolith in the centre of the temple began to slide across the floor to reveal Solomon rising from a lift from under the floor.

'I hope you are still blindfolded?' shouted Solomon.

'Yes, we are,' they said in unison.

'Good, keep them on and I will guide you to the archives.'

Guiding them both onto the lifting plate, Solomon used the controls to descend through the floor.

By the time the lift had stopped, both Gerald and Vaylor had no idea they had descended below. As far as they were concerned, when the blindfolds had been removed, they had just been guided to a new location at floor level.

'Right my friends,' said Solomon, 'you are now standing in the secret vault, where my ancestors have stored the archives through the millennia.'

'Wow!' whispered Gerald. 'This is amazing. It is so large. There must be thousands of books here?'

'There are over one million books actually,' remarked Solomon, puffing up his feathers. 'I take immense pride in them.'

'Outstanding...' said Vaylor.

'OK,' interrupted Solomon. 'Out of all these records, I have selected a selection of volumes to look at. They are the only ones that contain spells and ancient incantations. So, if we take three volumes each, we can search for anything that looks interesting. Once we have narrowed them down, we will try them one by one. OK?'

'Sounds good to me,' mumbled Gerald. 'Let's get started then,' rubbing his hands together in anticipation.

For two hours, they searched through the pages, but nothing jumped out at them.

'Well, that's me done,' said Gerald.

'Me too,' followed Vaylor. 'Plenty that seemed interesting, but not what we wanted.'

Only Solomon was reading the last few pages of his last book, shaking his head and looking very disappointed. 'I'm so sorry Gerald. It's starting to look as if our luck is running out... Oh! Just a minute...' he stuttered, flicking back through the previous page. 'Forget what I just said... I think I may have found something here.'

'Thank heavens for that,' sighed Gerald. 'Will it work?'

'I don't know,' answered Solomon shrugging his wings. 'It is a reversing incantation. It is very old, over a thousand years or so. However, whether it will work with the magic from the destroyed stone globe and the *Ouroboros* ring we found, is yet to be tested. Do you have it with you Gerald?'

'Yes.' he replied. 'It's in my shoulder bag.'

'We don't even know if the magic was permanent or reversible.' warned Solomon.

'I understand,' said Gerald, 'but let's not be negative about this. We can only try.'

'OK,' continued Solomon, 'it is a very short incantation to be repeated three times, whilst you hold this black candle and the *Ouroboros* ring between two mirrors.'

Vaylor found two large mirrors and placed them facing each other as instructed. Gerald just held the black candle in one hand and the *Ouroboros* ring in the other.

'Right,' continued Solomon. 'Cut the top of the candle to expose the wick and light it. As you do so, place the candle and *Ouroboros* ring between these two mirrors.'

'Like this,' replied Gerald, placing both objects in the correct place.

'Yes,' mumbled Solomon. 'Now please slowly read the incantation on this page.'

Gerald asked Solomon to turn the book around, so he could read the following hand-written words...

'The magic upon me
Be trapped this night
Between these mirrors
Never see light.

*

The magic upon me
Be trapped this night
Between these mirrors
Never see light.

*

The magic upon me
Be trapped this night
Between these mirrors
Never see light.'

As soon as Gerald had completed the three incantations, the ground started to tremble. Within seconds, a ring of bright lights began to envelope him, followed by a mysterious grey mist, that began to obscure his body.

'It seems to be doing something,' said Vaylor.

'Oh, do you think so?' remarked Solomon sarcastically.

There was no sign of Gerald, just a swirling ball of mist and bright lights, hovering precariously three feet above the floor.

This continued for a full five minutes without any change. Then with little warning, the ball descended to the floor in a burst of pale green light, but when the mist eventually cleared, Gerald lay unchanged, but covered with several deep lesions across his torso and unconscious on the floor.

'Oh shit,' blurted Vaylor. 'It hasn't worked! He will be distraught.'

'I can't wake him,' said Solomon, panicking about Gerald's life. 'I haven't got anything here to care for him... I...'

'Don't get yourself all in a flutter,' interrupted Vaylor. 'I've dealt with many

301

unconscious people on the battlefield. Granted, not in these unique magical circumstances, but unconscious nonetheless.'

'He desperately needs to have those wounds seen to,' said Solomon nervously.

'We'll have to take him back to Sarika,' suggested Vaylor, 'she will want to see to him herself.'

'I agree,' said Solomon. 'We'll have to go immediately.'

With no time to lose, Gerald, still unconscious, was secured tightly across the back of one griffin, making sure the Ouroboros ring was placed safely in his shoulder bag. Vaylor then mounted the front griffin with Gerald straddled in tow. Solomon secured the temple doors and flew ahead of the convoy.

***

Sarika, who was standing at the top of the Great Doors of her kingdom, was busy looking over the horizon, when she heard a disturbance below. Looking down, she saw a crowd of her people mingling around two griffins and several people carrying someone towards the entrance.

'Hey, you down there,' she shouted. 'What goes on?'

'It's Gerald Ma'am. He is wounded and unconscious.'

'Quick,' shouted Sarika. 'Bring him directly to my private quarters,' but just as she finished speaking, Solomon swooped in from behind and settled on the wall at her side.

'Sorry for startling you Your Majesty, but you need to attend to Gerald immediately. We tried to help him, but the incantation went terribly wrong.'

'What the hell happened?' she asked.

'It's far too complicated to explain right now,' squawked Solomon. 'Nor is it the right time. Let me just say that it wounded him and made him unconscious. Please, just attend to him. When we know he is safe, it will all be explained. I'm sorry to be rude, but you must go to him *NOW*!'

Running dangerously down the stone staircase, she guided those carrying Gerald to her quarters and had him laid on the bed.

Please leave now,' she ordered the people. 'I'll see to him from here.'

Tears in her eyes, she quickly grabbed her battlefield medical kit and carefully bathed and stitched his wounds. He was breathing, but no matter how she tried, he would not wake up.

For several days, she wiped his brow and changed his dressings. Feeding him was a nightmare, but she managed to feed a large hollow reed down his throat and trickle-fed him nourishing soups.

***

One evening, long after Solomon had explained what had happened, she lay by Gerald's side and cuddled him, placing her hand upon his chest. It wasn't long before she fell asleep but was soon awakened by someone holding her hand.

'How long have I been here?' asked Gerald. 'What happened to me?'

'Oh, thank heavens you are awake,' she said crying. 'I thought I had lost you forever,' but knew she had to tell him straight away. 'It didn't work Gerald! You are still one of us. The incantation went wrong! It cut you to shreds and you have been lying in my bed for days. It hurt you.' She sobbed, wiping the tears from her eyes.

'Damn,' he sighed. 'It was supposed to change me and send me home. That's it then, Solomon said it was my last chance. I have a terrible feeling that my body in my own world, is growing weak. I'm finding it harder to feel its presence.'

'You said you love me, Gerald! Don't you realise, I love you too. Stay with me? I will do anything to make your life with us happy.'

'*I don't think I may have a choice,*' he thought. 'I still must try Sarika. There still must be a way. I must admit I have grown to love you, but I must keep trying. I still miss my family and friends back home.'

'Then at least kiss me and show me you fool,' she said, placing the tip of her nose next to his.

Gerald did as she asked. Still feeling a little sore from his healing wounds, he kissed her and carefully positioned himself on top of her sleek body. He unbuttoned her clothing and immediately became aroused. Having no resistance, he started to caress her erogenous zones gently, by kissing her neck, stomach and thighs. Moaning and groaning at his touch, she gently indicated that the time was right, by positioning her legs around his waist and gently guided his manhood inside.

Back arched, Sarika gasped in ecstasy by each of his delicate movements, until he finally exploded, sinking slowly on top of her.

'Don't move,' she said, waiting for her involuntary spasms to subside. 'Just stay where you are for a minute.'

'I couldn't move if I tried,' he mumbled, his head buried in the pillow. 'Wow!'

'Well, I certainly wasn't expecting that,' she sighed. 'Nothing like I was led to believe.'

'What do you mean,' he asked, lifting his head from the pillow.

'You're my first my love.' she whispered. 'It was far better than I ever imagined... I love you.'

'*What have I done?*' he thought. 'I love you too.'

CHAPTER

THIRTY-ONE

Things were looking up for the following week or so and Gerald seemed to be making solid plans for his and Sarika's future, but then things took a sinister turn.

Gerald began to fall into a spiralling depression, constantly reminiscing on what he had left behind in his home world.

'Why can't you leave the past in the past Gerald?' screamed Sarika. 'This is your home world now.'

'I'm sorry. I just can't seem to get it out of my mind. Every time I think I'm moving forward; I seem to get thrown back in the past.'

'You have to stop this Gerald,' she cried. 'By the way, I have to tell you something.'

'What?'

'I'm pregnant!'

For a moment, his eyes sparkled with happiness and fear at the same time. Holding her tightly against his chest, he whispered, 'Are you sure?'

'As sure as you are green. Of course, I am pregnant. I hope it's a boy, so he can take after his father.'

'A boy, eh?'

'Yes,' she smiled. 'I would like to call him *Aldorin*, after my grandfather.'

'Well, that's a wonderful name,' he smiled. 'But what if it's a girl?'

'I'm not sure,' she replied. 'I'll have to think about that one.'

'Not sure how to take the news, he held her close. 'That's brilliant news,' kissing her gently on the lips. No sooner had he kissed her, his face looked solemn.

'What now?' She asked.

'Nothing,' he said, walking towards the door. 'Just those thoughts of my family flowing back in my head again. I need to go and clear my head.'

Sarika was now at the end of her tether. She had to do something. They were about to have a family of their own and that had to be saved. She knew she had to ask for the services of her trusted friends once more.

While Gerald was off on one of his guilt trips outside the kingdom grounds, Sarika quickly summoned Vaylor and Solomon. As soon as they arrived, she wasted no time in letting them know about her problem.

'I just don't know where to turn next!' she sobbed.

'Just a moment,' said Vaylor. 'Just slow down and start from the beginning.'

'What I am about to tell you, must stay within these walls for now,' she said, still sobbing.

'Yes, of course,' said Solomon. 'What is it?'

'I am afraid for Gerald's mind. As you well know, Gerald and I have been dating each other for some time now. However, there is something else!'

'What?' grumbled Vaylor impatiently.

'I'm... I'm pregnant with his child.'

'Oh!' remarked Solomon, flapping his wings. 'Well, congratulations and no doubt, it will change a few things around here, but you haven't yet mentioned what's worrying you about Gerald?'

'He is getting very depressed,' she said, wiping her tears with her handkerchief. 'He can't seem to get his past out of his mind. One minute he is happy and secure, then next minute he is feeling down and talking about what he's left behind. The problem is, each time it happens, the deeper his depression and the longer it lasts. He is the father of my unborn child and I can't have him like this after the birth. What the hell can we do? Can you help me, him... us?

I'm Sorry,' said Solomon, 'I don't have any other spells and because of what happened recently, I dare not subject him to anything else.'

'I can try to talk to him,' interrupted Vaylor.

'That won't work,' she sobbed. 'I have talked until the griffins come home. As soon as I think I'm making headway, he regresses within minutes.

'There still may be a way to help him,' Solomon interrupted. 'It's a bit of a long shot, but it could work.

'How?' she asked with tearful eyes.

'The Sea of Tranquillity!' he blurted.

'The Sea of Tranquillity!' she snapped. 'What the hell is that going to do?'

'When you were a child, your dear mother took you there. It was believed that if a child was washed in the waters of the Sea of Tranquillity, they would be protected against all evil.

After she had finished bathing you, the spirit of the sea spoke to her and presented you with that *Talisman,* to keep you safe from harm.'

'So that's where it came from,' she sobbed. 'I knew it was magical, that's why I gave it to Gerald when he left last time, but I always thought it was a family heirloom.'

Solomon flew from his perch and landed close to where Sarika was sitting. 'Right, listen carefully,' he said. 'The old scriptures also mention that if anyone returns to the Sea of Tranquillity with what had been given to them, it will take it back and return it to the sea, but that is not all,' he said looking very serious. 'Whosoever is bearing the gift on its return, shall also forget about its existence and memories associated with it.'

'What does that mean then?' she asked, looking a little worried. 'Does that mean if he is wearing it, he will forget all about what we have achieved with Mahabone and more worryingly, will he forget about me and what we have together?'

'I don't think so. He chirped. At least I think, I'm sure.'

'You just - *think* - you're sure,' she snapped.

'As I understand it, he will lose his memory of the *Talisman* and just any memories of where it originated from. As he was in constant possession of the Talisman when he went home last time, the Sea of Tranquillity will choose what is best for him.

'And what about here and now,' she asked, her eyes almost bulging from their sockets. 'He has had it in his possession ever since he came back and he still wears it around his neck now!'

'That is different,' interrupted Solomon. 'The *Talisman* is part of this world, not Gerald's. In this world, it is only meant to keep the bearer safe from harm. When you gave it to him last time he was here, you gave it out of love, in the hope that he would return. The Spirit of the sea would have recognised this and granted what you had asked for. Look, stranger things have happened! I mean since he has been here, look what has been achieved. What he has done for us, is beyond our wildest dreams.'

'I'm so confused Solomon,' she whimpered. I don't understand any of this.'

'Look my dear friend, you and Gerald can spend the rest of your lives as you are, with him going deeper into depression, or we can throw caution to the wind and step out in faith! It will either work, or it won't.'

Later that day, Gerald was seen sulking around in the great hall, when Vaylor pulled him to one side.

'Hey, my friend, what's up?' asked Vaylor. 'You're looking a little down in the mouth.'

'I'm OK,' replied Gerald, his mind elsewhere. 'I just can't stop thinking about my home world. I know this is hurting Sarika, but I just can't deal with this,' burying his head in his hands. I must find a way to return this *Ouroboros* ring to place with the last one I found. I need to complete my mission and find a way back to my family. I also must make sure the rings never fall into the wrong hands, free everyone from these objects of magic, once and for all. 'It's taking me over Vaylor and I don't know what to do!'

'Listen my friend,' whispered Vaylor. 'We are all very grateful for what you have done for us and I for one, cannot see you suffer like this.

Look, you have been working far too hard. Why don't you ask Sarika to go somewhere quiet for a few days of rest? A place that she might know of, where you can gather your thoughts in peace and quiet. Maybe then, you and Sarika might come up with innovative ideas. It will be a lot better than sitting around in this dusty old place. What do you say, eh?'

'I don't know,' he replied, shaking his head. 'I don't know what to think anymore.'

'Well at least think about it my friend. Go on, ask her, you'll make her feel a lot happier, you'll see.'

Sarika sat in their private quarters, hoping that Vaylor and Solomon can get through to the love of her life. She knows he is longing for his own world and that he is trying to hide his sad feelings from her, but she is frustrated and unhappy with their current situation.

'*I hope they know what they are doing,*' she thought. She knows he constantly wears the *Talisman* in the hope it will one day lead him to another way home. '*Why wouldn't he want to stay here with me?*' she thought, quietly sobbing to herself.

Moments later, Gerald came walking through the door, and parked himself in front of her. 'I'm so sorry darling,' he whispered. 'I've been such a selfish fool. I haven't even given any thought about how you are feeling about this.'

'It's alright,' she whispered, looking deep into his eyes. 'I love you Gerald and it hurts me to see you this way. Why can't we just be happy with what we have?'

'I know,' he replied sheepishly. 'I have had a thought. Vaylor had a word with me today, because he was also worried about the state of my mind, so I was wondering, would it be possible if you and I went for a little break somewhere? A place where we can relax together for a while. Maybe we can even thrash out ideas at some point, but mainly to get our relationship back to where it should be.'

'That would be nice,' she replied with a sigh of relief, that Vaylor had done his job well.

'Any ideas on where to go then?' he asked with a spark in his voice.

'Well, I do know of a wonderful place actually,' she said, fluttering her eyelids. 'If we use those griffins we captured, it will only take us a few days to get there, but I've not been there for a very long time.'

'Where is this place?' he asked.

'It is known as the Sea of Tranquillity. It is on the edge of our known land, just past the farthest horizon.

Apparently, when I was a child, my mother used to take me there. I can't remember anything about it, but I am led to believe it is a beautiful, tranquil place, hence its name,' she smiled, knowing that when she returned with the *Talisman*, the ocean that revealed it to her, would hopefully take it and all memories associated with it, back to where it came from.

At least that's what Solomon advised her would happen.

***

The following day, both the griffins were saddled up with enough provisions to last several days. Far more than what was needed, but they didn't want to take any chances.

An hour later, they had said their goodbyes, and were on their way to the *Sea of Tranquillity*. It was a very pleasant journey. Nothing that was out of the ordinary, it just seemed very peaceful, with a good lot of talking along the way. For once, Gerald seemed to keep a positive outlook for most of the journey.

'We should be almost there by nightfall,' said Sarika. 'We can set up camp and rest the griffins and ourselves of course.'

'That's good,' he grumbled. 'These bloody saddles. My backside feels like an open sore. Probably looks like one too.'

'We have a real chance to find out about ourselves out here,' she said smiling. 'Get to know who we really are together. No responsibility, no people, just you and me, together.'

'Don't forget the baby! There is three of us now, maybe more!'

'I hope not,' she said laughing. 'As it's my first pregnancy, one will do just nicely.'

'Oh, you're expecting more later then?'

'Well, you never know.' She smiled and started galloping ahead of him.

A brief time later, when the light was just beginning to diminish, the valley revealed the bay at the *Sea of Tranquillity*.

'Wow,' gasped Gerald. 'That looks beautiful.'

'I agree,' she whispered. 'Look, we can make camp there, just between those two trees. Then we can travel the last few miles in the morning.'

After making camp and securing the griffins, they both settled down for the night.

***

For a few days, Gerald had his ups and downs, yet still had time to pay attention to Sarika's needs. Although they made love every night, they spent hours talking to the baby and finding out about themselves as a couple. Nevertheless, even though he was trying very hard, he still had trouble dismissing the memories of his past, often falling into his depressive state.

Eventually, Sarika spotted a hollow log at the edge of the shore. It had been hollowed out to make a crude boat. Remembering what

315

Solomon had told her about the *Spirit,* who resides in the Sea, who takes mystical gifts back and chooses what is best for the bearer; this was her opportunity to get him and the *Talisman* onto the.

'Hey, look what I can see,' she said, grabbing his hand. Gerald grabbed his shoulder bag holding both *Ouroboros* rings and slung it across his chest.

'What are you taking that for,' she asked.

You know it never leaves my side. I can't afford to have someone steal it back.'

'If you must,' she said, leading him towards the shore.

'What now?' he panted, not knowing where she was taking him.

'It's a boat,' she squealed excitedly. 'We can experience the tranquillity of the sea together at close quarters.'

The makeshift boat was very heavy, but with a little perseverance, they managed to get it to float in the water.

'Do you think it is safe?' asked Gerald, looking a little worried.

'Well, we'll find out,' she smiled. 'What's the worst that could happen? Swimming, that's what. If it goes down, we will enjoy a good swim,' she laughed, jumping into the boat. 'See, it's still floating. Now jump in and use that piece of wood as a paddle.'

'As you wish, Your Bossiness.'

After only ten minutes paddling, Sarika asked Gerald to stop and take in the beauty of the calm sea. He thought it looked wonderful and peaceful. Unfortunately, as soon as he looked over the side of the boat, he could see the reflection of his past. The university where he once worked, the family he had lost, his mum, Tom and his friend and colleague, Sandy Williamson.

Suddenly, a horrendous pain stabbed him across his torso. Grabbing furiously at his chest to ease the pain, he dislodged the talisman from around his neck and dropped it over the side. As he watched it spin deeper towards the abyss, so did his memory of its existence and the reflections of his own world became more intense.

'Are you OK Gerald?' asked Sarika, looking very worried.

'I not sure,' he replied, feeling very confused.

'What happened there then?' she asked.

'I don't really know! I was thinking about home, but then I got a shooting pain across my chest.'

'I've got a drink for you to make you feel better,' she said, going through her bag.' But as she turned to give him his drink, he had vanished. Looking frantically around the clear waters to see if he had fallen in, she realised he was gone!

'GERALD,' she screamed. 'Where are you?

CHAPTER

THIRTY-TWO

Gerald's Home World ...

Sandy sat there in her university office, tapping a pen on the side of her glasses. She hadn't had any contact with Gerald for just over a week now and was getting a little concerned. He was only supposed to be taking a week off, but every attempt to contact him lately, had resulted in utter failure.

'I *must get myself over there. He should have been back well before now! He might even be in some sort of trouble,*' she thought. '*He should have returned to work by now!*'

She had become very friendly with Gerald, even closer than he would have liked at times and had something very important to tell him. She didn't have that many friends, but he seemed to press all the right buttons that many others failed to do.

Knowing what her friend had discussed with her about the strange world he believed in, she decides to jump in her car and go off road, risking damage to her car's suspension, whilst on route to his forest cabin.

The track to Gerald's cabin was slightly overgrown for an uneven forest roadway. It was obvious, that no vehicles had passed there for some time, but when Sandy got there, Gerald's car was still parked on the gravel drive.

'That's weird,' she thought, pulling up behind his car. *'He said he never goes anywhere without it. He must still be in there.'*

Stepping out of her car, she made her way to the front door. 'Hello, Gerald, are you in there?' she shouted, whilst knocking on his door. There was no answer. 'Maybe he is around the back,' she whispered to herself. So, she wandered around the back to where he usually hung out. 'Hello, are you around here Gerald?' Still no answer. *'Where the heck can he be then?'* she wondered. Just then, she noticed an open window at the rear of the house and stuck her head inside. 'Hello, anyone at home,' but still no reply.

Looking around the living area, she could see he had been in there, because his coat, wallet, pager and car keys were still lying on the coffee table. But then she noticed the front door was still bolted from the inside. Knowing that it was the only entrance and exit to the property, she concluded that he must still be inside. Then she saw him!

The reflection of his bedroom door could just be seen through the wall mirror and because it was ajar, part of one leg could be seen hanging at the side of his bed.

'Oh my God Gerald, are you alright?' she shouted frantically, whilst climbing through the window. Smashing several dishes and stumbling back to her feet, she ran into his bedroom. Immediately, Sandy looked upon his sleeping face and tried to wake him.

Gerald slowly opened his eyes to find himself very disoriented.

'Sarika, where the hell am I?' he asked, looking perplexed.

'Who?' asked Sandy.

'I was floating on the Sea of Tranquillity..."

'Where? Are you still dreaming? asked Sandy.

Gerald suddenly realised he was back. Lifting his hands, he was amazed they were no longer green, they looked normal.

'Thank Christ for that?' he shouted, startling Sandy.

'You scared the hell out of me Gerald,' said Sandy. 'I thought something terrible had happened to you. In fact, when I first laid my eyes on you, I thought you were dead!'

'DEAD!' he shouted, still trying to make sense of what had just happened to him. 'Oh, Sandy, you won't believe where I have been and what I have done.'

'Tell me in a minute,' she replied, 'because I also have something extremely important to tell you too.'

'By all means,' he said. 'You go first.'

'Thank you. I'm afraid it is of a very delicate nature.'

'Oh! he said looking a little confused. 'What is it?'

'Can you remember,' she said lowering her voice, 'when I came over to yours a little while back and ended up staying overnight.'

'Yes,' he replied, not knowing where this was leading to.

'We had a drink or two together,' she whispered. 'Then we ended up having sex together.'

'Erm, yes we did,' responding with a large lump in his throat.

'Well,' she said, taking a deep breath. 'I'm pregnant.'

'Oh! You're pregnant.' he replied, knowing that he had left Sarika in *Deawilder* with his unborn child and has no way to get back. Now he's found out that he is the father of Sandy's unborn child. 'Sorry, forgive me dear, I meant to say congratulations. It was just a bit of a shock for me.'

'A shock for you.' she snapped. 'It was a big shock for me too. I have not told anyone yet, as I thought it only right for you to be the first one to know.

'Don't get me wrong,' he said, 'I am over the moon. How do you feel about it?' he asked, feeling very nervous about her reply.

'Well, I'm certainly not going to get rid of the baby,' she snapped. 'It's totally against my principles.'

'You misunderstand me,' he replied. 'I wasn't meaning that. I just wanted to ask what your plans were.'

'What do you mean?'

'I mean between you and I. I would like to honour my responsibilities as a father. This is great news Sandy. Look, I like you very much and hope you like me.

'I do,' she smiled.

'Then can we not continue as a couple or if you agree, we can even make plans to get married. Not just for the baby's sake, but because we love and enjoy each other's company. I know I love you. I've had a crush on you since I saw you in that shop you worked in. I just never had the courage to say anything. What do you say?'

'Gerald,' she gasped. 'Did I hear that right. Are you asking me to marry you?'

'Yes, I suppose I am. If you'll have me that is.'

Sandy simply pondered for a moment, before smiling from ear-to-ear.

'YES!' she screamed with delight. 'Thank God for that. I was so scared in case you rejected everything. I more than like you Gerald, I love you too. I prayed you felt the same way. Of course, I will love to marry you.' Wiping her tears of joy away, she walked to his side and placed her moist lips on his.

'Now that we have settled that surprise,' she said excitedly. 'I must tell everyone.'

'Hold your horses, Sandy. Family always comes first. Once they know, then we can tell everyone else.'

'You're right of course,' she smiled. 'I seemed to get a little ahead of myself with excitement. I am so happy we are together now as a family and I do love you so. Now, tell me where you have been all this time?'

Gerald, sat up from his bed and rubbed his hands over his face.

'To be honest, I really don't know where to start,' he said, scratching his head. 'I remember going to bed that night you stayed. The next thing I remember is being by a river bank in the supernatural world we spoke about. You know, *Deawilder,* where Mahabone resides, or should I say resided.'

'You never did.' she gasped. 'You mean to tell me that you have been there all this time?'

'Well sort of,' he said cautiously. 'I seemed to have been there for weeks-on-end, but if you remember me telling you about the time difference between their world and ours, it must have only lasted just over a week in our world.'

'Yes, I remember you saying,' she replied, whilst looking a little bemused. 'So, tell me exactly what happened?'

Gerald continued to tell her what happened regarding the death of King Tubal'cain, how Mahabone had changed him into a *Triglotine* and Solomon's several attempts to change him back. Then there was the finding of the second *Ouroboros* ring.

With that, Gerald put his hand in his shoulder bag and showed her the *Ouroboros* ring.

'Wow,' she gasped, 'That looks amazing.'

'That's nothing,' he smiled. 'This is the second one I have found.' putting it back in the bag.

'Second?' she asked inquisitively.

'Yes. The first ring is in the safe. You haven't seen it yet, but I will show you later after finishing what happened.'

'OK then,' she smiled.

'I'm not going to tell her that Sarika was carrying my child.' he thought. *'It would really upset her. What she doesn't know, won't hurt her.'* He hoped!

''Finally,' he continued. 'I was on a small boat with Sarika, made from a hollow tree trunk, floating on the Sea of Tranquillity. I was looking at my reflection, thinking of home, whilst feeling terrible pains in my chest, making me drop my *Talisman* and watched it sink. The next thing I remember, is waking up here with you looking at me.'

Standing up, Gerald picked up his shoulder bag holding the second *Ouroboros* ring and beckoned Sandy to follow him to the fireplace in the living room.

'Right Sandy,' he said looking very serious. What I'm about to show you is a family secret. If anything should happen to me, you will know where everything is hidden.'

'What do you mean – hidden?' she asked, looking a little perplexed.

'These things must never be made public. They are dangerous! The fire place used to hide the Mahabone's old wooden toolbox and the *Sleeper* bell, but both were destroyed when I visited *Deawilder.* However, I have now retrieved the second of the three *Ouroboros* rings for safe keeping.'

'Why keep them now that Mahabone is dead?' she asked.

'All three rings are needed to complete the sacred sword Shibboleth but no one knows where the third is hidden, but with me retaining two of them, no-one can have enough magical power to become a threat to anyone. We know that Mahabone has a brother called *Orobas* living elsewhere, but no-one knows where.'

Gerald pointed Sandy towards the painting beside the fireplace and pulled one side of the frame away from the wall, revealing the hidden wall safe.

'That's neat,' she whispered.

'OK Sandy, you must memorise the following key code. It is: 5, 2, 6, 3, 6, 0, A.' After watching him punch in the keys, she spends a few seconds running the numbers through her head.

'Got it,' she replied.

Gerald slowly opened the safe to reveal the large first *Ouroboros* ring.

'Look, here is the first ring I retrieved several years ago,' placing the first ring on the coffee table, he reached into his bag and pulled out the second, placing them side-by-side.

'They're massive and beautiful,' she gasped.

'Yes, they are,' he smiled. 'But look at the difference. The dragons on both rings are different.'

'Oh yes,' she said 'They are.'

'I bet if the third ever comes to light,' he said, 'it will be different again. So, now that you have seen them and up to speed about their significance, they must be kept under lock and key. Never to be revealed to anyone. Understood?'

'Yes, my darling,' she smiled. 'Never to be revealed.'

***

A week or so later, Gerald and Sandy, who were now settled in their cabin in *Wyre Forest*, had resurfaced the uneven road leading to the cabin for visitors, before arranging a surprise family meal for their parents at their local *Royal Forester* restaurant near Bewdley.

'What's all this about?' asked Wendy when they arrived.

'You'll soon see.' smiled Gerald. 'Just sit yourself down at the table I booked.

Tom never said a word. He just patted Gerald on the back and grumbled as he sat down next to Sandy.

'Mum, Tom, this is Sandy. The woman I was telling you about, from the university.'

'We're pleased to eventually meet you Sandy,' smiled Wendy. 'He has said so much about you. Helping him with his work and what-not.'

'Oh, has he now?' she smiled, looking at Gerald. 'I'm also pleased to meet his mother and his Uncle Tom of course. He has told me so much about his family too.'

'He has, has he,' said Tom staring at Gerald.

Look, never mind all that,' interrupted Gerald. 'We are still waiting for Sandy's parents to arrive, so we can have a nice meal together as a group.'

Gerald beckoned the waiter over and ordered a few drinks, just as Sandy's parents walked through the door. Gerald immediately stood up to greet them, leading them to the table.

'Hi darling,' said Sandy's mother. 'What's going on?'

'Just take a seat both of you.' she smiled. 'This is Gerald, his mum Wendy and his Uncle Tom.'

'Pleased to meet you all. My name is Joy, and this is my husband, Martin.'

'Right,' said Gerald. 'Now that we have all been introduced. We have invited you here for a celebration meal.'

'What celebration?' asked Martin.

'I want to ask you,' said Gerald holding Sandy's hand. 'I want to ask for your daughter's hand in marriage. We work together at the university and have been living together for a few weeks now. I thought it only right to inform you of our plans, and ask your permission.' Both Wendy and Joy burst into tears.

'Well,' said Martin, looking at his daughter nodding. 'If this is what she really wants and that she loves you, then I have no objections.'

'There is something else I have to tell you all,' said Sandy looking sheepish. 'I hope you won't be mad at us. I'm pregnant with Geralds child.'

'Mad! of course we're not,' said Joy.

'I must say we are a little shocked, but not mad,' said Martin. 'As long as you are both happy and are financially sound to look after your family, then let's all celebrate.'

'I couldn't have put it better myself,' said Wendy. Tom just sat there expressionless.

'Then let's order our meals,' said Tom. 'I'm bloody starving.'

'Here-here,' they all shouted.

***

Their marriage arrangements were put in place very quickly, as the last thing Sandy wanted to do, was to walk down the aisle showing her bump.

Long after the wedding festivities and honeymoon was over, life returned to normal, until it was time for Sandy to take her maternity leave. Heavily pregnant, it wasn't long before she went into labour, where she gave birth to a beautiful baby boy, called *David*.

Chapter

Thirty-Three

Kings College Hospital - Present Day ...

Seventeen-year-old David sat there aghast, after hearing the past events his father had just told him...

'So, there you have it son.' whispered Gerald. 'When you went to the cabin after your visit yesterday, did you check everything I asked you?'

'Sorry dad,' replied David. 'It completely slipped my mind.'

'Then write this down before you forget again and don't show it to anyone.' instructed Gerald.

David borrowed the pen attached to his fathers notes at the bottom of his bed, before tearing a thin strip of blank paper from the notes.

'When you leave here,' whispered Gerald, 'go back to the cabin, there is a safe hidden behind the painting at the fireplace and look at the artifacts inside. The combination to the safe is 5, 2, 6, 3, 6, 0, A. You will then see what I have told you is real. Remember, keep what you find under lock and key. Look for yourself, but don't allow anyone else, and I mean anyone, to know about them. Do you understand?'

'Yes dad, got it,' smiled David.

'Now put it in your wallet son, and promise me you won't forget to look.'

'Don't worry dad. I will remember.'

'I've never tried this myself, but may I suggest you hold onto these rings when you go to bed.'

'Why?' asked David.

'I would like you to try dreaming of the events I have told you about. Try not to think of your past dreams as nightmares. Just think of a place, or a person in *Deawilder*. As they are magical, the rings may help you to get a deeper feel of the place, providing they work of course.'

'Why the hell would I want to do that dad?'

'Because I don't think I'll be around long enough to go back. Don't forget, you may end up there for real, whether you like it or not.'

'Not bloody likely,' snapped David. 'How's that?'

'Because you are my first born, and it's not over yet. Were you not listening to what I told you about my past endeavours? At least you may have the chance to experience the places I have told you about in your dreams. It is inevitable you will end up there one day.'

'OK, OK, I'll give it a try, if you insist.'

R. L. Barnes.

'Thank you, son. All I want is for you to have a little heads-up. Just in case anything really happens. I don't want you to go through what I had to. At least you are now aware of everything I know.'

'OK. But what about mum and her parents, my grandparents?' asked David. 'You never mentioned them. You promised me. You said you would tell me the truth about why I never met them.'

'Oh yes,' said Gerald, not sure how to break the truth to his son. 'You did meet them all son, when you were a baby. The sad truth is, your mum and her parents were in a terrible accident. Please understand I had to protect you. They were tragically killed by a drunken lorry driver. Which is why I had to bring you up myself. I did have a little help from grandma Wendy and Uncle Tom in the early years. At least grandma Wendy is still here, but Uncle Tom is a bit of a mystery.'

'A mystery? asked David, looking perplexed.

'It was strange,' said Gerald. 'He was there one minute, then disappeared from the face of the earth. We have not heard a peep from him for several years!'

'I remember great Uncle Tom. So, why can't I remember mum, grandma Joy and grandad Martin?'

'You were far too young to understand the circumstances of the accident,' said Gerald. 'As

332

I said before, I had to protect you from what happened through your younger years.'

'But why wait until now?'

'I don't know son. I just didn't know when it was the right time to tell you. You wouldn't have fully understood, until now.'

I understand dad. You could have told me before now. Look, I must go, they're calling time on visiting.'

'Here,' said Gerald, putting his hand in the bedside cabinet. 'Please take my wallet. It has over two hundred in it,' whispered Gerald. 'Go home in Afghan Road, Take the car and fill it up with the cash in the wallet. That should give you enough to get to the cabin and back.'

'Are you sure?' asked David.

'Yes, I'm sure, you're my son, aren't you?

David kissed his dad on the forehead, gave him a squeeze and waved farewell.

'Don't forget son,' shouted Gerald. 'When you try tonight, don't let anyone see the rings. Always keep them safe, and take a bag with you, just in case.'

Chapter

Thirty-Four

Back at the wooden cabin after his supper, David sat pondering about what his father had told him over the last two days. Opening his wallet, he slowly removed the slip of paper he had written the combination on, before making his way over to the fireplace painting.

'I have seen this painting all my life, whilst I was growing up.' he thought. *'But I never gave it much thought. As far as I was concerned, it was just another grubby old painting. Only now when my father ill. does tell me it has secrets hidden behind it.'*

Pulling the side of the hinged painting to one side, it revealed the hidden door and combination keys of the wall safe.

One by one, he slowly pushed the keys in the order he was told.

'5, 2, 6, 3, 6, 0, A. That should do it.'

The mechanism inside the door *clicked*, allowing him to open the door. There in full view, was two golden rings, each made from two different dragons.

"Christ,' he gasped. 'I would never have believed it, if I hadn't seen them with my own eyes. The old bugger was telling me the truth after all.'

Being late in the evening, David took the rings to his bedroom and placed them neatly on the table.

'Go *to sleep holding the Ouroboros rings and think of a place in Deawilder, Oh, and not forgetting the bag,*' he thought, remembering what his father instructed him to do.

Lying on his bed, he carefully placed his shoulder bag around his neck, laid on his bed and held both rings across his chest.

Thinking hard about Sarika and her supernatural kingdom, the *Ouroboros* rings started to make his hands tingle. They made him feel so lightheaded, he quickly drifted into a deep sleep.

***

David miraculously stood in the corner of an immense courtyard.

'How the hell did you get in?' shouted a funny green guard from the top of the battlement. 'Sound the alarm, we have another human intruder.'

David did not know what to say, and remembered his father's description of these funny green people. Swiftly putting the *Ouroboros* rings in his shoulder bag for safe keeping, David answered the guard.

'Sorry sir,' he shouted. I didn't mean to intrude. You see my father said…'

'Never mind what your father said,' sneered the guard, as the alarm sounded in the background. 'Who the hell do you think you are, wandering in here like this? Don't you realise this is Queen Sarika's' underground kingdom? Her private home if you will.'

Just out of Davids peripheral vision, a well-dressed green man smiled with spiky teeth, and approached David from one of the doorways.

'Forgive our guards,' said the well dress man, 'they can be a little zealous at time. But that is not a bad thing.'

'OK,' said David, turning around nervously.

'How rude of me. Let me introduce myself. I am Prince Aldorin, son of Queen Sarika. And who are you, may I ask?'

'I am David Lindsell,' he whispered. 'Son of Gerald Lindsell.'

Aldorin pondered for a moment, rubbing his chin. 'Gerald, you say?' he asked. 'And where did you come from?'

'I'm a little confused at the moment,' said David. 'My father asked me to see if I could see

Deawilder in my dreams, but this seems so real!'

'I think you better have an audience with the queen,' said Aldorin. She may be able to help you more than I can.' He told the guards to stop the intruder alarm, then led David to the inner chambers.

Walking through the corridors, David couldn't believe he was witnessing everything his father explained with attention to detail, until they stopped outside a large set of doors.

'The queens chambers David,' said Aldorin. 'Please wait here until her footman asks you to enter.'

'May I ask if I'm in trouble?' asked David.

'Not at all,' replied Aldorin. 'However, I do suggest you treat her with respect.'

Aldorin knocked three times on the chamber door, then left David to wait on his own.

After several minutes standing around, David could hear bolts being unlocked from the other side of the doors. A small footman, dressed in what looked like overalls made from sackcloth, peered gingerly through the half open door.

'The queen will see you now sir,' whispered the footman. 'Who should I say asking for an audience?'

'I didn't ask,' replied David. 'I was brought here by Prince Aldorin.'

'Oh, I see, sir.'

'And not to sound rude,' said David. 'My name is David. David Lindsell.'

'Very good sir. Please follow me.'

David followed the footman down a short narrow corridor, until they stopped at an open doorway.

'Excuse me Your Majesty,' said the footman. 'I have a Mr David Lindsell, directed to you by Prince Aldorin.'

'What name did you say?' asked Sarika.

'David Lindsell, Your Majesty.'

'Send him in.'

'As you wish, Your Majesty.'

David watched as the footman beckoned him into the queen's private quarters.

Sarika stood there staring at him, then indicated to David to sit down by pointing her finger to a chair in front of her. David just nodded and walked over and sat nervously.

'Well, Mr Lindsell, or can I call you David?' asked Sarika.

'David will be fine, Your Majesty.'

'Good.' she smiled. 'Please feel free to call me Sarika.'

'Oh, you must be the woman my dad told me about.'

'Did he really?' she smiled. 'I was just about to ask if you were any relation to Gerald. Now that I look at you, I can see the uncanny resemblance. It was a sad day when I lost him many years ago.'

'Lost! What do you mean?' asked David looking a little confused.

'I remember we were sailing on the sea of tranquillity,' she said. 'I was talking to him one minute, but when I turned around, he had vanished.'

Oh, I remember,' he replied. 'Dad did mention that.'

'It took me a long time to accept he had gone,' she said with a sad expression. 'I eventually assumed he had made it back home.'

He did,' he said smiling. 'Otherwise, I would not have been born. Anyway, all of this still seems a little surreal to me.'

'How do you mean David?'

My dad told me about the family curse he had to deal with and that I would have to come here one day, because he stole the *Ouroboros* rings.'

Oh, yes,' she whispered. 'I certainly remember those things. Even to this day, we have never been able to find the third ring. Only when we have all three, can we assemble the full power of our sacred sword, *Shibboleth*. You are aware of *Shibboleth*?'

'Yes,' he said, whilst rolling his eyes. 'He had mentioned it several times in his stories. Dad also said for me to use both rings, to see if their magic could let me see your kingdom in my dreams. However, they did more than that! They apparently brought me here instead.'

'They certainly have David,' she smiled. 'So, he must have told you about me carrying his child when he disappeared?'

'He mentioned it, I'm sure,' he replied.

'Well then, I take it you met your half-brother?' she said smiling.

'I have a brother?' he gasped.

'Yes. He introduced himself to you when you arrived. My son, Prince Aldorin.'

'Yes, but he's Gree...'

'Green, you were going to say?' she cut in. 'Mahabone had already transformed your dad into a *Triglotine* at the time of my conception.

'Oh, I see,' he whispered. So, tell me David, how is Gerald, your dad?

David filled his lungs and breathed a deep sigh. 'He's dying. He has a cancer eating him from the inside.'

'What is a cancer?' she asked inquisitively.

'It's a terrible disease, and in my dad's case, incurable.'

'Nonsense,' she laughed. 'Although it is terrible news in your world, we have always found a way to treat people with magic.'

'With Magic?' he asked.

'Yes. When you came here using the rings, do you still have them with you?'

'Yes,' he replied, opening his shoulder bag to show the rings.'

'It's been a long time since I have set eyes on these. Then I will summon Solomon, our wise owl, to see what can be done.' She then sent her messenger to get Solomon.

***

Half a day later, Solomon arrived, soaring over the battlement walls and into the courtyard.

'Where's this son of Gerald?' he squawked. 'I must speak with him now.'

'Hello my friend,' shouted Aldorin, from one of the doorways. 'Come through to the queens' private chambers. You'll find him there.'

After Solomon had introduced himself, Sarika explained how David had arrived using the *Ouroboros* rings, and how Gerald is dying from a disease in his home world.

'Solomon, is there anything we can do for Gerald?' asked Sarika.

'Well,' said Solomon. 'We know the two Ouroboros rings are not at full strength without the third. But wow that he has two of the rings with him, David can use their magic to take him home, by resting and thinking of home. Just as he did to get here.

If all's well, he can take the rings to the hospital in his own world, where Gerald can hold one on each hand, whilst reciting the following incantation.'

341

R. L. Barnes.

Plene tuere hunc hominem -
Cancer eius sanatur et non revertetur
Nunc vive cum immortalitate

'OK,' said David. 'But will it save him?'

'Let's hope so,' said Sarika.

'You will have to be quick David,' said Solomon. 'Because the longer you take to carry out this spell, the less effect it will have on him.'

'I understand,' said David.

'Remember this also,' warned Solomon. 'If you return home post-haste, Gerald will have a good chance of recovery, but may not see any changes for a few days. It will renew his life-force.'

After hearing this, David thanked them for all their help and understanding, then asked if he could have a private place to rest, for him to make his way home.

CHAPTER

THIRTY-FIVE

David's Cabin – Present day ...

David woke up startled, then quickly leaped out of bed.

'I'm back!' he screamed. 'Holy shit, that was terrifying and exciting all at the same time,' whilst looking around the cabin bedroom.

Checking to see if he still possessed the *Ouroboros* rings, he searched around the bed until he spotted them tangled between the bed sheets, breathing a sigh of relief.

'I must get these to the hospital as soon as possible;' he thought

Quickly putting the rings in his bag, he got dressed, then made his way to his dad's car.

***

Gerald sat in his bed, as David walked through the ward doors.

'Hello son.'

'Hi dad. I did what you asked me to do last night.'

'And did anything happen,' asked Gerald.

343

Yes, it did,' whispered David. 'I did exactly as you instructed, but it didn't just let me see *Deawilder*. The rings sent me there.'

'Really,' replied Gerald, looking surprised.

'Yes. I met everyone, but there is no time to explain everything now. Solomon gave me instructions to help you. It will make you better he said. But it's imperative that it happens now for it to work.'

David pulled the curtains around Gerald's bed for privacy, before removing the rings from inside his bag and placed them on Gerald's bed.

'What the hell have you brought these for?' shouted Gerald. 'I told you to keep them under lock and key!'

'For once in your life, shut up and trust me.' David took a piece of paper out of his pocket, where he had written the words of the spell.

Gerald was taken aback at his son's authority, then nodded in agreement.

'You must hold one *Ouroboros* ring in each hand,' instructed David. 'Now you must recite the following words on this paper. Don't ask. Just do it!'

Knowing that his son had spoken to his trusted friend Solomon, he held both rings, and recited the words of the incantation:

Plene tuere hunc hominem -
Cancer eius sanatur et non revertetur
Nunc vive cum immortalitate

There was a moment of stillness before the rings began to vibrate and glow blue. There was a brief feeling of static air around Gerald, making his hair stand on end. Then nothing.

'What happened?' asked David. 'Solomon said it might take a day or two for it to work.'

'I'm not sure son. I noticed the spell was written in Latin. I could feel something weird going through my body. Let's just wait and see.'

'Let's keep everything crossed, eh?' said David, returning the rings to the safety of his shoulder bag.

CHAPTER

THIRTY-SIX

Deawilder – Present day ...

Many years had passed since Mahabone's body was buried under the grounds of his stronghold. His old guards had been freed and were starting to enjoy their new life, as well as working together with their new friends, the Queen Sarika and the Triglotines.

'What the hell is that Janus?' asked Elara to her husband, whilst pointing to the sky.

'I don't rightly know. I've never seen anything like it before,' he replied.

Floating on the horizon, was a very large black cloud. It did not look normal, as it looked so dense and black. Dark as the night itself. It certainly wasn't following the rest of the clouds. In fact, it was moving quickly in the opposite direction, straight towards the stronghold.

'It's getting very close now,' said Janus. 'In fact, I can hear a crackling noise getting louder as it approaches.'

Janus turned, leaving Elara still staring at the black object. Running to warn the other members of their community, he arrived to see the others already standing in a crowd and looking to the sky.

There was an immediate sense of panic, as the black cloud slowed to a halt, and with an ear-piercing crack, gently lowered itself into the main courtyard, causing the crowd to run in all directions to the perimeters.

'What is it?' shouted a young boy.

'We don't know,' shouted one of the elders. 'We have never seen anything like this before.'

Everyone gasped in disbelief, as the cloud emitted a blinding blue flash of lightning, proceeded by the materialisation of a large, tall and musclebound figure.

All the people looked on in fear. The large stranger held a similar sorcerer's staff, that had been broken and buried with Mahabone.

'I have not heard from your master in a while.' shouted the large stranger. 'Where is he?

'We don't know who you mean.' said another woman. 'What do you call him?'

'His name is Mahabone.'

'Sorry, but Mahabone has been dead for years,' said one of the elders.

'He is what?' boomed the stranger.

'Everyone knows he was killed in battle long ago by a human warrior called Gerald,' said another elder. 'What is your name sir?'

'My name is *Orobas.*' he boomed. 'I'm the eldest brother of Mahabone and master of my own distant realm. However, if what you tell me is true, and that my brother is dead, then I claim this realm as my own. Let it be known to all, that I'm now the new master of this realm.'

'But we have been free of servitude for years Orobas. We have children that has never known the oppression of our past.' said a young father.

Come here young man. kneel in front of me!'

The young father made his way through the crown and stood defiant in front of Orobas.'

'I said kneel!' sneered Orobas.

'No,' said the man. 'I stand for our freedom. Our fathers fought bravely to make it so. We don't want you here.'

'You are either very brave,' said Orobas. 'Or very stupid.' With that, he pointed his staff at the young man's head, and with a blinding flash, decapitated him. 'The crowd was in uproar

'So, now that you have witnessed what happens if you disobey me, be sure to warn people across your lands.

Stepping away from the headless body, he demanded where he can find Gerald.'

Scared of what this necromancer would do, one of the elders approached him.

'He's not here,' said the elder, quivering at the knees. 'He is no longer of this world.'

'Why is that?' replied Orobas.

'Because he returned to his own world many years ago.'

'And what world is that?'

'Earth,' replied the elder.

'Then he won't be there for long.' he sneered. 'I think it's time I should go to Earth, and pay this Gerald a visit.'

R. L. Barnes.

You have come to the end,
but it's not over yet! ...

Book Three

COMING NEXT

Book One	Book Two	Book 3
		COMING
		NEXT

Go to the Series link on

Amazon

or visit his website at:

https://www.robert-barnes.com/

ABOUT THE AUTHOR

Robert L. Barnes - Author

Robert was born in June 1960 at St Mary's Hospital in the City of Newcastle upon Tyne, England.

In the early 1980's, he gained his first set of qualifications in the subjects of Freelance Journalism and Authorship. He has since written several articles for local tabloids over those early years, such as the Shields Gazette, The Northern Echo and the Sunderland Echo, for example.

However, in his later years, he ebbed away from freelance journalism by showing an interest in technical writing, as well as short stories for his many readers to enjoy.

Now living in Durham in the United Kingdom, he now enjoys gaining inspiration from his varied travels, where he can put his imagination onto pages of fantasy and fiction for his readers enjoyment.

Please visit his website for other books.

https://www.robert-barnes.com/

Printed in Great Britain
by Amazon

38388525R00205